MEMOIRS OF A MODERN SHE NOODLE

Wynn Frolley

NeoPoiesisPress.com

Neo Poiesis Press, LLC

2775 Harbor Ave SW, Suite D, Seattle, WA
Info@NeoPoiesisPress.com
NeoPoiesisPress.com

Wynn Frolley– Memoirs of a Modern She-Noodle

ISBN 978-0-9975021-0-7 (paperback: alk. paper)
1. Fiction. I. Wynn Frolley. II. Memoirs of a Modern She-Noodle.
III. Erotica

Library of Congress Control Number: 2018937907

Design, art direction & typography: Milo Duffin and Stephen Roxborough
Cover illustration by Anthony Bloch

Printed in the United States of America

This book is dedicated to anyone I ever loved.
Without you, this fictive evocation would be empty as air.

Also, to my mother, *sine qua non,*
who will never read this book,
and to my one and only husband, David,
who has read every word more than once.

***

I sing the body electric,
The armies of those I love engirth me and I engirth them,
They will not let me off till I go with them, respond to them,
And discorrupt them, and charge them full with the charge
of the soul.

Walt Whitman,
Leaves of Grass

THE STORIES

Why She-Noodle? i

Ballooning in Perris 1

A Moment in Moab 25

The Way of the Cookie 29

Up in the Hills 31

Barrage of Breasts 41

The Occasional VSOP 45

My Dinner at Musso's 49

Penis Pastiche 53

Foreign Secrets 55

Faking it 61

Libertarian Lust 65

Happy, Happy Birthday, Baby 75

Meditation Music 85

That Night on Mount Pinos 95

Blue Movie at Dodger Stadium 115

Talking Men 133

Tapas Dancing 135

Mixed Doubles at Bluebeard's Castle 143

Ginger Noodle with Wild Mushroom 179

Smoke and Mirrors 189

Moving Day 201

Out of Body 211

Lift-off 215

Getaway 221

Acknowledgments 226

About the Author 227

Enrichments 229

Why She-Noodle?

I'm not sure you'd know this about me if we bumped into each other at the grocery store, bending over the frozen macaroni and cheese or wheeling kids in shopping carts up and down the aisles foraging for milk and toilet paper, but truth be known—I was a She-Noodle, back when everybody had sex and they loved it and they loved each other (or they didn't love each other, but they still loved the sex)! Those of us girls who went that free love way, together or alone; I call us all "She-noodles" because what better name to conjure steamy days and warm, buttery nights that melted our hearts and between our thighs and taught us all to fly?

Originally, that expression—"she-noodle"— was a general term of endearment, suggestive of the naughty fun found in a Victorian periodical of erotica called The Pearl, which I discovered sequestered in the Special Collections Department of the university library where, among the musty stacks, I was buried in heaps of legal-sized, lined yellow pads and unscalable mountains of 3x5 cards. I was trying to find my way to an idea big and new enough to write about for years to come; hence, I was researching an academic paper which would later define my PhD thesis: "The Rhetoric of Sex in Victorian Literature and The Uses of Sex in Contemporary American Fiction."

The first part examined how the Victorians observed and described the sex act; it was all about voyeurism, euphemisms, and epithets, while reviling moral hypocrisy and revealing sexual taboos. The second part considered how writers including Nabokov, Roth, Updike, and most especially Jong, used sex as the defining action—the centrifugal force of their characters' story. In, out, arc, and af-

termath—most of it seems to have been about the sex. Who, what, where, when, and why—doing it was the all!

Ah, Ms. Jong! What a superb champion of women's sexual freedom of the moment you were! In glittering literary tropes as euphonious as the "zipless fuck," she gave a generation of women permission to find their own G-spots and notice the difference between that and the other kind of orgasm, or even if there was another kind! Thank you, Erica, for opening the portal!

I discussed this sexual shift in detail in the seminar paper I wrote back then. Alas, the dissertation, the extended leap from that first idea, never saw the light of day outside the library in which I was writing it. I left it where I wrote it, hand-scrawled, hidden back in the stacks, where it seemed to belong, behind a first edition of Fanny Hill.

When I'd decided to leave graduate school for the scenic route through life, it seemed fitting to bequeath my last, best academic idea to someone unknown to me, stashed in the future somewhere. Perhaps a graduate student in the next century might find these notes and musings useful in reconstructing who we were and how and why we were She-noodles in our 20ᵗʰ Century youths.

It was a heady, hot topic then and I found much to mull over in that tattered monthly magazine, The Pearl, first published in July of 1879 and then suddenly gone—vanished without a trace—by December of 1880. Stories were "to be continued" installments, serialized over multiple issues, with enticing titles like "Lady Pokingham, or They All Do It," "Miss Coote's Confession or the Voluptuous Experiences of an Old Maid," and the guilty party of inspiration, "Sub-Umbra, or Sport Among the She-Noodles," which gave rise to my personal lexicon for the real *mothers of invention in our time of self-discovered liberation. We were, and maybe still are, women who made up their own rules and played by them: She-noodles! All sorts!*

It was an entirely different time from now—we modern She-noodles flourished out of the shadow of the Victorian closet, both at home and abroad, sunbathing bare-breasted on beaches worldwide. A lot of us had taken the bulls by the horns and other bodily parts and declared ourselves sexual beings, in contrast to our mothers, who were told and so told us, "Good girls don't like it," and, "You only do it for the man," or, "It's the messy but necessary business of making babies."

Some of us, a lot of us, found out it was more than that - plenty more than that - and so good, in fact, that "the first time with your one and only" would never be enough. So, we took our clothes off and went skinny-dipping in the possibilities, threw our bras to the wind, and had our own excessive adventures on the road to Wisdom.

I began on my own She-noodling path at a fairly young age. It must have been the summers on Fire Island which we spent mostly naked, ocean-salted, and basted in coconut oil. I might have been all of twelve when my first boyfriend and I set out to sail a short distance and were blown off course by sudden winds and heavy petting.

But I want to be completely clear on this point right from the start: I am not a victim. I made my own choices. Some were not wise. Some were downright awful, but they were my own. I made them. I survived them. If I'm lucky, I've learned from them. I won't deny them. They are part of the sum total of me, along with the shape of my ear lobe or the mole on my hip.

The tales scribed here are figments of a She-noodle's

imagination, based on times and places that have gone the way of Schwab's Lunch counter and the Brown Derby, as well as body-painting parties and tie-died bell-bottoms. No matter, they are some of what makes a life, captured in a time between time, in the mid-1970s, Los Angeles, beginning and ending, overlapping in a Yeatsian gyre, the spiral that connects the points between the past, the present, the future—all at once. The real point is, whatever you do from here on out—stop and smell the roses! And try to get it while you can, because believe you me, nothing lasts—just ask Ozymandias!

BALLOONING IN PERRIS

There is that moment when a lot of things are coming to an end when one feels compelled, in the midst of so much ending, to force a bulb and make something new and fresh and fragrant. It may only last for the duration of its blossom, but while it lasts, it is *sweet*.

I don't begrudge myself those few brief blooms I've had along the way which have showered me with plenty, tickled my fancy, and then let me loose where the milkweed seed flies its own merry way. That last one, just before I got in the Little Green Car and drove north for good, leaving L.A., the Land of Hungry Ghosts and the too-sunny angst enshrouding the hills and flats of it—that *final affair* was worth its weight in a mountain of hyacinth.

The odd thing about it was that I really didn't mean to get into it in the first place. The guy was dating a friend of mine. She lived halfway across the country and seemed an unlikely match for him in any case. She was strictly blue blood from out of town and a long way back and he was an original Lebanese street vendor twice removed, made good, better, Big Time in the States. He was swarthy, with a lot of hair, and a good deal of funny money to play with. She was a pale, thin-skinned blonde who never toyed with her considerable wealth, and that was how she kept it.

I had dinner with them before she left to go back to Connecticut. We met in a Mexican restaurant near where I lived in Silver Lake. It was Barragan's, a favorite neighborhood spot. I didn't think too much about him and I guess he thought even less of me. On immediate first take, both of us could leave it. But I was working on a freelance story for which he had some contacts. It was a

1

not-very-significant article about the gem trade and the revitalization of downtown L.A. He knew everyone in the wholesale jewelry biz and offered to introduce me around.

When I went downtown a few days later, dressed to chat and take notes, he told me over drinks that when I approached him in his office, he had absolutely no idea who I was. He was quite surprised to realize it was me, the one he'd met and written off as "a potato", as he put it. I don't know why he thought that or what a potato actually looks like in clothes, but I wore what amused me, not what made me look glamorous or pseudo-starlet, or whatever was normal protocol for women in their 20s in Los Angeles in the mid-'70s.

I didn't know about the "potato" part of his thinking until later, when we actually had our clothes off. And I'm glad I didn't because I might have gotten pissed and stomped off, the way I did one day when some male person at Zuma Beach came up to me just as I had gotten out of the ocean and told me that I was wearing the wrong kind of bathing suit. I was wearing, in fact, a dance leotard. He informed me that it really was very unbecoming, as it covered up too much and with a body like mine I should at least have the courtesy to wear a bikini. Others might have been flattered in a Playboy-Dumb-Bunny sort of way. Not me! I verbally slugged the guy and walked off.

Anyway, *this* guy didn't say anything *that* stupid until much later on, when suddenly it didn't matter anymore. By that time, we were already lovers and knew intuitively that it was a temporal thing. We could just go around with each other for a fast, fun ride and enjoy our differences, instead of engaging in the endless and often fruitless process of rewriting and editing your lover. We didn't bother with any of that. We floated freely in the present tense and on course to the day of my departure, suspended out there in some indefinite future pluperfect moment.

But *that* day, in downtown buildings made bright and shiny with new money, he took me around and introduced me to the best precious gemstones in Los Angeles.

In one many-mirrored shop, I held in my hand a sapphire the color of Caribbean water and as big as a half dollar. When I closed my fingers around it, a warm spot glowed in my palm, which instinctively craved what it held. I had never really experienced that kind of physical desire, the one for magnificent and impossibly expensive baubles. The feeling is quite a bit like carnal lust as there's a similar, almost uncontrollable urge to have *it*, have that one precious thing all to yourself.

At the end of the day of interviewing, note-taking, and witnessing one lust-inducing object after another, Gem-Man, who was landlord to all this glistening glory, invited me to have a drink and wait out the first crush of rush hour. We did that, at the steel-and-glass, exceedingly postmodern bar in the Bonaventura.

I explained to him in great detail that I had almost definitively decided to pack up and move to Minnesota, where there was a person I thought I would finally marry after years of indecisive flirtation with the concept; in fact, I had just spent the day before packing boxes of books and manuscripts and graduate school notebooks which I had sent to this person's mother, who would hold them until I got out there. I explained all this so that he knew where I stood. I've always known when someone was lighting up to me and I felt I should set it straight at the get-go. He didn't seem too fazed by it and asked me to go to dinner the following night.

"Sure," I said, "I'm always up for dinner!"

He paid the tab for the gin and tonics and I went back to my house in Silver Lake. I typed up my notes, wrote a few snappy paragraphs on gemstone culture and posted them to my editor at the glossy rag I freelanced for. I continued to pack more boxes for *The Move to the Midwest* and *Happily Ever After*, which were the chapter heads I had in mind for the next part of my sub-vocalized, unwritten autobiography.

Then I got the phone call. It wasn't the man I thought I was going to marry. It was his brother. I had been leaving messages one place and another for "my intended," letting him know what sort of time-table I might be on, driving across country with the car and the dog while shipping everything else. Then I had gotten a great idea. I'd fly out and surprise him for his birthday and have the car shipped with the rest of my stuff. I hadn't heard back from him yet, but I wanted to get his brother to pick me up at the airport the day of the birthday party. I'd left a message with the plane's arrival time and said not to contact me unless there was a problem.

When the phone call came, it caught me off guard and worried me. I assumed something had happened, an accident or something, and I was being reached on an emergency basis.

"Harry!" I shouted, once I recognized his voice. "What's wrong? "

"Nothing, really. I mean nothing in *that* way."

"Well, where is he, then, I've been calling for days. Is he out of town, sailing or something?"

The pseudo-fiancé in question was one of a group of boy-men who grew up on the shores of

White Bear Lake and sailed with the dedicated fervor of religious fanatics in the Church of the Topsail. Now they were men (well, were at least as old as men might be) and their sailing talents were readily employed by older boy-men whose age and success allowed them to purchase bigger, better, faster, sleeker vessels, requiring crews of six or seven additional boy-men to run them. He was one of those, a sailor boy-man in demand on big boats, another in a long line of the same, looking after each other over a very long haul – Trans-Atlantic or Trans-Pacific, they were in it together.

I wanted to marry him mostly because he was my beloved girlfriend's oldest friend and he was somehow familiar to me like the boy-next-door I never lived next door to. He had a long, complicated family name which ended in a *the III* but everyone called him Chip, which I suppose was better than Junior. He was, I believed, going to make a fortune and I had hoped to be along for the ride and even put some cash in the pot to seed my up-and-coming money tree.

The first deal was in spec homes along undeveloped lake front, south of St. Paul. I knew nothing of business. I was an artist and wanted to stay that way. I had inherited a small legacy and threw away money enthusiastically like colourful confetti, showering it on friends in whom I just believed in for no particular reason. It was my hope that one of these persons would magically make my investment grow from the handful of beans I started with into a giant stalk dropping golden coins just outside my window or more consistently via quarterly checks in the mail—either way would suit me. Of course, Chip wasn't just some person; he was the person I thought I would end up with, in a blaze of ...what? Fate? A bolt out of the blue?

5

A Disney moment? Investing in him, I thought, was like investing in a truer kind of Futures Market—ours together.

There was a long pause on the telephone before Harry finally said, "Chip's over at the development. He's moved in over there, in fact."

"Well that's great!" I enthused. "That means we won't have to look for a place. You got the message I'm flying out there to surprise him on his birthday? Do you think you could pick me up?"

There was another long pause and then he said, "Actually, he's moved in, *with* someone."

I still didn't get it. "So, he got a roommate! That's okay! We can work around it." I went on a little dizzily, "I can't wait to see the place! I only saw the excavation and then the plans, of course. It'll be great to see it all together. We had a wonderful time picking all those colors and carpets, even though we might not live in it long, since, after all, we're just planning on selling the thing and reinvesting in something else and..."

I noticed, suddenly, the continuing dank silence on the other end of the line.

"Harry? Is there something I'm missing here?"

"Well, *yah.*"

"So? You've got my attention. What's the deal?"

"Chip's moved into the place with a *girlfriend.*" He paused and let it sink in.

"A girlfriend." I said the word like it was foreign and new on my lips.

"*Yah,*" he said again, using the Minnesota catch-all phrase diminutive of "*Yah, sure, you betcha,*" which could mean anything from "Have a nice day!" to "No shit!" and his use of it here was more or less a plea for me to not kill the messenger.

"Well," I said, thinking for a moment of Jack Benny and the beautiful black-and-white '50s which did not in any way prepare me for the sex, drugs, rock and roll, or unrealism of my own personal Roaring Twenties, now epitomized by this utter betrayal: Chip-the-Boy-next-door, a blue-eyed, blond-haired, perfectly Episcopalian person becomes a sudden sort of Frankensteinian Fred-MacMurray-in-*The-Apartment*-type-of-louse? It was hard to fathom!

"I guess my little birthday surprise would be a *real* surprise. I'm coming anyway."

"Oh, come on," pleaded Harry, "that's not going to solve anything! It's just going to make a scene."

Those Minnesota men weren't big on making scenes. Actually, that's not really true. They like to "make the fun scene" or "make the sailing scene" or "make the country club scene" or any one of those standard recognizable scenes that everybody like them likes to make. But a real scene, with real humans saying real things, not necessarily pleasant or jocular or man-to-man, those big tall Scandinavian blonds don't go in for *that* kind of scene at all.

"If I decide to come," I went on, between clenched teeth, "don't bother about the ride. I'll get there on my own."

I hung up. He was mid-sentence in what was about to be, I could tell by the sliding pitch up, a male dithyramb on why to leave well enough alone.

He did try to ring me back a couple of times over the next hour or so. I didn't answer the phone. I sat and stared with considerable dejection at my half-packed life scattered around me.

My roommate at that moment had once been my childhood boyfriend from another time and place entirely. When my grad school roommate, Skinny, moved East to go to law school, my friend Green-Eyes moved in. As we had been lovers once, we had an intensely disinterested perspective on each other which exceeded that of the usual non-

7

romantic roommates of mixed sexes. When he came home that afternoon and found me in a stupor on the couch he asked in the usual disinterested way, "Bad day?"

I hated to tell him about it. He never liked the guy from Minnesota. He openly snickered at the idea of me playing tennis at the country club. It was utterly against the grain of his essentially Marxist aesthetic. Sailboats, green lawns, and tennis togs made him want to throw up on someone else's white Keds.

"I don't think I'll be going to Minnesota as soon as I thought."

"Oh?" he asked with even more than the usual disinterest, "How come?"

"I don't think it's going to work out," I threw back, casually, like a professional liar. "Instead," I went on, "I think I might have to go to the South of France and find Old-What's-His-Name."

Old-What's-His-Name, my Eveready-Heartbreak, The-Devil-by Any-Other-Name, Dr. Faustus, Destroyer-of-Serenity, aka. My-Old-Flame, or just Flame for short. I tried to forget him, moved from one coast to the other to get away, and I had been just about ready, after all these years, to finally sever the tie and take the leap of faith into the arms of Chip-the Boy-next-door. Now, I felt certain, I had to rekindle that Flame and find *him*—the guy who tore me to pieces every time I saw him. If I could just embrace him, I'd cleanse my soul of all sub-umbra longings for The Great White Way—no, not Broadway—*The Suburbs*!

I thought at the time My-Old-Flame remained the only one who could really rock my soul and throb my heart. This upset in my plans, I took as a sign: Go unto Marseilles!

That's where he was, currently traveling

around on a sabbatical. He'd written me a number of touching notes, asking me to join him there, on the road, where he would gladly show me the world of ancient truth and contemplative beauty. I hadn't known what to write back. I was making my mind up to write him a fond farewell letter, go the straight and narrow to the Land of 10,000 Lakes, and buy a wedding trousseau from Lord & Taylor's on the way, when this sudden little snag put a run in my stocking.

The fact of the matter was, I was nearly out of money. It was a modest inheritance from my father which had allowed me to buy a used sports car, pay cheap rent in Silver Lake, maintain a sublet in New York, and commute to my ongoing relationships, the one in Minnesota and the other in Upstate New York. Now, we were coming to the end of the fat. Maybe I had enough for this one last gasp to Europe. Maybe not. I told my roommate, "I'll be booking a flight and getting a passport in the morning, so we might as well go out and celebrate tonight!"

Green-Eyes looked a little surprised and amused but said, "Sure, whatever you say, let's go shoot some pool and throw a few down."

Patrick's Four Leaf Clover was a literal smoky dive on Hollywood Boulevard where my friend went often and knew and was known by the regulars. They had names like Pete, Sally, Jack, and Jolene. Names I knew I'd never remember, so I didn't even try.

I ordered Chivas with lemon peel on the rocks and played pool, which I don't do very well. It didn't matter. I was distracting myself—that was all. I drank another round and shot another round of pool. It went on like that for some time. When the room was black and blue with smoke, my friend finally noticed I was drinking seriously and asked,

"So...about Minnesota?"

"Well, there are 10,000 lakes and they make a lot of butter which is lucky because people eat a lot of it out there, what with Eggs Benedict in the morning and hot buttered rum in the afternoon." I missed another shot on the pool table.

Some guy, vaguely familiar to my friend, kept putting quarters on the table I was playing and challenging me. It was ridiculous, really. He thought he was hustling me. I kept losing but he kept playing me nonetheless. I kept drinking. Soon I was seeing triple and cueing up to the illusory balls rather than the actual ones. That's when Green-Eyes said it was time to go.

"Come on, kid," he said like Bogart, "it's time to put your lips together and blow."

I knew it was time, but the question was, would I make it home *before* I blew everything all over my own shoes? Meanwhile the schmoo who had been stacking the quarters up and, I guess, had bought me a number of the straight shots I was throwing down, seemed to feel he was entitled to take me home now. I stared at him in disbelief when, out in the parking lot, he came at my friend with his hands poised in a pugilistic stance to take a few pot shots and prove his point.

To his credit, my friend, who is a slight man with an utterly pacifist frame of reference, was able to talk the loudmouthed lout back into a reasonable point of view. He said, "Look pal, she's got to go home, she's got the flu and never should have come out tonight. She's been throwing up all day as it is and I don't think she'll be much fun anyway. Right?"

And he looked at me and I shook my head and said, "Right, throwing up all day, might throw up right now, if I can't get home to my own bed," which happened to be absolutely true. The guy backed off and staggered into the bleak Los Angeles night, shouting a rant of angry, nasty incoherence.

We drove slowly down side streets and criss-crossed our way to the little bungalow we shared at the base of the Silver Lake hills. My friend helped me up the long flight of steps and then folded me into my bed. I didn't stay prone long. I was up sick in a kind of relentless way for the rest of the night. I had poisoned myself and it wasn't funny.

I thought of all those youthful moments in which people laugh and recount their tales of alcoholic binges and the consequences and they laugh, and everyone laughs as though it's this great joke we should all share, as though it's some kind of terrific initiation into an exclusive secret club. Really, it's not funny. It's far from secret. Anyone can get it and having gotten it, should know better than to get it like that again. But that's alcohol for you—readily available brain thinner. The more you get it, the more you lose it, the more you lose it, the more you get it—a self-perpetuating intelligence solvent. And it's legal and everything!

The next morning, I was flat on my back and still very ill. The phone rang and from the depths of my disturbed brain I thought it was a fire alarm. I started up, thinking I had to run out of the house, realized I had no clothes on just as I hit the front porch, realized then that it was the phone, picked up the receiver, said, "Hello, hold on please," ran to the bathroom, puked hard the remainder of my stomach lining, rinsed my mouth, fell back into bed with the phone beside me, its cord curled round and round itself in a ferocious knot, and growled in a voice that was down in the basement with Lauren Bacall, "Yeeeesssss?"

"Hi there!" said a voice out of left field. "Still up

for dinner?"

"Up for dinner?" I echoed listlessly, flat on my back. It was Gem-Man. I had of course completely forgotten we'd made a date. "Uh, I'm a little down and out at the moment."

"Anything I can help with?" he asked with the slide in his voice heading upwards like the slow traipse of a roller coaster ascending the first hill.

"Got a good remedy for a hangover the size of Manhattan?"

I was weak and lightheaded. I knew some major disaster had struck me down but I wasn't sure whether the villain was the Scotch or the lost dream of happily ever after by the lake. I was vulnerable, whichever it was. I guess he sensed the possibility, an opening where there wasn't one before, with the instinct of a cat that knows where in the bushes a bird's nest is built.

"Oh," he cooed sympathetically, "like *that* huh?"

"Umm-hmmm" I growled back.

"Sure, I've got a list as long as my arm but at the top of the list is a sauna, a swim, and potion of fresh juices."

I had been prepared to "shine this guy on", as the expression of the moment went. But he caught my attention with a pleasant suggestion which my whole sick body caved into, in that instant. "You know where such can be had?" I croaked, still under the floorboards with Bacall.

"Sure." His voice slid again, this time the downside of the roller coaster hill. "We'll just drop in at Dirty Lil's. She's got it all at her place in Beverly Hills."

"Do I have to drive?" I was still half inclined to ditch, if there was the least bit of effort required on my part.

"Would I do that? Make a sick lady drive the

freeways by herself? Nah. I'll come get you. How soon can you pull yourself together?"

Now there was no excuse. I told him to give me an hour. I needed to shower and bend my body in some yoga poses and get the blood flowing towards my swizzled brain.

Our backyard had been someone's little paradise once, in the '30s, when the place was first built. There were tall banks of hibiscus fenced in on two sides with the intermittent burst of bougainvillea growing up and over and around a now-buried fence of bamboo sticks. A grapefruit tree grew on one side of the yard and a black walnut filled the other and stood between the back door of the house and the small room-sized studio where I had sat and studied and read and crashed through big long waves of intellectual conjecture for the last couple of years of graduate school.

At the back, a wildly overgrown bush of faded pink and fragrant roses draped like tumbled silk over thorns, down to the edge of a small paved patio, under a cluster of loquat, apricot, and palm trees. In the center of the yard there was a circular concrete fixture which might have been a fish pond or even a small fountain once, but it had long since cracked and been neglected. I had been filling it in with bags of potting soil and planting succulents and desert flowers in it, in hopes it would fill out and transform from something clearly falling apart to a miniature landscape I could tend with nail scissors and careful hands.

This is where I did my yoga, day in and day out, on this small patch of hand-poured concrete in the sun. It was private and often I could lie there completely naked and put my feet over my head and forget about everything. I lay there now, flat on my back in a bikini, letting sad thoughts

13

evaporate in the aching gold light of late springtime in Los Angeles. I thought about the boy-man in Minnesota and his new girlfriend breaking in the cute little planned housing unit I had helped build, if only with money. It smarted. But, in all fairness to him, I could see how it happened.

I'd been going back and forth across the country, up and down both coasts, and side to side in between, deciding first one thing and then the other, first one man and then the other, for three, going on four, years. When Chip fell for me at first, he fell hard, and he was sweet and kind and doting. He asked me to marry him about a year into it, late one night after too much cognac. I hedged the question back then, but clearly I'd been thinking about it ever since. In the meantime, I still saw my My-Old -Flame, Heart-throb-cum-heartbreak, whenever I could, as often as possible, considering we lived on opposite coasts. Sometimes I would fly to St. Paul, spend a few weeks with Chip, then fly on to the East to spend a good part of the rest of the summer with *him*.

Chip knew it and said very little about it. I thought it showed good sense on his part, but a lot I knew. What was really happening, which I didn't know and never would have guessed, was that I was setting myself up for this: the moment at which I finally decide to let the old stuff go and start a new life in lime green and eyelet curtains, he's got the spot filled with something new and different.

Well, I guess it served me right. On that thought, I arched my back in a final salute to the sun and went inside to change. I kept my bathing suit on but put a wraparound skirt and a skinny T-shirt over it, packed underwear, a towel, suntan lotion and dark glasses. I poked at my eyes with a little mascara, so as not to look too faded.

I just had time to throw down a couple of aspirin with some ginger ale before he pulled up in front of the house in his yellow Mercedes and I slid down the stairs to the street to meet him.

We whisked out the Santa Monica Freeway with the sunroof open and soft cool jazz on the stereo. Gem-Man was open and easy and solicitous for my well-being. By the time we turned up somewhere roughly in back of and up into the hills from the Beverly Hills Hotel, I'd told him most of the whole story and he'd told me a little more of his.

"Dirty Lil," it turned out, was his mother.

I was a bit stunned. I wasn't used to meeting somebody's mother on a first date with a hangover formerly the size of Manhattan, now receding to something closer to the Bronx, but still pounding like bad traffic on the Long Island Expressway. All those sunny days in SoCal had yet to cure me of my New York State of metaphors.

I started to say to him, "Look, no way, turn around or let me out!" but he was quick to reassure me.

"Don't worry about her. Lil's been and done it all. That's why we call her Dirty Lil. She was a professional card player once, so don't ever play poker with her. She'll empty your pockets. She knows every cure in the book and then some, for hangovers."

The house we pulled into was an older stucco monolith of a white elephant behind a tall hedge with years of landscape shaping behind it. It was found for her by his older brother who bought and sold real estate for Middle Eastern millionaires, billionaires, and heads of state. This one had been previously owned by a trade lobbyist for the Lebanese government. It was sold fast and cheap when war broke in Beirut and the rep and his family had to leave the country for diplomatic

15

reasons. His older brother was in the right place at the right time to finesse the sale, which was a real steal, literally.

The house was great. It was wall-to-wall antiques from everywhere. Louis Quatorze side by side with Sixteenth-century Century Islam. Gem-Man let himself in and then brayed up the front hall stairs, "Lil! Where the hell are ya?"

A rather short and mildly wide woman toddled down the front staircase, which was actual Venetian marble. "Honey," she squawked back, "no place I'm tellin' *you* about!"

Her hair was cut in a short modish style and died a brandy-colored brown. Her eyebrows were waxy with penciled color and black half-lashes were glued to the edges of her lids. Orangey-red lips grinned around a big pair of gap toothed uppers. She had on a persimmon-colored cashmere leisure suit and stood with one hand on her hip and the other on the banister, Mae West style, half way down the stairs.

"So," she said shortly, turning her brown cow eyes to me, "the kid says you tied one on, big time! Don't worry, we'll fix it. The sauna's cookin' and the shakes are in the freezer. Myself, I gotta go get a pedicure. I'm leaving for Vegas tomorrow and my toes are a mess."

You could see she was on a trajectory and couldn't be stopped. A Gucci bag the size of a small suitcase was thrown over her shoulder.

"See ya, Lil. Keep yer nose clean!" Gem-Man affectionately called after her.

"She was a belly-dancer in Beirut and the old man fell for her hard," he told me later. "He sold carpets and hookahs in the streets. His family forbade the marriage, so they ran away to the U.S. together to start a new life. All was forgiven when he made a fortune importing foreign handicrafts and she made him three sons, the *only* grandsons in the family."

These details unraveled one by one as we melted the day away, first dripping small hot rivers of body salts in a good-sized, severely hot sauna built into a mini-monolithic pool house. The pool itself was a huge rectangular affair, built the way they made them in the '50s, to last an ostentatiously long time.

We got hot, then stood under a cold shower and cooled and got hot and then cooled again for some amount of time I lost track of. Then I flopped in the pool, sopped up the sun, and drank large amounts of mineral water on ice. Finally, Gem-Man brought out the shakes his mother had made up and left in the freezer for us.

"Here it is." He smiled at me and handed me a frosted tall glass of a pumpkin-colored liquid, "Dirty Lil's Secret Recipe for the Day After Whoopsies."

It looked awful. It tasted ambrosial—fresh oranges and pineapples juiced, mangoes and papayas pureed, spices mixed in flavors ancient and Asian, ginger and cardamom, nutmeg and clove, and then something a little bitter, possibly ginseng, with the added oomph of blue sea kelp.

"I watched her make it once," he said, "and stopped counting at thirty-nine ingredients. Royal jelly, bee pollen, red clover and acidophilus, you name it, it's in there."

I didn't mind drinking it. I was ready to try anything to kick over my engine.

"A little sleep," I mumbled. "I'll be fine."

Gem-Man smiled that enigmatic smile of white teeth and tan, hairy skin. Without my asking, he dribbled sun-tan lotion on my back and massaged the shoulders, the back, the thighs and the calves, as he spread the goop evenly down my backside. I dozed and groaned and dozed.

17

Something must have worked. When I woke up, all I could think of eating was a Pink's chili dog with onions. Sick as I had been, this was a strange food idea. And yet, there it was, a blatant yen for a long dog smothered in greasy meaty Tomato-paste chili with handfuls of cheese and spoonfuls of chopped sweet white onion. And a cream soda to wash it down. We dressed and went to that monument on Melrose, the giant Hot Dog Stand of hot dog stands –Pink's. What a place!

We laughed at the ironies of the cure, the healthy shake that gives you the strength to eat industrial-grade junk good. We laughed, and I knew I was going to make it to the other side of a bad moment. We laughed and I was glad this American-born Middle Eastern palooka was shining his onyx eyes on me.

When he dropped me back at my place, I slept the sleep of empty blank pages for fourteen hours and woke refreshed, with a new determination. I decided that neither would I go to France and chase down ancient one-way streets, nor would I force my way into a White Bear Lake model home, not too far from the shores of Lake Superior. Instead, I'd pack my bags and boxes, hire a mover, and hit the Pacific Coast Highway, all the way to Seattle.

It was a beautiful city, sparkling clean and evergreen and surrounded by water, mountains, and beauty. I'd been there a couple of times and each time, I thought *what a place to start a life!* That was it, then, neither backwards, nor sideways— I was on the move up and onward to a new city, a new life outside the mouldering groves of academe. I was finally just going to be an artist after all and I'd be damned if I was going to look back.

The sun was silver yellow and the sky was native turquoise that next morning when I got up and put on Bonnie Raitt to begin the big pack up. The phone rang at lunch time and it was Gem-Man. I told him my plan and he said, "Well, why don't you come out to my place and we'll have dinner and toast your future on the open road?"

Dinner—always a weakness on my part—I just can't resist those guys who just want to feed me dinner. I've always felt if someone was kind enough to buy me dinner, the least I could do was to go out and eat it! I'd spent the day sorting the detritus of paper stuff everywhere around me and now there was the promise of fresh seafood and an ocean view out in Venice, near where he lived. I jumped in my Little Green Car and hit the freeway before rush hour froze all movement.

His place was a great little '30s beach house, nestled in a tiny alley street between Ocean Park and Venice. It was the vintage equivalent of my place in Silver Lake, but of course it was in much better shape. He owned the joint and knew how to increase its value by careful maintenance. And luckily for him, he had the capital to pour into it and keep making improvements. "Look," he confided, as he showed me around the place, "I've been taught to think of these things in a very basic way, from thousands of years of experience. I ask, "How much am I spending?" and "What's the return?" If the return isn't the greater part, I get out of it, fold, cut losses and collect outstanding debts, one way or another. I'd do it with this house, or that car, or any business proposition that went sour or sold me short."

"And women?" I prodded him with a touchy jibe. "Do you cut your losses and fold there too?"

His white teeth gleamed in the oceanic afternoon sunshine and he smiled like a boy with cookies on his mind, and asked me "Would you like a gin and tonic and a lawn chair while I shower and change?"

A G&T. My favorite! Sure. Why not. All the while I was thinking, when I was looking at him directly, right into those same brown cow eyes of his mother's, I was thinking, there was something explicitly sexual about him. His lips parted a certain way; they were a kind of vaginal color. He had hair every place which was black and lavishly, pubicly curly. I looked at him and realized I couldn't see him without thinking about having sex. I mused on that phenomena and sipped a big tall gin bubbling in not too much tonic with half a lime squeezed and floating in the ice. It might be nice, I thought, to spend more time at the beach, before leaving town forever.

The restaurant was right on the breezeway in Venice. It was famous for its fresh fish and he was surprised I'd never been there before. "This place is a landmark out here, like Pink's is on Melrose. How could you miss it?"

I explained I'd missed a lot of the scenery while I was beating my way through graduate school and teaching a full course load. With the minimum thousand pages of reading each week combined with several hundred composition papers to grade, there wasn't a lot of time for extracurricular eating. But lately, having given up the academic grind, I was happy to dine out whenever possible.

This was part of his opening, his leveraged buyout of my remaining days in Southern California. He offered to point out every classic L.A. trip, place, restaurant, you name it, and send me off with "The Best of L.A." firmly in mind.

"How 'bout Musso and Frank's?"

I shook my head. "Nope."

"Well, there you have it! How can you leave L.A. before you have lamb chops and creamed spinach at Musso's? It's a Hollywood tradition since 1919!"

And Gem went on like that and made plans for

dinners and drives and expeditions which promised to occupy my every waking hour up until the moment I got in the car and drove away. But I wasn't thinking about *that* moment, just then. Instead, I was drifting off into an eddy of Lotus Eater's rapture. I could see his lips move, but the words began to blur. Finally, I leaned across the table and said, very softly, "You have very nice lips."

For one instant, Gem was surprised, then quick smiled his way into a next move in the same direction. He paid the bill, quite easily, as though he'd been doing it most of his life, and we walked back to where the car was parked, along the beach walk. We wrapped arms around arms and I slipped my hand in his back hip pocket. He slipped his thumb inside the waistband of my skirt. I noticed I wasn't thinking about sex with other people, the way I normally did when making love with someone for the first time. Usually, I have an out of body experience, remembering every lover I've had before. It takes me time to know someone and really be there with just them. This had a different feeling.

We were just touching, barely touching, and I was thinking about sex with him, just him. I liked that he could grab me that way.

We drove slowly, carefully, on small back streets, to the bungalow off Rose Avenue. In low pink lights, we smoked hashish and drank Pernod before we told little tiny stories of ourselves to each other. He told me of standing on the rooftop of his hotel in Beirut, the night the bombs started. There they all were, himself and a few others like him, stuck on a business trip in the middle of someone else's war. They all huddled together on the roof and drank up the best booze in the house, keeping score in an endless game of poker they were playing to keep their minds off the real live bombs going off over their heads.

21

"I kept thinking it was the Fourth of July, but then suddenly I'd wake up in a cold sweat in my hotel room, realizing the sound effects were built to kill. I swore to myself, if I got out of there ok, I'd get back to the States and stay put. I was out of it only long enough to skip the draft anyway. Now, every Fourth of July, I think of night-time in Beirut and I kiss the ground hello instead of my sweet ass good-bye!"

I borrowed his robe and took a shower, washing every private place I had, from between my toes to the back of my neck. When I came out of the bathroom, steam rolled with me into the bedroom, which he had lit like a shrine with votive candles. The covers were pulled back to very fine, oxford blue cotton sheets, which I slid onto, from a puddle of thick, white terry cloth on the floor. I loved the shadows on his walls, the little licking motions of flames which quivered in a beach house breeze.

He sucked, licked, and oiled me for hours it seemed. I wanted to get into his parts but he held me back. "Lie back," he said, "I want to touch you everywhere."

So I let him. I utterly surrendered. He sucked my toes and stroked the bottoms of my feet, massaging the bones and the tissue that was always aching in the curve of my very high arch. He kissed the back of my knees and I thought of the opening of Godard's *Le Mépris*, in which Brigitte Bardot and Michel Piccoli, map out the parts and territory of her body for adoration and objectification. In French, it all sounds so yummy. The very word Mépris, with its accent over the "e", leaps from the back of the mouth like a gasp during a sudden sex act. In English, their sensuous call and response is reduced to a catalogue of parts, but the exchange between Bardot's "Tu les aimes mes genoux

22

aussi?" *You love my knees also?* to Piccoli's "Oui, j'aime beaucoup tes genoux" *Yes, I very much love your knees* came vividly to mind—a touchstone of a kind of lust, as the Gem touched and tucked into me like food he couldn't wait to put on a plate and so tore into with his bare hands.

He'd rolled me over on my stomach and then grabbed each cheek of my ass and squeezed hard, found the bone at the bottom of each and rubbed the spot until I gave way and let each muscle held tight go; at last, let the knot untie and I sighed into a deeper and deeper place of relaxation at the same time I felt a little hotter, a little brighter, a little wetter.

I was ready to have him, right then and there, but he wouldn't give. Instead he continued to torture every erogenous zone I had and a few I didn't know were possible. Deep under my arm, he rubbed and licked and then stuck himself in, and I went wild, while he held me down with the flat of his hand against my pubic bone. My toes curled up and I might have screamed except he took his prick out from my arm pit and put it in my mouth. He held me like that and wouldn't let me move except to suck him. He got wide and full and pulled himself out and held himself and me still for a moment, waiting out the urge to come.

He moved me sidewise and onto my stomach. He drew my ass over the side of the bed, my arms stretched out and holding the other edge. Slowly, very slowly, he slid his hand between my legs and touched my lips lightly, dipping a finger in quickly, stirring the wetness up, until I let down a flow of juice he used to wet his hand and then himself. He lay his chest onto my back and positioned himself for penetration. I wanted it now. It was a widening, then a fullness, and a heat to boil water between those legs, in there, in the recesses of my rosy center. He mixed it up good in *there*. At the same time, he paid attention to the on-switch, the hot clit spot which was already swollen and humming and buzzing with live current. It was the jewels, his red and purple jewels, that kept me at melting temperatures and a good touch, a gem cutter's touch, with fingers that knew where to find my own stashed rubies. When he came he finally pushed me over the edge with a fresh slap on my ass cheek and said "Go! Go!" And I went, loud and clear and pulsing like a strobe. We were done and done in. Completely finished and almost unable to move in any direction. We rolled up and in and then flat out onto the cool, blue sheets, folded into each other's sides and dozed out into the ether.

A MOMENT IN MOAB

Long before leaving Los Angles, I was moving to California, sight unseen, and leaving that same Old-Flame, Old-What's-his-name, who had fractured my heart into uncountable pieces. Yes, I was leaving him behind! But as dumb irony would have it, that same Flame was helping me leave him, by driving with me from New York to the Pacific Coast, where he would be checking into an artist colony to finish his novel and I would be checking into the rental listings to start my new life. We were practicing the end, we were considering our vocabulary for the future. We had 3,000 miles of silence and sex to figure it out. The radio was dead in the maroon Mustang, which was my car at that time and the one we were taking across country. If we didn't talk to each other, there was nothing to listen to but the wind blowing through the windows which were wide open and roaring with furnace heat bouncing off the black-top highway running out like a ticker tape behind us.

We took Route 80 to 71 to 70, all the way to Colorado. The last thing I remember before we hit the memorable magnitude of the Rocky Mountains was the startling, crazy green lushness of western Pennsylvania—unimaginably beautiful following the worn-out dreariness of what came before and then again just after, across Ohio and beyond.

Vague impressions of dirty cities gave way to the amnesia brought on by repetitious flat fields of pale green corn and yellow wheat, cross-hatching the thick midriff of this country. Out of its center, there were long stretches of road so barren, so bleak, that you'd think Dante walked along them, imagining *The Inferno*, imagining a hot asphalt road with nothingness on either side, that went on forever—Hell on the Highway.

Our means of breaking up the monotony was to have relentless car sex. He drove. I sucked. He drove. I lay back while he stuck fingers in and around the hot red pocket between my legs. He drove and drove into the night and through the earliest part of morning before we stopped for coffee and gas and then drove on.

The plateaus which lead up to the Rockies are empty as the road in *Purgatorio*–the higher you go, the slower it goes over the steppes where little grows but survivalist mountain scrub and the twisted bodies of bristle cone pines. Even though it's been a gradual sort of ascent, your first real view of mountain peaks seems sudden, vertiginous. I still think of Redstone, where we went after turning left off 70, out of Glenwood Springs, as being iron-red and frosted with late spring snow. Winding up and winding down the vast solid mass of those mountains is a humbling experience. All the things inside your head which seem bigger-than-life are made as nothing in comparison to the facts which those Rocky Mountains are.

When we got to Ouray, just before the Red Mountain Pass, we stopped in a coffee shop where a Dale Evans lookalike served us plain coffee and the realest piece of red cherry pie I'd ever had, with red skins and tart red juice I couldn't get enough of. I finished it and scraped the plate and was sorry later on that I hadn't ordered up a piece to go.

We drove, drove on, up and up and over Red Mountain Pass and, at something like 11,000 feet, stared longingly out at the spectacle of Redcloud Peak, its big red face staring down at us from mythologically inspired clouds, 3,000 feet above us still, where the shining lights of "Paradiso" glinted in that mountain's icy mirror of the melting sun.

Then suddenly it was Silverton, a real Western town with swinging doors on the local saloon and cowboys with spurs strolling down Main Street. Down and down again we rolled to the town *actually* called Purgatory, past Electra Lake and on to Durango after we tumbled out of the Lemon Reservation.

It had been that kind of a rollercoaster from north to south, but outside of Durango we made a right-hand turn, headed west again, and crossed the border into Utah on Route 666.

I can't remember where we stopped or if we stopped or if we just kept driving the way we had been, like insomniacs escaping reality on the open road. It just seems like one minute we were up there scraping the sky, bathed in one kind of red, and the next minute, we were barreling into the desert, the dead red desert, dusty, clay-red with still-green stubble and listless tumbleweeds marking contours like charcoal pencil.

I gasped. I had never seen anything like it before. We had driven on an alternate route to the only highway out of Monticello, Utah. Part of it was still being paved. Flagmen signaled us off to the side of the road and forgot us. We forgot ourselves and sat and marveled in the colors of this wild, desolate place, this reddest desert I'd never seen before.

Everything about it reminded me of sex—red, hot, flat-out sex with a capital *X*. We parked behind a dense patch of scrub brush which protected us from the unpaved by-way. The sight of the Moab Desert everywhere made me both thirsty and dripping between the legs. Nearby, the sound of giant earth movers, making a road in the midst of this dead wildness, groaned and sputtered on. I couldn't wait any longer. I made him come around to my side of the car, I opened the door and pulled my shorts and panties down. I turned and slid my rump over the side of the seat, so he could come at me from behind. I watched out the window as cars drove by, unaware we were hidden there. The desert stared back.

We dripped great drops of head sweat in the shadow of that red, red rock. We dripped and melted body salts each into each, my shorts twirled round my ankle carelessly, and just when I thought I would pop, he did. We groveled in the red dust and sobbed something guttural, some glad, sad grasping at the truth between us which was broken and could not be fixed. This was the beginning of the end of all that came before.

We pulled ourselves together to drive on and on, through the cooler mauve desert night. The road ahead unfolding its uncertainties, the road behind vanishing in the illusion of the linear, all the while memory ran in circles alongside the car; wherever we were, the past was present, unfurling in a spiral, like a moon shell behind my eyes, while the moon itself followed us everywhere.

THE WAY OF THE COOKIE

After years of observation and plenty of reflection I have developed what I refer to as "The Cookie Theory of Consciousness: The Real Difference Between Men and Women Finally Defined."

It goes like this. Women tend to think about things in the same way that they eat their cookies, known in inner pop-psyche circles as "spiraletic processing." *Videlicet*, a woman pursues an idea as she nibbles the cookie, starting at the outer edge and working her way round and round, crumb by crumb, point by point, in the way of all spirals, covering all random points in the field of the cookie, in a universe of infinite possibilities of and for that cookie, until she gets to the final bite, that one concentrated nugget of wisdom at the heart of it all, which she pops like a piece of melting chocolate, dissolving its final flavors across the galaxy of her taste buds.

Men, on the other hand, like to eat their cookies in chunks. Serialized, well-defined chunks. CRUNCH: The Beginning. CRUNCH: The Middle. CRUNCH: The End. It's simple, it's tidy, it's easy to finish.

This is not to say that some girls don't eat cookies like boys, or that some boys don't run in circles with girls—A and NOT A are both true. Creative people of both sexes have been known to make much of their individual and specific cookies, albeit with boys generally making little guns in one or two bites, and little girls nibbling theirs into careful heart shapes, over time. The point is, human consciousness has these completely separate and opposite directions that it can go in, simultaneously. At the same time it occupies the same space, the same object, the same "energy field" of the cookie—*das Ding an sich*—its consumption

29

is the thumb print of the mind which consumes it.

Some would argue that in either case, the fate of the cookie is sealed in utter annihilation. Others profess that while the cookie–the *reality* of the cookie–is altered, its essence remains unalterable, as in the Shadow of a Cookie in THE Jar on a Shelf in Plato's Cave.

One way or the other, we all take our bites. As a confirmed spiraletic nibbler, I believe I am doing my part for the unification of all disparate points on a flowing continuum. I like to imagine that every time I *think* a thing through, I am in fact getting to the heart of the matter by covering all points surrounding and concentric to its *essence*.

I eat my cookies round and round, making them last and last, until that final long-anticipated bite is done and I wallow in the aftermath of its totality: how no two points are ever *identical*, how it is only the *sum of all points* which coincide in the *single cookie* I am which tells the *whole* of me.

UP IN THE HILLS

Gem-Man was driving me up into the Hollywood Hills, cornering round curves, turning again and again into the incline, winding up and up into their glittering heights. We were taking a back-road route to find the sign that spelled it all out–HOLLYWOOD–in humongous, showbiz-sized letters. He planned to snap nude photos of me in various poses there, mimicking the shape of the letters. He thought it would be fun and I thought it would be funny! Another last-minute memory for the book, another lens on L.A. from afar.

In fact, that first turn onto Laurel Canyon off Sunset left me on the mental curb side, lost in the dusty clouds of remembrance, reminding me of the beginning of that first affair in Los Angeles, after My-Old-Flame left and my life as a student of Rhetorical devices began. *That* affair was a surprise from start to end.

It was complicated, with many moving metonymic parts. Synecdoche, toponyms, littotes-the works! Part for whole and whole for part, we had them all! Compelling, curvaceous metaphors for confusions of time and place as we drove too fast through a limited number of long nights that turned into short days, before vanishing utterly, like a mirage of water in the desert light. As Democritus so aptly put it, "Metonymy–that is the fact that words and meanings change."

She was a woman who dyed her hair red to match the brandied peach and cream of her skin. They went perfectly together, her skin and her hair, which is why I didn't know for quite a while that she actually dyed it. She's probably dyed it several times since then. I wonder if I'd recognize her, if I saw her on the street? Perhaps I would, if I saw her eyes. They were huge, the color of tortoise shell, with flecks of green and gold. I couldn't *stop* looking into them, once I had looked. I wanted to stay right there with her and listen to her stories, incredible stories she told me about her father, her mother, her grandmother, her life which had already been through so many turns of fortune, I lost track of them all.

Yes, she was very intricate and I was drawn to her, to the light which shone out of her eyes when she laughed and filled the room with it.

We met in a graduate seminar in Linguistic Theory and Practice. We spent a lot of time figuring out how to read Chompsky, build sentence diagrams based on his transformational grammar model, and analyze the speech patterns of non-native speakers. We talked down and dirty about Speech Acts and, without a doubt, the most interesting thing about the class was this woman and her eyes, glowing a certain she-noodle light from the depths.

I'm vague on our first meeting outside of class. I think, in fact, she asked me to grab a bite to eat with her, before our "Ling. Grad. Sem. 601." We went to the commissary. She ordered a chopped liver sandwich from which she removed half the bread and then ate half of the half and offered the other half to me.

"Chopped liver," I said, "reminds me of eternal torture."

She laughed and spilled, "It reminds me of my grandmother. She always made me chopped liver sandwiches when I got home from school. Other kids got cookies and milk. Me, I got chopped liver on rye with a little onion."

We giggled like fillies neighing and ran off to class discussing the T+1 Theory of Language Acquisition, drank large coffees, New York style, with two sugars and cream, and smoked lots of cigarettes on the breaks.

Afterwards she invited me up to the place she was staying for a drink.

It was a house way up in the Hollywood Hills, at the top of Laurel Canyon. I drove behind her and she led me up the canyon road, curving and turning, turning and curving, until we ultimately couldn't go anywhere but into the driveway of the house we'd finally arrived at. It wasn't a particularly grand place—a shop-worn, mid-'50s steel and glass affair, an architect's modest idea stuck on top of the mountain, and a temporary place-holder for someone's future mansion. At that moment, it was a rental.

She took me inside and introduced me to her friends who seemed to me very *unlikely* associates for her, based on my twenty-minute intimate conversation over chopped liver.

One was a tall, extra-large guy with hair that was thinning on top but was still long and straggly at the sides. The other was a swarthy, wiry, nervous person in his 30s, with a quiet, angry way about him.

I don't think we ever actually had dinner. I remember a vague cocktail and then the feeling that I really had to go home. I had hundreds of pages to plow through in a single night, my roommate was peeved when I called since she'd already made dinner, and I felt a kind of uneasiness there, as though they were just waiting for me to leave to do something or say something. I never figured it out. It was one of those ongoing questions which never got resolved in our own brief, mysterious relationship.

We never went back to that house, since she moved shortly afterwards into an apartment on Sunset Plaza Drive, up in the hills behind the Boulevard. We used to go to Greenblatt's deli, which was as close as you could get to home-cooked New York Jewish food out there in Hollywood, with roasted kosher chickens and deviled eggs and take-out blintzes to die for. We would get a bunch of stuff from there and then hole up in her apartment for days, enjoying ourselves, each other, and sometimes others.

The first time we made love, I can't even tell you how it happened. I knew that I had something going for her. Every time I saw her at school after that time I followed her home up into the hills, she lit up inside and spilled out her eyes and I could have ripped her clothes off right there in the middle of campus, or, more likely, locked in a stall in the library girls' room. But we didn't do that. We just waited it out, wading gently in, testing the waters, getting used to it, before taking the plunge.

In a gradual peeling away of layers through days of sunbathing, nights of studying, exam prep, and paper grading, interspersed with nights of drinking and talking and smoking long, thin Benson and Hedges, we lay down together. Half the night had already faded away; I remember most vividly the color of an early dawn sky and the sound of birds, as we wrapped she-noodle arms around each other and entwined lengths of aching, noodling legs.

She'd been telling me one of her stories, just before. It was about how she'd been in Greece at a time in her life when everything was up for grabs. Her father had died suddenly, a statistic of bungled doctoring. "It was odd," she told me, "the same statistic took my mother out too, in childbirth."

She flew her father's body back to Israel, where he was buried in the desert he'd come from. "He was born in a Bedouin tent. From there, all the way to Cleveland, Ohio to be a dentist—it was a long way for him!" She said this with a smile and not without some irony.

She had taken him back to Israel because his mother, the grandmother who raised her after her mother's untimely death, lived there now, in a house built by the grandfather she'd never known. She knew that to return him to where he came from was the right thing to do. She stayed on a while longer to comfort and be comforted by her grandmother and then took off, on her inheritance, to see the world.

She'd been in her first year at college when her life unraveled. It took a long time to get back there, finish her degree and move onto this, which was to become a certified teacher of English as a Second Language. She touted this as the ideal profession for a compulsive itinerant such as herself. "Then I can be anywhere in the world and have a job skill that translates into money!" she said, sending up TV ads for correspondence schools.

She was very particular about having a mobile plan of operation. She'd sold the family house in Cleveland and pretty much squandered the money, all the money, including the life insurance, the investments, the works. Now it was up to her to pull something together for the purposes of making a livelihood; it was either that or find money to marry. She'd had the chance at that more than once, but passed it up, holding out for something more like love.

She had been married once, she confided, to a musician. It ended in tears and empty pockets.

"After my father was gone, nothing held me to any one place or another. I drifted, lived in hotels, some of the best, some of the worst, all over the world. I didn't care about the money. I wanted my father back. So I spent myself and everything I had trying to bury the loss."

Black night sky and distant Los Angeles city lights collapsed to diamond points in cobalt. Still, the story went on.

"I was in Greece," she told me, "staying in a small hotel near the beach on Minos. Nearby, there was an exquisite villa owned by a wealthy European woman. She must have been in her late forties. Very stylish, very expensive, perfect face, skinny body. She was a widow of a very wealthy industrialist. She married him when she was twenty and he was fifty-something. He had a massive coronary on the eve of their twentieth wedding anniversary, and left her one of the richest single women in the world, at forty. She had this tremendously deep soul and I thought she was the most interesting person I'd ever met.

"We started talking in the bar in my hotel, where she came for dinner and a round of backgammon with some friends. She invited me over to her villa for dinner one night and of course I went. It was an absolutely beautiful place, with exquisite folk art on the walls, hand-carved furniture, and a garden full of wild roses and red poppies. We had drinks in the garden and then it really got interesting."

Up-in-the-Hills smiled her huge smile and her tortoiseshell eyes gleamed and spilled their lights. "She had this beautiful little dinner made just for the two of us and there was only one other person there, her housekeeper, whom she sent home after the dinner was on the table. We ate stuffed grape leaves and drank retsina and she told me this remarkable story of how she had a friend, a special friend, a girl she'd helped out of a difficult and compromising situation in her own hometown. She'd taken the girl under her wing, sent her to good schools, paid for all her expenses and when the girl came to spend holidays, this woman, Helena, gradually found she had fallen in love with her protege

36

and soon couldn't bear to be without her.

"She took the young woman with her then, every-where that she and her husband traveled. He chalked it up to unfulfilled motherhood. She wasn't able to have children. But she knew better; she knew she was in love with the girl.

"Finally, finally, one night Helena could not contain herself any longer. She went to the girl's room and confessed her feelings and tried to kiss her, just once, on the mouth. The girl was repulsed. She packed her suitcase and left in the night, not to be heard from again."

All this Helena told my friend, who was now telling it to me. She went on, "When she finished her story, I went over to her and put my arms around her and kissed her, intentionally, on the mouth. I wanted to tell her that I would be that girl for her. I was ready and willing and incredibly turned on by her. And just when I thought it was going to happen for me, Helena burst into tears and told me to go, go away and leave her and never come back!

"I tried to make her see that I wanted to be there with her but she insisted. So, I never got to find out what it would be like, to make love with a woman."

And that's how I found out that she was as drawn to me as I had been to her, like a magnet, like a bee buzzing honey out of flowers, like She-noodles finding each other out.

She had beautiful hands with long beautiful fingers and peach pink toes to match. I kissed each finger and sucked her thumb. She had a big expressive mouth fixed in an elated smile and breasts with rosy toast-colored aureoles the size of silver dollars with large cinnamon nubs for nipples. They were lickable and pinchable. Mine were smaller and a paler pink with little inverted nipples. They were hard to fetch out of their hiding place, but once they were found out, they sent a tingling feeling that went down my spine and straight between my legs. She licked me like a kitten licks a paw, and shiny wetness poured out of me. She climbed me and rocked back and forth, back and forth, rubbing pubic bone to pubic bone, clit to clit. We gasped and juiced on each other and came first one and then the other in shakes and heaves, within arms' and breasts' reach of each other. I slid my thumb inside of her; she slid the same in me.

We were softly rounded, drowsy noodles then, heaped upon the pillows of her bed. As we drifted off at dawn, she sighed and laughed a low rolling ripple, as though the punch line of some long-forgotten joke had just come to her.

The morning came as it always does and makes us look at ourselves, each other, the room, the company, and consider the effect of waking up together.

The best is when you wake up laughing. The worst? The worst is when you don't know how you got there or who this person is or what you've said or what you've done to whom. I won't own up to *that* bad of a morning, but I've been close, *very* close, to the edge. And the times I've been closest to *over* the edge were all mostly with Up-in-the-Hills. I wanted to go there, way out, on, and over, all the time with her and did, as often as I could, in the brief time we had. Always to the edge and back, back to a thin margin of safety.

We got up and went out for breakfast, down to the restaurant at the Tropicana Motel. It was an authentic California motel kitsch coffee shop, with fantastic French toast—huge deep fried slices covered with fresh fruit and a spritz of powdered sugar. We were sleepy-eyed but wired the way lovers are on first discovery, high on each other and laughing out loud. We were trying to figure out what it was going to be with each other but neither one of us was willing to put out a list of rules and regulations, parameters, expectations—nothing outside the immediate moment was mentioned. We just took it for ourselves—a day, a night, a morning to be exclusive with each other in the present.

Besides, she already knew that half my heart belonged to some man back East. I told her that somewhere earlier on. I always did, back then, put a road block between myself and anyone not *him.*

I could be 3,000 miles away from the guy and still feel as though he were in the next room. It was kind of a problem with me. Unable to sever the relationship, I lived with it by telephone, by mail, by mental telepathy, and by a variety of obsessive behaviors.

She knew that about me and it seemed to be all right with her. Or maybe, as so often is the case at the *beginning* of things, she didn't know what she really felt about it, or what she was *going* to feel about it, later, the deeper we went with each other. It's the natural path of infatuation to transform all flaws into charming idiosyncrasies and interesting contrasts to our own peccadilloes. It's later, when infatuation wears thin and expectations are tired of being disappointed that some is not enough and *more* is not enough, and finally enough is *enough—*and it's over.

No, lost in laughter and something like love over enormous strawberries, we weren't wondering about the end, the rules, the limits. The sun was shining California gold, and two shiny She-noodles were making yum-yum noises all through breakfast.

A BARRAGE OF BREASTS

I don't think women feel the same about breasts as men do. And they certainly don't feel about their breasts the way that men feel about their penises. Women may want their breasts to be a certain way—bigger, smaller, fuller, firmer, whatever—but I doubt there is a common consensus of what that way ought to be, nor is there a single hot button which touches off anxiety in how they ought to be, except in the valley of the shadow of breast cancer, in which case most would choose to have them over losing them, but if it came to that, would prefer to lose them and live rather than keep them and die.

For men, I believe, it is quite a bit different. It does seem to be the size of the thing which has them all worked up and worried. Most heterosexual men, I have been told by reliable sources, have never seen an erect penis in the flesh, so to speak, other than their own. So there is a kind of mystique as to what size might be the standard. The sensitive point in question boils down to this: is it big enough? Conversely, how many men who are actually fixed with really big schlongs hang out in front of the mirror and think, "Gee, maybe I should get a penis reduction?"

Women who have big breasts which are out of proportion to the rest of their bodies do think about breast reduction. One friend of mine who at 13 had a size 38D chest confided that if she got as big as her sister (a size 45EE) she would absolutely have hers reduced. "You can't believe what a pain it is," she said. "You can't sleep on your stomach, all your clothes have to be custom fitted, it's really hard to climb trees, and really, really revolting to walk down the street in New York City."

Both she and her sister rode American Saddle-

41

bred horses, known in the horse trade vernacular as "Shaky Tails." Whenever they showed their horses in Madison Square Garden, crowds gathered to gawk when the ringmaster called out to the Five-gaited classes, "Rack on!" and those blond beauties with the huge hooters scooted their racy Shaky Tails at high speeds around the ring. In the end, I think they both got theirs fixed.

"Hooters." There's one of those words which women mostly don't use to describe their breasts. It comes, presumably, from the sounds emitted by male voyeurs upon glimpsing a pair of "really big ones." I guess they hoot, instead of grabbing their crotches in public like the guys in hard hats tearing up the streets of New York. I'm not sure which I prefer less.

"Tits," on the other hand, is a word we all use. "Great tits!" is an expression I remember hearing from both sides of the gender gap throughout both my pregnancies and nursing cycles. Sure, I breast-fed! I figured, with boobs like mine, they were going to go south regardless, so I might as well use them for what they were built for—the nurturing of another human being.

That seemed to me like a good enough reason to swear off vanity and media hype. And, of course, it felt absolutely divine. Though not at first. At first it was kind of like torture. A hungry little animal tears at your breast with a sucking pressure that can pull a blister in a matter of moments. Then you go through hell every time you nurse, for the next week or so, while the nipple is cracked and chapped, repairs itself, and then toughens. After that, it's kind of like heaven. It certainly is true love.

That's why it's not as hard as I thought it might be to let go of my own personal stereotypes with regard to my own personal breasts. When I was *fifteen, they were one sort of breast. I know that. They had a different purpose back then. Then they were the hummingbird's red syrup flowers. They were fashioned to draw those birds with their big, long, pecker-beaks down into the red folds of the flowery vulva where the seed is planted to grow human beans—because that's what they are, little beans that sprout into beings in a blush of one- plus- one worth of sparks.*

Now that I am older, my breasts are something else again. They are smaller than they used to be, shrunken a bit from their milk-producing career. Also, one of them has a scar where a lump was removed. I'm not the least bit sorry the scar is there. It gave me back my life. It is its own kind of war wound and I feel it like my personal little red badge of courage. Others have not been as fortunate.

From here on out, I'll celebrate having them by using them to their fullest extent. I'll ask my lover to pinch them and tweak them and lick them and gently nibble their nippleness while I sigh with utmost pleasure. Because I want to use them as much as possible while they're here to use. I don't want to go to my grave or face mastectomy feeling, "Why me? They've barely been touched!"

I want to use them and use them and use them, so that if I should turn out to be that one in whatever number of women to lose, in order to live, I'll know they were done and done well.

So, to get back to my original point, I really don't think that women feel the same about breasts as men do.

When you take a close look at how men speak about them among themselves, call them privately in their own minds, or describe them in print, you start to get the picture of just how fixated their thinking is.

"Cantaloupe-cantilevered," "cupcake breasts," and then just plain old "jugs," all sustain an underlying food and nourishment connection, although, in the case of "cupcakes," I always think of frivolous, hugely-frosted affairs, with the classic cherry on top, cementing a desirous dessert affiliation.

As for those "pointy perky breasts," "bodaciously bosomed" ones, and the "nicely rounded" sets—they're all about personalities—being the Cheerleader, the Nightclub Singer, and the Campus Coed, respectively. "Marble mounds" are awfully romantic, while the "lushly curved" are pure lust in a flowered sarong. "Formidable, conical breasts" are severe, dressed in black, a little dangerous, promising a possible tattoo. What about "bazongas?" Well now, "bazongas" will never let you down. If you capsized at sea, you could float to shore with them, wrapped around your neck.

"Balconies" are for admiring from afar and "bubbies" are your best friends. "Chichis" are a sweet drink that knocks you on your ass. "Headlights" are for those lost in the dark. "Chestnuts" are for roasting, "lollos" for licking, "muffins" for munching with butter; "marshmallows" melt when heat is applied and a good old-fashioned "bust" just wants its bodice ripped and ravished because otherwise, the silly "ninnies" will just make a fool of you. But don't be sad because the "flip-flaps" are bound to cheer you up. "Maracas" and "kettle-drums" will let the beat go on, until you're so absolutely exhausted, you just have to put your head down on the "baby pillows," have a nice "feeding bottle," cuddle up with your "nubbies," and go to sleep.

The Breast. She's a beaut, is she not? Be glad. Squeeze hard. Sleep well. Goodnight.

THE OCCASIONAL VSOP

I love cognac. I order it in good restaurants and late-night bars and dream of snifters I have cherished and the kisses that went with them. Oh yes, I think of boys, young men in their twenties around whose waists I wrapped a slender She-noodle tendril and drew them to me, into my cloud of French cigarettes, strong black coffee, and good cognac in a thin-lipped, well-warmed glass.

It was VSOP and I bought it for myself and those certain He-noodles I fancied. I picked out the boy and purchased the bottle and brought them both home with me to my bungalow in Silver Lake, or the fourth-floor walk-up in Manhattan, or any place, really, where I found them and it and me together in the same moment. I drew them into the boudoir in my mind and I had my way with them, those steamy He-noodles of yore. Some were Yum-Yum boys, others were not. They were all VSOP to me.

One who was a bit older than a callow youth threw the gauntlet at my feet in the graduate English department where we jockeyed for position against each other. We savaged each other's remarks in classes we shared; we had terrible public arguments about ideas of critical theory, rhetorical posturing, and what constituted literary merit in a post-modern era, as though it mattered, *really* mattered, in the larger schemata of Things in the World. Everyone thought we hated each other's guts.

The fact was, I asked him very early in the quarter to join me with a bottle of cognac and see what might happen. He took me up on it, betraying the girlfriend who had moved across the country and into his same apartment building in order to be near him. He lived two floors above her, and somehow managed to slip me and others in and

45

out of his bed and shower, between his sheets and reading assignments.

Whenever I went to his place, there was always the danger that his girlfriend might show up unexpectedly at the door. That sometimes bothered me but mostly it gave us an edge, a sexy, dangerous edge to work against, while we pulled back the layers of our animal natures and scratched at the lust itching between us.

He would always go down to her apartment, early in the evening, to ward off a nighttime visit. I would take a shower, while I waited. It had tremendous water pressure and a good pulsing shower massage head. I opened my lips to it, planted my feet firmly on the shower floor, and waited to feel the hot rolling wave of something electrical exploding off my pudenda, and just before I reached that ecstasy, I stopped myself, and dried off, pausing only to slide a finger in, to feel the ripening wetness.

I lay in his bed, with the light down to a candle and my cognac resting in a cup of hot water, its perfume opening the nasal passages. When he came in, he took a fast shower and hurried to bed and I hurried to make his yard arm hard and ready to poke my pink and wet spot. He was sweet and clean and I sucked him in the dark under the covers. He had a good figure, about which he was a little too vain, but I didn't really care. In fact, I enjoyed fanning the flames of his ego, because it seemed to make him a more enduring lover.

He smelled of soap, a simple men's soap. His ginger-colored hair was not too distant from my own Botticelli batch. Our pubic regions melded coppery-ginger to red-gold, in a harmony of matching parts. In many respects, ours was a surrogate sister-brother affair. We were happy to sleep secretly with each other, whenever possible. We did it whenever we could and never blamed one another for the times in between with others. We liked to have long, hot bouts of sex between heated arguments which pitted Postmodern Deconstruction against the straw dogs of an aging New Criticism.

I loved it when he just put it in me and stroked and stroked away at my G-spot, a hour or more, until I came by the spontaneous combustion caused by the friction of moving parts. Nobody can quite believe it when it happens like that and I was certainly astounded when we flew off into carnal ecstasy that very first time with no other stimulation than the thrust and pull of a Ginger He-noodle working it off inside me.

I was working it off too—the many circumlocutions of mind over body, Aristotle on lists and Ezra Pound on poetics, Joyce rolling through Dublin reinventing the novel with Ulysses in mind, and Noam Chomsky who just had to explode syntax beyond recognition for our own good and mystification. It was all very-very and we both needed that occasional VSOP in a siege of good sex to forget about the smog and the freeways, the haves and the have-nots, the dreamers and their dreams. We felt we could survive it and win, survive it, rise above the noise and the fray, and revel in it, besides.

Yeah, it was good steamy noodles and hot cognac which cured anything, up to and including the last day before it just, finally, didn't.

MY DINNER AT MUSSO'S

We were hooked on each other after that first night of transcendent sex, Gem-Man and I. We had a long breakfast at The Rose Café, the neighbourhood spot, and then I drove dreamily back to Silver Lake to pick up a tooth brush and my dog and some clean underwear. I didn't need much. I'd already borrowed a pair of running shorts and a candy plaid man-tailored Polo shirt from him. I know it was a big move to make overnight, moving into his clothes like that, but we were working on deadline. I was planning to leave town the first of July and arrive in Seattle by the Fourth. Considering it was the third of June, I had little time to spare.

I didn't care. I was on a whirlwind tour of Los Angeles landmarks. We went to the Griffith Park Observatory and saw the show and then went to Musso and Frank's Grill for dinner. I wore my white, three-piece suit with no blouse on. Just a black lace bra under the vest, under the wide-lapeled, '70s jacket. Nothing else but a strand of tiny cultured pearls around the neck. He ordered me the current fad aperitif, a Kir–white wine with a splash of cassis mixed with mineral water, because I still couldn't stomach scotch. He was having a giant tumbler of Chivas over lots of ice, the way they make them at Musso's. We watched the waiters in their matching cutaway jackets move quickly and elegantly with trays of steaks and veal cutlets with roasted potatoes or cottage fries. There was the feeling that a lot of old Hollywood was eating dinner there that night, or maybe just their ghosts.

Gem-Man assured me it was that way every night. We got one of the leather banquette booths in the back room and sat next to each other, looking out at the dinner crowd. He was showing me

49

off and I didn't care. I too played it as it lay.

Across from us sat a couple of young hand-tailored suits with hip haircuts and gold Rolexes peeping out from under French cuffs. One of them caught my eye and I guess I caught his as well. Through the Caesar salad followed by the medium rare lamb chops and creamed spinach, Gem watched me being watched and watching someone else. Between courses, he slipped a hand between my thighs, stroking my crack.

By dessert, I had to pee, badly. As I shuffled my bottom to the end of the banquette, I was aware of the one suit, the one with the red beard and the prep school hair, watch my breasts closely, to see if they moved or showed their shape. I stood up slowly, without looking at anyone. I carefully slid off my white jacket and folded it, sleeves together and then in half, to avoid creases. I bent slightly at the waist, my ass towards the suits, my breasts beneath the vest, cleavage cupped into black lace rolling towards Gem-Man.

I walked, looking straight ahead, to the ladies' room.

When I got back, I was careful to turn the other way and bend slightly towards the suits this time. I knew they couldn't see much, just the cleavage line and maybe a hint of the black lace arm straps. I picked up my jacket and slipped it over my shoulders, with my arms folded across my chest. I used them, along with the jacket sliding off or down a single shoulder, in an erotic ballet of bare arms, nude shoulders, and naked hands.

I had the house specialty for dessert–Diplomat Pudding topped with fresh strawberry sauce. I ate it like it was sex, licking the spoon and pursing my lips around the berries. I knew they were watching and I ran my tongue around my lips at the end of each bite, just right, like we saw it done in sexy close-ups in Playboy and Penthouse. All the while, Gem was stroking my thigh with his black eyes glowing in the dining room dimness.

When it was time to get up and go, I stood up and was prepared to leave quickly and pseudo-demurely with my jacket slung over one shoulder, but he stopped me.

"Here," he said, grabbing my bare forearm in his hirsute hands, squeezing it, a bit hard, a cuff on my wrist, "let me help you on with your jacket."

He stood me square in front of the suits and he slipped it on me and squeezed my shoulders, possessively, while he let them have a good look at me. I was wet between the legs and looking straight ahead.

We drove up into the hills after dinner. I made him go by the apartment on Sunset Plaza Drive where *she* used to live. She was gone now, without a trace, and no one knew where to. I didn't tell him much about her, only that she was a woman he would have liked and I would have liked to introduce them.

I let him think about that and was silent and we drove on and up further and further, until there was only the dirt road at the end of Mulholland where we parked and looked out over the Valley. The lights were brighter than Christmas and made the stars in the sky look skimpy by comparison.

Without touching me, he said, "Get in the back seat. Take your pants off. Leave your panties on."

I did it. I took my white pants off and rolled them up, to put under my neck. I wore just the white vest now, and a pair of black silk panties which were more like a G-string. I learned from experience that black underwear is what you wear under white pants, if you don't want them to show. I know it's counterintuitive, but it works. I picked the G-string pair out because I knew he'd like them.

He got out of the front seat and came around to open the back-seat door where my knees were bent and waiting. I heard him unzip his fly. He got in and pulled the door behind him. He handled himself while he handled me, pulling on the panties, pulling them between my slit and wrapping my pubic hair around his finger and pulling it, He was teasing me, the way he'd been doing all night under the table at Musso's. He opened my legs, pushed one leg to the floor, and positioned himself to enter me. He pushed in, around the black silk which he continued to pull on and use to work at my clitoris. When he knew I was coming, he let himself go and there on the wide back seat of Gem's yellow Mercedes, we had an orgasm which would have jumpstarted anyone's dead battery, if a person just knew where to put the cables.

PENIS PASTICHE

Because we were secret lovers and no topic was taboo, I asked my friend, the Ginger-Noodle, if he thought a good many men felt themselves judged on the basis of their penises. He said most, if not all. I had to ask him this question because I had never really considered the issue from that standpoint— the male angle on how they might be perceived, vis- à-vis their organs. I could always tell that it was important to them, though, both as an object of self-satisfaction as well as a subject fraught with apprehension.

You can judge its status in their world view by its lexiconic redundancy, e.g. the sheer number of different names it's called, from "Aaron's Rod" to "Zubrick." Though not commonly heard in recent parlance, "Yard" was the word of choice for several hundred years, starting in about 1400 A.D. and falling into obscurity by the mid-1800s. That old and long association gives a whole new meaning to "marking territory in yards" with perhaps "yard arms" giving rise to the military appellation "short arms," and what does this do to our mental picture of "Scotland Yard" on the one hand, and the "arms race" on the other?

As for Bushwacker, Bum-tickler, Giggle-Stick, and Jigger, Toggle Switch, and Trigger, I can't answer for them. They're all out there somewhere, crashing around in fast cars down mean streets and even further out there, alone in a home on the range.

Meanwhile, the One-eyed Milk Man is an old friend of the family who, along with Old Hornington, Tug Mutton, and Uncle Nudinnudo, all take lunch once a week in a French café where there is always an accordion playing.

Each in his own way was the Top Dog in the

bun. There's no sense in having regrets over the likes of Plugtail, or Plowshare, Johnnie, or Jacques. And Old King Priapus, let's face it—there was a Schmuck! So, whether it's a Nine-inch Knocker, a Sausage or a Nippy, a Pestle or a Peter, a Pup or a Putz, or whatever you want to call that thing, there are other things a woman thinks of which have nothing to do with what might look like It to the male member in question.

She might be thinking of shopping for dinner or folding the laundry or counting backwards from one hundred. She might be just beginning to sense the sunrise on her feet and the cold between her toes start to leak away. She might be feeling something in- and something outside of herself at the same time that she's feeling you and it and him and herself again. She might feel an utter blank, a white piece of paper, something to scribble on and on, and fill with color.

She might be escaping into a dream of tropical nights and the exposed flesh of someone else's body; she might be having an actual out-of-body experience; she might be starting to come and feeling ripple after ripple of something hot and freeing, something salt and breathing, radiating and heating front and back, side to side while humming a sweet high song like little first birds or last whippoorwills.

These might be the thoughts she was having, which undoubtedly would have drowned out the din of any noisy obsession some might suspect of her, while contemplating the Man Root's Pondsniping Quim-wedge.

FOREIGN SECRETS

I was sitting in traffic on the 10. I had an appointment for the Little Green Car at Imported Auto of Santa Monica, and then another mad cap adventure planned with my final fling in L.A. We were going to ride the Ferris wheel at the Pier and then eat sand dabs and hand cut potato chips. A car crash up ahead brought everything to a halt just past Robertson. I clicked on the radio and tried to dial something in, but got the static that comes between frequencies until, BLAM—there it was, loud and clear—horns, bass guitar riffs galore, chirpy flute, shakers, dumb drums, "Do it! Do it! Do it! Ooooooooooo—Do the hustle!" The Hustle! And it all came back in a flash of line dancing and spinning disco balls...balls...balls...

Up-in-the-Hills invited me over to meet some friends of hers. Well actually, one was a friend of hers and the other was a friend of *his* who spoke very little English. They were from Israel. The one she did know was in fact an old boyfriend of hers from the time she lived there with her Grandmother. He had been very high in the Diplomatic Corps there, but now he was doing something else, something, it was subtly suggested, having to do with the Secret Service. His friend was either his body guard, or really just a friend. He was supposedly involved in the manufacture of prosthetic limbs. Later in the night, when we lay down together after they'd gone, Hills was quite hilarious as she attempted to re-enact his description of the fake hand he manufactured – how it went *fleep fleep* instead of *flap flap*.

To me, he just smiled and flashed his white teeth across the table of the nightclub we went to and said "*I hlove hAmerica. I hlove dhis about dhit! Dhe moosic, dhe hlights, dhese tchiney dhings*" and he pointed to the sequins on the hand-embroidered tank top Hills was wearing.

It was The Rainbow on Sunset where we went and drank and danced the Hustle that night. She was set on giving me to her old friend and giving him to me. We knew the whole night, in fact, that eventually they would leave and we would have each other. It was a conspiracy of She-noodles, as sometimes is the case.

We started at her place, with a few drinks. Since the last time I'd visited there, she'd specifically bought a bottle of Jack Daniels, which was what I was drinking back then. The lights in her apartment were low and candles were lit. We danced there first. I could see that her friend, Foreign-Secrets, was a formalist, with a very specific idea of how the dance should go, not the sort of free form, fake-the-moves style I was used to. I didn't care too much about it, but we worked on our steps anyway—one, two, three, dip, one two three, turn... *The Hustle* whispering in the background with the beat that put a spin back on the spin!

By the time we actually got to the club, I think we were quite high. The men kept buying us drinks, because I think that's what they thought we expected them to do. And I suppose we did. I remember us dancing in a line, Hills, Foreign-Secrets, Mr. Prosthesis, and me. I kept thinking about Ingmar Bergman's *The Seventh Seal* and those figures, in weird silhouette, lurching across the hillside, dragging one another along to the end of the world. But here, it was just Hollywood and foreign men with very white teeth and bronzed skin. Secrets had almost honey-colored hair, which was in tight circular curls all over his head which made me think perhaps he'd had a permanent and a rinse besides. There was something in the way he danced with me; his mind made up, about how he was going to have me. Hills smiled and laughed and spilled lights out her eyes across the dance floor at me. We knew the real story and we weren't telling.

Later, back at her place, we split into couples and he led me into our She-noodle lair, while Hills went into her guest room with the man of a certain expertise, he of the fleeps over the flaps. We were apart from each other, then, and behind closed doors.

Foreign-Secrets was quite strict in what he wanted from me. He lay back on the bed, stretching his tight athletic body out, beckoning. We were naked and I don't know how we got our clothes off. Perhaps we just took them off. Unashamedly, just ready to have it from each other. His body was gold all over, as though he lay nude in the sun regularly. His cock was long and thick and standing straight up at me. Of course, he wanted me to suck him, which I did, as he did me, so that by the time he got it in me, I was wet and sweet like an open mango. I landed on top of him and we became exotic cats dancing.

Meanwhile, in the next room, the Hills was getting a prosthetic demonstration and, presumably, fucked by same.

And then suddenly, like a clock struck midnight—Cinderella-like—but at 3:00 a.m. instead, it was time for them to leave. They got up, put on their designer label disco pants, and were out the door. Secrets was driving a very expensive, leased car—a two-seater, white Lamborghini Miura with doors that opened up like angel wings. As they got in, the vehicle looked like some crazy combo of toreador macho and Jetson lingerie seductively hugging the curb under the pink vapor lamps— an over-the-top set decoration. When the guy with all his foreign secrets intact turned the key and

the engine went vroom-vroom, like a cartoon, we
She-noodles waved our tendrils in fond farewells,
left finally—gladly—to each other. She laughed and
I laughed and we took a shower together, washed
each other's necks and hard to reach back places,
and used the shower massage creatively. I wonder
if the apartment next door heard us, up so late and
laughing uproariously in the pulsing water?

Dry, we went out into the big studio living room
which faced the East and the rising sun, and we lay
down on the extra mattress which was her couch. It
was covered with mink coats and giant pillows with
Middle Eastern fabrics on them. The minks, she
explained, were the last of her inheritance. She'd
gotten everyone's mink coat and she could neither
bear to wear them nor part with them—her grandmother's coat, her great aunt's coat, and the one
her father gave her mother when they were first
married. We lay down naked on those furs and gave
each other deep massages. She said to me, "Your
back is the color of cinnamon toast—light brown
with cinnamon speckles. It reminds me of garnets."

"Garnets? "

"My mother's garnet necklace. It was very beautiful. Hand cut, in an antique gold setting. They'd
been in the family for—well nobody knows how
long—*centuries*. My grandmother was saving them
for me. She wouldn't give them to me after I brought
my father home to be buried. I begged her for them
but she wouldn't let me have them. She was sure
I would lose them, and of course she was saving
them for my dowry. *'I'll gif dem to you on your ved-
ding day,'* she said, squeezing my cheek between
two crooked knuckles.

"Then, when I *did* get married and married a *goy*
from Greenwich instead of her hand-picked rebbish
boy, well, then she thought she'd better keep hold

58

of the necklace a little longer, hoping I suppose, that her dream-come-true version of my life could happen still, if this one fell apart as she predicted it would.

"Of course, it *did* fall apart. He was a musician who couldn't make a living and I was back in school to finish my B.A. I was writing a lot of poetry. It was pretty much all I wanted to do, so I took an independent study in the alternative program and wrote my way to a degree. We were living marginally on my inheritance, which was rapidly dwindling. And probably if she had given me the necklace, it ultimately would have been hocked, since that's what my husband specialized in, for raising cash between gigs. But really the clincher happened after I finally realized we had to call it a day and I got to where I could build up enough confidence to walk out the door on my own and mean it: *nobody's* girl!"

All this time, she had been rubbing my back, my legs, my arms, my hands, my fingers, every square inch of knot was ironed out and laid to rest, down to the tips of my toes.

"So I finally did. It was a Sunday morning after a late Saturday night. I'd packed the essentials while he was playing a gig and I locked myself in the guest room. He made a big ruckus, dead drunk as usual at 4 a.m. He banged on my door and I told him to just go to bed. I would see him later, after he'd slept it off. He recognized that kind of talk. We'd had other nights like this.

"In the morning, I got up and made a pot of coffee and drank half of it before I went in the room. He was *such* a slob. Cigarette butts in old spilled Coke cans; banana peels under the bed, I mean, the *pits* (which is one of the reasons I moved into the guest room)! It was *my* study anyway. It was my one bar held against chaos. He stayed out of my room and I stayed out of his way, with his practice and his friends and his friend's friends and girlfriends and, you know, the whole crowd that tags along with "the band." But when I went in and sat him up and told him I was leaving him, that day, and I'd be back in three days with some guys and a moving van to get the rest of my stuff, he went wild. He started shouting at me about how worthless and pathetic I was and how, (and this was the worst) my poetry was trite."

"It killed me. I folded in two. I cried. He knew he'd hit a nerve and went in for the kill. He said, 'Yeah, It's a joke. We all read it out loud when you're not around and laugh over it.' And then he began quoting lines to me that had stuck in his head. And I realized that it was true. It all sounded like Hallmark greeting cards, it sounded like romantic drivel, only worse, in la-dee-da rhymes. He destroyed it for me. He destroyed me. I hated him. And that was good because I didn't waver. I picked up my bag and left. I went back to Cleveland and took over my Dad's house which had been rented out all that time I was living in Israel and moldering in Yellow Springs."

"So," I wanted to know, "what happened to the garnets?"

"aah. hmmmmm." she hummed, "that's another story."

It was already past dawn. We had to sleep. The sun rolled in through the window in a howl of orange and yellow. We closed ourselves into a circle of sun and slept, a girlish heap of naked noodles wrapped in musky minks.

FAKING IT

It may be that men have it over women with their equipage to pee in the woods, but women have it made in the area of face-saving in the sex pen.

No matter how well-intentioned, or vividly painted, or even front-loaded with sales market appeal a guy's pitch for himself and his sexual prowess may be, if he can't deliver as promised, there is no way, unless he's fantastically creative, that he can fake an orgasm he never had.

Women, on the other hand, have it within their power to make any man feel like a sex god, like Elvis, only better. It's all in the flexing of the muscles, or in the palm of her hand, or the tips of her fingers. But chiefly it's in the muscles in the pelvic floor. These are the muscles which flex when she holds or releases her pee stream. These are the ones which if you keep them in good shape, will keep your sex life in good shape for the long haul.

All you have to do to keep them strong is flex them, which you can do any time, any place. No one knows when you're doing it, so it's very useful for times when you're tied up in grocery check-out lines or stuck in rush-hour traffic. You can flex your pelvic wall and know that you're doing something good for yourself and someone you love or might love someday.

These are the muscles which help a woman get over, even if she's not getting off. And she might not be getting off for a variety of reasons: too much to drink, not enough to drink, sad thoughts of some ex-lover she's trying to kick, or maybe the guy is there for the first time and he hasn't found her magic places yet. Or maybe he just doesn't know where, let alone how, to look!

Whatever it is, she can choose to let him think

she came anyway. She can choose to protect the inner secrets and utmost privacy of her sexuality until she decides to reveal herself in that way. It's one good method for preserving that power of herself, the fervid sexual power of her most private self. Women are just lucky that way—they can do that, if they choose to.

Guys cannot. If they had too much to drink, or cocaine cut with Novocain, or a numb heart, and can no longer feel their own cock, never mind letting someone else feel it, they are stuck.

Though some to whom this may happen may be quick to make a mountain out of a molehill and develop a whole impotence complex around an incident or two, wiser guys have a backup plan in place ahead of time.

The backup plan might include a variety of techniques and/or tools which most certainly will draw attention away from a half mast flag pole and may in fact have the positive result of stirring the woman up into a frenzy which she might not have gotten to on the standard plan.

For instance, prolonged licking and fingering of the clitoris and simultaneous massage of the G-spot with fingers or vibrator will get anyone's attention. Some heterosexual men have the misconception that only single, lonely woman and lesbians use dildos and vibrators.

In fact, many a married woman would be delightfully surprised to receive a birthday present or a Valentine in the shape of a sex toy of some sort. Receipt of such might inspire her to dig down to the bottom of her underwear drawer and pull out some black lace thing, or silk and shiny other, to whet the appetite of the bedfellow of however many years. And when she's wet, whether wife or first-time lover, and starts clawing at the covers and groaning in that low girl-dog way, the guy who can't fake it suddenly finds he doesn't have to, while that wild woman let loose in the bed forgets why she started faking it in the first place!

LIBERTARIAN LUST

It seems crazy that I could have been in L.A. for going on four years without seeing the La Brea Tar Pits. All I can say is, when I saw it I felt inexplicably sad watching the slow black goo burp bubbles from the depths, seeing how this whole silly city was built on the bones and ghosts of the past—all varieties of the past—pre-historic to pre-pavement to pre-tract homes to pre-postmodern architectural wonders. As Joni Mitchell sang: "Everything comes and goes/Marked by lovers and styles of clothes/Things that you held high/And told yourself were true/Lost or changing as the days come down to you..."

It *was* coming down to me, and I knew it. After the Pits, Gem-Man took me to Canter's on Fairfax for hot pastrami, L.A. style. I got lost in uffish thought somewhere between the coleslaw and steamy meat on rye with Russian on the side. In a booth just short of the waiter's station, I thought I saw a pale, bald pate I'd seen before, ghostlike, floating just over the top of the banquet booth. I didn't want to be caught looking hard at another man in public by the one I was with, so I stared at my plate instead, remembering where I last saw that shining crown.

I'd gone to a party in the Wilshire District with my favorite Ginger-flavored He-noodle. It was a huge brawling affair—the end of the semester before summer break.

People were tending to drink quite a bit and the music got louder and louder as the night wore on. There was a crowd in the next room trying to get the underpants off the big blonde from Hawaii. In the kitchen, a Jesuit apostate was teaching a small crowd to hang tea-spoons from their noses. In dark corners, all over the house, people were coming on to each other, or trashing someone's thesis, or talking tenure track to nowhere.

Although the Ginger-He and I arrived together in his or my car, we always made it a point to stagger our entrances, to appear to *not* be together. Some of it had to do with his old girlfriend but most of it was that we just preferred the edge of a secret affair. I loved the feeling of moving behind the scenes, adjusting props and tilting mirrors just so, planning perfect sleight-of-hand tricks—*now you see him and now you don't, there she is and there she isn't*. And I must have been in one of those moods that night.

The host's wife was named Dragon and she spoke very little English. She was from Taiwan. She was fantastically exotic, and I wondered how it was that the nerd in the white shirt and tie had married her. He was so entirely conventional it was hard to believe he would make such a distinctive choice in a bride. She had prepared wonderful party food and a horde of hungry graduate students were consuming everything in sight. I drank glasses of white wine and kept moving restlessly through the crowd. I stopped only when I thought something might surprise me or make me laugh.

I had a conversation with a woman who had recently dyed her hair red. I told her I was developing a theory about redheadedness. Being one myself, I thought it was important to have a position on the state of the gene pool. I asked her, "Do you want to be the only redhead in the room or do you naturally seek out other redheads?"

She was Australian, and had that great wide sound to her vowels which made you listen closely to everything she said. "Well, I do like to be the only redhead in the room, but I do naturally seek out other redheads, which I suppose is why I went red in the first place."

I had been maintaining that people who dyed their hair red wanted to be the only red in any given room, while natural reds were always glad to find others like themselves and naturally gravitated towards each other through the rarefied magnetism of primal recessive genes.

She proposed something quite different, a sort of teleology for redheaded adaptation of the human species whereby everyone becomes red-headed, at one time or another, in order to understand the nature of red-headedness and empathize with the condition inherent in expressing a deeply recessive gene. We agreed that if all of humanity made up the whole of the possible human corpus, then redheads comprised the nervous system for that oversized physical manifestation. People became redheaded as an outward symptom of an inner tuning of their nervous energies into the network of redheaded synergy. It resonated with some far-fetched truth, but would it hold up under facetious cross examination? I didn't hang around to find out. I pushed on and worked the crowd.

Sometime after that, I recall seeing the Libertarian for the first time. He was a thin, wiry, blond-going-bald guy, almost albino, with mean, thin lips and very little laughter in his eyes. He didn't smile. He just looked around seriously and blinked, as though he were continuously sizing the situation up. I have no idea what I saw in him. It kind of makes me want to throw up that I actually fucked him, thinking back on it now. But it had to do with some research I was doing into the essential qualities of Bad Men and the nature of their corruption. There was a point at which I believed that you could transform someone merely by the act of sleeping with them, earnestly and with fervor. In this way, I was waging a personal war against those I felt certain were perpetrators of high crimes and misdemeanors.

It was my Roaring '20s, and I was still trying everything I could think of to change the world for the better. And I think there were a lot of us who thought we already had. We stopped a war. We ended the draft. We noticed the rivers were dying and the air was dirty, so we tried to fix it. These were the things we were thinking about and becoming somewhat under the influence of. We hadn't figured out how to swindle, bilk, and pillage for our own self-interest yet, that was still to come. Back then we were mere beautiful dreamers who had yet to come to grief against those well-known hard facts: Men, Money, and Power.

But I'm not even sure if *that's* that whole of what got me going with this guy. I think it was something else. I think my animal nature knew something about him that the rest of me didn't want to know. Whatever it was, suddenly, there I was driving across Los Angeles in his yellow Karmann Ghia, way out to his condo in Thousand Oaks. I'd left my secret lover unexpectedly behind and simply driven off with this complete stranger. To this day, Ginger-Noodle has never forgotten or quite forgiven my disappearing act that night. But I was on a quest and couldn't be stopped.

His name was something like Ernie or Arnie and he had recently run the election campaign of one of the more famous Republican Conservatives of our times. He himself was a Libertarian. Back then, mid-seventies, I'd never heard of it as a political party. He smelled a live one and went in for the kill. He somehow got me to believe that the Libertarian Party stood for everything I'd ever cared about, only more so. For a long time, or at least most of the ride over to his place, I was trying to figure out how a guy who professed to believe everything I believed could run a candidate as rapacious and self-serving as the one he had.

"It doesn't really matter," he said, "what the candidate is like. What counts are the people who put him in office. Those are the people I work for. Those are the people who run things."

"And who are *they* exactly?" I wanted to know. I was halfway across the city and deep into the night with this person.

He smiled a wicked gapped-tooth smile, "Oh, a bunch of guys in suits."

By the time we got to his condo, it must have been midnight and I realized I had gotten in over my head. I'd told him, somewhere just after the Harbor Freeway interchange, when I realized he was far closer to a Neo-Nazi than to my kind of Utopian Anarchist, that under no circumstances would I consider having sex with him. As far as I was concerned we were going out to his place to continue our scintillating discussion and drink some wine. He said, "I've got some terrific pot, a Thai stick. You'll love it."

Everyone smoked pot then–Libertarians, Republicans, Democrats, and Independents alike —so I wasn't surprised. But I got out my verbal high-lighting pen and went over in depth the limits of our "date." He made average male noises like he got the point and yet, once we got out there, I could see how it was going to be.

His condo was spacious, with all the pretense and none of the substance of luxury. I guess it was just how they were built back then, in the '70s. It was especially spacious as it had almost no furniture anywhere to be seen. But there was one room with a grand piano, a bar, and a stereo system with four speakers positioned around it. Quadraphonic sound. "Wow," I said, "you're a serious listener. Are you a serious pianist, too?"

"Not serious enough, I guess, or I wouldn't be running political campaigns, I'd be playing national concert tours. So, I guess I'm not serious. He smiled and his thin lips revealed little, gapped teeth, sharp and ready to bite. But he didn't bite. Instead he opened a bottle of white wine, a Pouilly-Fuissé, and handing me a glass, he said, "This is a very expensive bottle of wine. I hope you enjoy it."

Then he took out a little bone pipe and put some sticky Thai buds in it. Two tastes later and my mind took off in the opposite direction from my body. My mind was wrestling with the vagaries of political corruption, but my body was contemplating exotic places it had never been before.

He said to me, "Just let me lick you. I won't touch you any place else. I promise. Just let me put my tongue between your thighs."

I'd been leaning on the piano, when he fell on his knees and stuck his head under my skirt. He pulled my panties down with his teeth. I wasn't wearing stockings. Just smooth bare legs in an Indian print wrap-around skirt which he peeled back and then dove into. He made me move my feet apart and then held them in place with his hands, one around each ankle. He stuck his tongue in and around my clit until it became its rosy swollen self and liquid thrills began dripping down my leg.

But I said to him, "You don't interest me in the least. You don't turn me on and I don't care about what you think."

"I like that in a female stranger," he said. "It makes me feel like I can trust you."

"Oh yeah? Well, I don't trust you, up close or at a distance."

"That's too bad," he said. "I know some fun games we could play," and he stuck his tongue through his gap-toothed grin.

The wine had hit me, the pot had overwhelmed me, and now this Libertarian had some "creative" ideas. He moved me in the direction of his bar, where there was a single bar stool. He turned me to face it, still on his knees, then he pulled something from his pocket which I didn't see but then felt. He tied my ankles together quickly and suddenly with some sheer black silk stockings.

"What the hell are you doing?" I barked at him.

He stood up, like he'd practiced this before and pushed me over, stomach to seat, and grabbed my wrists, which again he was prepared for with another black stocking. He bound them together and then tied them down to a wrung of the stool which was like a '50s soda shop model, chrome and vinyl. And then before I could say anything else, he had a gag in my mouth, white gauze and masking tape. "Oh shit," I thought. "I'm going to die here, in Thousand Oaks, and nobody will ever find me." I began to get very frightened and my cunt got tight and dry.

He'd had my pants off by the piano and now he lifted my skirt up and over my back.

"That's some ass you've got there. Like a boy's ass, only rounded. I bet it's hot in there." He jammed a couple of fingers in and began to play with what he found. A tight, frightened hole in the wall. But there was something about it that was getting to me. Something wet was happening without my even being able to help it. *This is horrible,* I thought, *here I am with a thoroughly despicable human being who has completely taken advantage of me and whom I wouldn't have given the time of day in the light of day, now that I knew better, and here he was pushing buttons I didn't know I had.*

After his fingers began to slide in and out on my repressed excitement, he took the flats of his hands and spanked my bottom while I twitched

71

against the chair. He dropped his pants and pulled his poker out. I couldn't see what it looked like but then he put it in me, jammed it hard, like he was making a political statement inside of me. He was going to have me, whether I wanted him or not, whether I agreed with him or not, whether I voted for his candidate or not, this guy—Arnie or Ernie or whatever the hell his name was, was determined to have me every which way. He fucked me like that for a long time, until he came spasmodically, the way some men do, and collapsed over my back, over the bar stool.

But that wasn't enough for him, no. He went back into my hole for some juice for his fingers which he got good and wet and then jammed into my ass. Others had tried to get in that spot before, but I was always too tight. He didn't care. He found it; he took it. When he'd gotten it worked loose a little, he jammed his re-upped poker in and I screamed hard inside my throat. But I was dripping down my legs again and I hated the son of a bitch for it. I came anyway. Came to light up Thousand Oaks with a giant burst of something ruby red and hot inside. "Good Grief," I muttered in the aftermath, reminded of Candy, accidentally fucking an archetype in the dark.

After that, he untied me and poured me a glass of pear brandy which hit me like White Lightning. He showed me to the bathroom which was luxurious but bare of anything personal or even appealing. There were some big towels hung on a rack and after turning on the taps in the giant Jacuzzi bath tub, and adding some alpine scented suds, he left me alone to think it over.

We slept on a futon on the floor of his living room, not touching. The next morning, I made him drive me back to where I'd left my car. No breakfast, no coffee, no conversation. It was what it was. That pale domed head in Canter's had come and gone like Banquo's ghost, evaporated into the steam rising from so many bowls of matzo ball soup. I never saw him again.

HAPPY, HAPPY BIRTHDAY, BABY!

I found a souvenir menu among the paper products I was sorting between boxes and trash bags—the in-out filing system of the detritus I had accumulated over four years of coming and going, coast to coast and side to side. There it was, at the bottom of a heap, the menu from Tiny Naylor's, its crazy, wavy, post-'50s modern drive-in building design on one side and a menu of its classic fare on the other—my favorite being "Little Thin Hot Cakes...With Hot Syrup and Melted Butter."

Essence of she-noodle food! Just the thought of it evoked an episode I hadn't exactly forgotten, but certainly had buried in the stack of my short-term memorabilia.

Far-Rockaway had called to say he was coming to L.A. for a visit. He was staying in Beverly Hills with his old school friend, whose father had written incredibly famous screenplays. Reportedly, his friend's father skulked about the house at all hours, between scenes and segues, while pecking away intermittently on an old Remington typewriter. It was assumed he was conjuring things funny, sad, or otherwise, with major star talent in mind. He appeared in a continuous state of distraction. Far-Rockaway had been there before and knew how to behave—never ask questions about what he was working on, or how it was going, or what the title might be. No questions. Period.

"I'll call you when I get in," he'd said, from a safe enough distance of 3,000 miles.

We'd been through a few episodes since the rough stuff between us went down. He'd finished an M.A. in Political Science and was shuffling the deck to see what turned up next. He was determined to go to law school but it was a matter of which coast to pledge allegiance to. He was coming out west to visit a few distinguished campuses, see how it felt to be that far away from the Brooklyn Bridge and mend a brand new fractured heart from someone I'd never met—all in one whirlwind trip to Los Angeles and its illustrious environs!

I was at the height of my unleashed Hollywood libido, whose philosophy was summarized by James Joyce's Molly's gasping groan: "Yes I said yes I will Yes." Perhaps I thought that more than enough sex, in as many varieties as possible, would eventually get me over My-Old-Flame and a lingering case of left-over, *broken-hearted blues*. If I didn't believe it, I was at least practicing a good imitation of someone who did. I was in the thick of it, with that woman, Up-in-the-Hills. I told her Far-Rockaway might come to town, asked her, was she interested?

"The three of us?" A little wicked smile flickered across her face. "Only if I like him. Do you think I'll like him?"

"Well, when I *did* like him, there was a lot of him to like."

"You mean he's fat? There's a lot to grab onto?"

"Not at all! Long and lean, except for where he's not. Where he's fat and long."

"Uh huh," she drawled and smiled like a crocodile.

Far-Rockaway came over to my bungalow in Silver Lake. He was going to drop in on the campus where my roommate and I were doing our graduate school time. He got dropped off by *Son of Famous*, who didn't come up to see us, afraid, I guess, of how most of *us* actually lived.

Far-Rockaway came up the stairs and grinned out from under his jazzman hat and dark glasses. My grad-school roommate, Skinny, was in class all day. This was my home-alone reading and class-prep time, when I could grade papers and get set

76

for the week. He grinned and I laughed. I wanted it as soon as I saw him, and he did too.

We made love on the hard daybed in my studio, my one room alone with a desk, a typewriter, and windows facing the flowering hibiscus and a small pruned fig tree. We just tore each other's clothes off and buried time and space into the flesh and sex act. And I remembered all about him, then, from before, when we were really lovers and played games like lovers play. He was long and knobby, like a French tickler or some specialized sexual device made of latex, only it was him. He reached way, way back into my pelvis and made it sing a long sultry song. Sure. I remembered how it was, when it was *something* between us. The leaves turned red and fell and broke my heart every day and he'd pick up the pieces of my soul at night and try to make a picture with them. I was writing a lot of poetry, smoking packs of cigarettes, and having nightly angst about life after college. It was my senior year.

He was the bartender, hired from last year's graduating class. It was his "year off" before grad school. I remembered cold October nights and snowy December mornings, black coffee and not much else. A kiss. A good fuck. A way to start the morning.

I remembered all this as we went at it, in the white spring light of March in L.A., a kind of white gold glimmering in the sky and the smell of pink roses which fell in long-overgrown thorny boughs at the back of our yard, like a waterfall of pale pink feathers, shabby and sadly beautiful in that bright light.

I didn't have much on to begin with—a pair of shorts, a tight T-shirt; I couldn't get it off fast enough. He dropped his pants and just put it in me. He warmed me up and flew me like a kite in a new March gale. Love-making before noon, a plate full of figs, slices of oranges, and handfuls of roses, roses, roses, faded the patches of former cold winters which blew up from the bottom of my mind. It was a good time to be in the present.

It was, in fact, his birthday. That's what made it extra special. A birthday surprise for him and fun and games for us. It had potential: *Far-Rockaway and the Two Red-heads*.

I took him over there, took him up into the hills, to *her* place. She looked fine, in extremely tight jeans and a slip of a pink silk chemise under a black, loose knit V-neck. We went to Donte's, the jazz club on Lankersheim in North Hollywood, together and drank and listened to a young whiz kid on the sax named Scotty Hamilton, just out from Rhode Island. I could tell my girlfriend was liking my boyfriend and I liked the way it made me feel - like something warm was sliding around the lips of my vagina.

I thought of how we would lie, and what we would do to each other and to him. All the while Scotty played beautiful blue notes and we all smiled, wondering who were the cats and who were the mice.

Back at her place, Up-in-the-Hills, Far-Rockaway, and I lay down under her family furs, and became naked bit by bit, socks and pants, panties and shirts. The bra pulled down and breasts lifted up, exposed, admired. I sucked her nipples so that he would know that I meant her to be excited, that in fact I wanted him to really fuck her well and I'd help him make her come. I didn't have to encourage him much. He wanted to get inside of her as soon as he'd met her. I liked that about him. I was glad she welcomed him into our animal furs. He did her and then me and then her and then me, without coming in either. I wondered how it must have felt to him, going from one to the other like that. It must have felt good because it kept him hard for a long time. She sat on him and I held his arms while she rammed him up deep in her cunt and ground her finger nails into the palms of her hands and sighed, "I feel as though I've just seen Pavlova dance."

She was about to peak and pulled herself off him and he became frantic to come. She pushed me over and made him do it to me doggy because she knew I liked it that way. She played with my clit until I came, and I licked her red and throbbing while Far-Rockaway jumped me from behind. He came and she did as I had and nobody wasn't wet and sticky. We all groaned together and rolled over in a heap.

I don't know if we dozed. I do remember that Hills roused herself first. She said, "There's a party up the street, let's go!"

I couldn't imagine leaving here and going someplace else *not* here. She bribed me with the promise of a swimming pool heated to a hot bath temperature. "You'll love it," she said. "It's covered with a big wombish tent."

Far-Rockaway didn't care. It was his birthday and he was already having the party of a lifetime. "Sure. Why not. Let's go."

And we did. We climbed into my maroon Mustang and drove very slowly up, up, further up into the hills, where big sprawls of mansions at the ends of gated roads took you by surprise. The one we went to was newer, though a little shabbier for wear. It was a single bachelor lawyer's place with black leather pillows and couches and arm chairs.

We walked in and there were the remains of a party—some spilled bottles and a covey of naked girls. Some hugely loud music brayed at us from all sides. Hills said, "I'll find our host and see if we missed the party."

"Wow!" said Far-Rockaway. "So, this is L.A.?"

At that moment, a naked woman fell onto him and pulled his pants off. I walked off, looking for Hills. Everyone around me had pupils the size of quarters. A woman with short blonde hair and little breasts and nothing on but her bikini under-pants asked me, "Have you been here before or is this your first time?"

She spoke in a flat voice as though she were about to have a tooth extracted and was sitting in the waiting room, waiting for the painkillers to kick in, with a wad of cotton stuffed in her cheek.

"First time what?" I asked

"Here, your first time here," she said without expression.

"This is my first time," I said, nodding like a bobble-head.

"Oh, I thought I saw you here before, but maybe that was just somebody who looked like you."

I was so struck by the empty resonance in her voice and the distracted stare of eyes slightly out of focus, I couldn't hear what she said after that. I was only aware of how odd it was, all these girls with blank stares and no clothes.

Hills finally reappeared from nowhere, wearing that dazzling grin, like a girl having fun with trouble. "Well, of course, he's very annoyed we showed up so late. He has trouble sleeping alone, so he's throwing a sleepover for the leftovers. The pool's out back."

We walked over a few couples of bodies entwined and doing things to each other, and out the sliding glass door. The cool night air stung my ankles under the wraparound skirt I was wearing. The Lawyer joined us from some unseen back room.

He was short and built and moved his hands a lot as he went on and on, needling away at Hills, but she threw it back at him every time. I knew then they *were* lovers. They had that way about them. I didn't care. It was the thing we had between us that mattered. He was strictly extracurricular.

We stepped inside the black rubber tent over the pool and it felt like a tropical rain forest at night: humid, moist, and close to the skin.

"Now for God's sake, don't anybody drown," chided The Lawyer, "I hate pulling bodies out the morning after. It spoils my day."

And he left us alone there, except that it turned out there was somebody there, already, just there, hanging around in the water. It was so dark, we could only vaguely see each other, even very close up. The water was perfectly warm and black. Bath tub warm, as promised. I was *so* warm, I could have closed my eyes in it and I think I did. I swam dreamily from one side to the other and let the water ripple against me like hot silk.

When I came up, I felt out the corner in which Hills and Far-Rockaway were nuzzling each other. I wrapped languid noodle arms around their necks and began to French kiss one and then the other. They in turn held me close between them and played with tits and clit together until I came. It was so relaxing, to let go. I did and then felt myself sinking and sinking.

A siren sang a song from the bottom of the pool and I let myself float down to meet her. Except there was a nagging feeling that I had forgotten something, something very important which I *needed* to remember. Something jerked at me from up above. A thought, a prayer, a hand grabbed me, pulled me up and I gasped, coughing chlorine.

I had almost gone to sleep and done the unforgivable: died naked in a stranger's swimming pool. Who pulled me up? Was it him or her? I'm not sure. I think it was the stranger. We were vaguely aware of having escaped a near-death disaster, but moved like dreamers in a dream, into the next scene.

We three got our clothes back on and left. Far-Rockaway admitted he'd been molested, back at the party, before we went into the pool.

"She pulled my pants down and jumped my bones! I had nothing to do with it, except to stand there and watch. Except for when I came, which I couldn't help either."

We laughed at the idea of some unknown nude just jumping on his cock, until he spilled and then moved on to find some other straight hard thing sticking out in the haze. Who knew, perhaps the door knob would be next?

We laughed all the way down the hill and out onto Sunset where we cruised to Tiny Naylor's last drive-in on Hollywood and Vine. What a place! Girls on roller skates delivering shakes, burgers, and hand-cut fries on trays they hung from rolled-down windows. At 4 a.m. Pacific Standard Time, they had the best breakfast in the neighborhood. Oh, those melt-in-your-mouth thin little pancakes! With warmed, real maple syrup and melted, real butter on top! Yum-yum!

We dropped Hills off at her place, afterwards. She was sleepy and had work to catch up on. I drove Far-Rockaway back to Beverly Hills, where even at 6 a.m., everyone was up and, apparently, *writing*. *The Famous Screenwriter* was still skulking about. *Son of Famous* was also there, drinking coffee and thinking about writing. *Mrs. Famous* was in the living room, reading the paper, drinking coffee, and editing yesterday's copy. Everything seemed lovely, except it was 6 o'clock in the morning and I was on the other end of their spectrum. They were all crisp as dry toast and I was limp as wilted lettuce smothered in blue cheese dressing. We hadn't slept and a hangover the color of bad smog was rapidly wrapping its creepy layers around our heads, even as the sun was rising.

"Happy, Happy Birthday!" I said to Far-Rockaway, and gave him a dry kiss on the lips, then left. I drove the surface streets all the way from Beverly Hills back to Silver Lake, where tall Egyptian Palms scrubbed the lightening sky with their bottle-washer tops. Upon arrival and finding my own empty bed, I collapsed with a sigh, rapidly faded to black, and slept until noon the next day.

MEDITATION MUSIC

I don't normally get into it with a girlfriend's boy-friend or other people's husbands. Experience has taught me that the risks are high and, generally, the losses great. Unless you're convinced it's your one true love, it's mostly not worth doing. Except, maybe, sometimes.

I wouldn't have done it *that* time, though, for all the right reasons. But it was just *too damn hot*, that one August in L.A.—100 to 110 degrees Fahrenheit every day, day-in, day-out. We were all wearing almost nothing, all the time. We kept our blinds pulled and the doors closed during the day, to keep the heat out. At night, we used electric fans to pull in the desert chill along with the smell of dry euca-lyptus mingling with night-blooming jasmine—the smell of the hills behind the city which wafted down when the sky turned lavender. In the evening, even the concrete courtyards off Vermont turned into sensuous ladies, dripping with yellow-lit jade trees, intoxicated with that crazy, heavy jasmine stuff, drifting in the cooling air.

I had taken to wearing nightgowns as dresses and slips as nightgowns or under-dresses from the '30s and '40s which could have been either, with their transparencies of organza and layers of the sheerest Chinese silk. I found such things in hos-pital thrift stores in chic neighborhoods, or else in the bottom of my grandmother's drawers. She had so many silk slips trimmed in lace she never wore—she had saved them up for a special occa-sion that never came. I liberated them and gave them a life they never dreamed of. The pink one with the hand-stitched rosettes on the straps, that was my favorite. It was my go-to garment in the hot desert air that blew in with the Santa Anas.

I was working on being an artist late at night, not only because it was so much cooler and the air so much sweeter, but because I just felt better about that time of night for riding creative thoughts to shore. Day brain waves felt so much more cluttered with people thinking their thoughts and yammering at each other with the blah blah blah of Los Angeles deals and dues and don'ts, while the night brain waves rolled free and cool like jazz and I could hear myself think, even through the occasional interruption of helicopters with spotlights patrolling the neighborhood. Yeah, I just naturally gravitated towards those empty late-night hours, with the same compunction I still have for seeking out the emptiest spot on the beach. I'll walk a mile to be alone.

I was wearing that pink silk slip, no bra, no underwear, working those hot, summer nights, doing freelance graphics at home and imagining my rendition of *Portrait of Another Artist as a Young Woman.* The hard part was to hold the picture of that artist, someday, after the moment of being discovered had already occurred—holding that wonderful, colorful picture of what life might be like, basking in the light of public acknowledgment—all the while surviving the daily noise of rejection after rejection. I sustained the necessary suspension of disbelief required for that task with the help of a wonderful dancer whom we all thought of as a swatch of Isadora Duncan's soul.

We were collaborating on odd and interesting projects which were the innocent roots of Performance Art. Isadora-the-Dancer choreographed a long poem which I had written and a variety of textual, visual, kinetic concoctions, like room-sized Sumi paintings. She thought in large, archetypal images and felt *everything* she did, down to the arches of her feet.

86

She carried on the life of the Modern Romantic, limitlessly pursuing true love while managing her own massage business, persisting in a determined dream to make a dance company of international renown. Simultaneously, she was becoming a shamaness of a of a brand-new, but none-the-less ancient, matriarchal "spiritual collective," a term she preferred to "religion," with its patriarchal connotations. She really was *something else.*

Sometimes when she talked I didn't know whether she was telling me something that had actually happened to her, something she had dreamed the night before, or something she imagined to be possible. All the while she talked, she worked her body through one set pattern of gestures after another, thinking about the deeper meaning, the message in the movement of each gesture.

We were going to make a sound track that summer for my long poem for dancers which she'd choreographed that past spring. It was based on an old Irish fairy tale "The Fairy Thorn" from the W.B. Yeats collection. I thought it was a fine thing, just as it was—a poem written and read by the poet, while dancers moved to the meter of the language. We'd performed it that way several times publicly and it seemed to work. People seemed to enjoy it! But she wanted something on tape to take on the road with her, when the company she imagined toured nationally, and if we were going to record it anyway, we might as well think of adding music at the same time and making it an actual score for the performance.

Later, when Isadora thought it would be a good idea to accomplish this theatrical transformation with an original musical composition by her boyfriend of the moment, I felt a certain hesitancy, if not actual foreboding, of a mistake yet to take place. She spent a good bit of time trying to put me at ease, and insisted she would drive me over to his apartment in Glendale to meet with him and talk through some ideas for the piece. I remember thinking about him, when I first saw him, that there was something in his pale, yellow-blond, fine-boned looks, which reminded me of someone, someplace else I couldn't quite recall. He already seemed so familiar to me, I tried to pin it down to an occasion when we might have met but, really, we hadn't. It was that he was just like some mad, glad, and gifted music boy-man I might have known, if fate had played a different hand.

Finally, I figured the familiarity was a product of having heard so much about him from Isadora. She'd gone into great detail about what a fantastic lover he was. I couldn't care too much about it, though, since I was there to talk about art and words and music and the permutations thereof. He had a great razz-a-ma-tazz rap of "processed sound technique" and was knowledgeable on the glories of modern multi-tracking. He talked a good game of it and had a certain magnetism besides. He played tapes of his compositions which sounded like meditation music for traveling to alien worlds. We listened and thought our dreams out loud with one another.

Afterwards, we shared a Happiness Chinese Buffet meal together, complete with fortune cookies which said such things as: "To get what you want you must commit yourself to something!" and "Make up your mind and do what you know is right!" and "You will be successful at your work!"

It was a sign, we felt, to seize the day. *Carpe Diem!* We all three agreed— clearly, we had vital life's work to do together and in the eve of that melting hot day somewhere in Glendale, we com-

mitted ourselves to it. We made our plan. While
Isadora would be away on her once-a-year trip to
see her parents in Costa Rica, the two of us would
move ahead on the immediate project: setting my
long poem to his musical score. That way she
would have a "scratch tape" to work with when she
got back, for a proposed September tour. Caught
up in the fever dream of the emerging artist, be-
lieving the next big break is going to happen, any
day, to any one of us, we pitched ourselves into
the ongoing moment of our imminent success. We
were roaring through our twenties, pedal to the
metal, in a steamy, souped-up jalopy of a life, and
all the possibilities glimmered like mirages on the
hot pavement ahead.

It *was* hot enough to fry an egg on the sidewalk the day Isadora set off on her trip, swathed
in flowered skirts and flowing scarves. With a kiss
and a wave, she left her lemon-honey lover behind.
Bleached, hot days melted into purple crayon
nights and he and I talked late into those indigo
hours when we were both up working on "things."
I liked having one person I could call during the
Late Late Show, someone to think out loud around,
with only the slightest tinge of sex floating up from
beneath the surface.

Meditation-Music tweaked electronics for re-
cording studios on a freelance basis, so he could
set his own schedule and compose music during
the cooler hours. We decided to have a production
meeting, one of those nights when it finally cooled
down to a sultry simmering from the raging sizzle
it had been all day.

He called me and said he'd really put his mind
on it and had sketched a few things out he wanted
me to hear. Was I up?

It was midnight, but for me it was the mid-afternoon. I got out of my slip, put on a soft, hand-kerchief-weight Indian print dress with a halter top over skinny bikini bottoms, and drove with all the windows down in the Little Green Car, letting the night air blow in and around my hair flying out behind me. Harvey, my half-coyote, dribbled sweat off his tongue in the back seat as the wind blew his ears back.

I brought a bottle of cold white wine, a bunch of cold white grapes, a box of Ak-maks, and a piece of melting brie. I was thinking words and music in variously tempting arrays. Sex may have been lingering in the air, but I didn't let myself notice it and instead looked right past it, into the garden where Art grows its own little fragrant flowers called "Truth" and "Beauty."

It was hotter on the other side of the hill from Silver Lake, where Glendale edged its way toward Highland Park and beyond. Meditation-Music's place was already fighting the heat emitted from the full rack of electronics in the living room. He had fans in all the windows.

"I'm going to have to get an air conditioner in here if this keeps up. Or else I've got to move, which is probably a better idea, except that I want to buy this other piece of equipment for the system and if I do that, I can't move," he said with the half smile of someone knowingly living a conundrum.

The white wine was still cold, but I was beginning to drip in a hot buttered-noodle sort of way.

I'd been there about an hour while he was fiddling with his electronic boxes and keyboards, turning dials and flipping switches, trying to find some sound he'd found before, but couldn't recreate now. Suddenly, he just stopped everything and sat in silence for a moment and then announced, "There's a rhinoceros in the room."

90

"A rhinoceros?" I asked.

"Yes, a rhinoceros and it's making a lot of un-heard-of noises, like "*Brrrrrrrrrrrrr*" and "*BRP-PPPPPPPP*," not to mention "*RAHHHHHHHGGGG-GGGG*."

"Is that so?" I asked, a little astonished by this display.

"That's right. Only silently, louder and louder, until finally it's the only thing you can't hear in the room."

"I see," I said. "I think I don't hear it too," having noticed the same viscosity of feeling in the room but afraid to square up to it, eye to eye. "But I am wondering," I went on, pushing the litotes to the limit, "what would happen if I *did* hear it and that worries me not a little."

"Uh huhhhh," he said, in the pause between one thought and another, "I'm not a little unafraid myself. But sometimes, with some people, the only way *over* is *through*."

"And what happens after that?" I asked. "After we are *through*, what happens after that?"

"We turn the lights out and go to sleep," he smiled and kissed me, lightly, a little wet, on the lips.

It was not an unfamiliar feeling, wanting to be intimate, *inamorata*, with my creative playmates.

Why not? Making things, creating things, doing works of imagination are inherently sexy sorts of things to do with and around other creative people. I admit it: there *is* something in shared creative fervor which hits an inner G-spot like no other. It is wonderful stuff—irresistible any time it happens. Creative juice mixed with underlying attraction is a mood elevator beyond any synthesized substitutes, including a double-layered box of fine, Belgian chocolates.

This is the stuff of which stars are made and then fall nova. This is the juice that launched a thousand ships of fools. For that one brief instant, we were convinced, *it was meant to be*, in some cosmic way that was greater than ourselves, and couldn't be denied. It was a *former life*, a *karmic debt*, a *connection from another dimension*! Somehow, we thought, because we had no ill intentions, no ill would come of this meeting of cosmic forces between us—this hugely familiar feeling, this crazy-craving heat viscerally glowing between us, surely this was harmless. Right?

We made love over and over and over to endless tapes of his sound-processed compositions and acoustic ambiences. The whole time, I had the distinct impression that we were making love on other planets, in other worlds, in a fifth dimension. And the orgasm! The orgasm was a blinding inner flash of blue-white light, right in the old third eye.

We rested. And then he got creative. He got out a small PZM microphone which he slapped on the wall next to us. It was the kind of microphone which could pick up a room full of noise, pin-drop by pin-drop. This mic he fed to an early sound processing, electronic keyboard in an interesting loop of delays and sampled bits of our love making. He used another hand-held microphone as a sensory investigation device, rubbing it very gently, delicately, across parts of my body, which first he named and then touched.

He said "Breast" and the word rippled apart into its phonic elements, *"BRRRRRREEHHHHHSSSSSSST-TTTTT..."* through the kind of sound processor he had rigged up. And each contour of my body he touched with this very slender, very sensitive microphone, each contour had a sound, a shape to its sound, a quality of softness around the nipples, a coarseness across the hairs of my mound, something like silk ripping, as he ran it down the inside of my thigh.

He came into me again, with that long honey cock, that beautiful, ivory thing which made me sigh and sing all night. We got lost in his self-generated music for cosmic orgasm. We spun into distant inner space, finding answers to the questions bigger than ourselves. *Are* we recreating the Big Bang effect *every* time we *do it*? Or, is this simple act, in fact, the simple truth behind nuclear *fusion*? Could we harness this stuff like solar energy and have enough juice to fly to Pluto and back, fueling jet propulsion with orgasmic explosions?

We went way out there and in there and back there and along the way, we made love like aliens with tentacles—toes became extensions of noses, belly sucked belly like giant mouths wide open, and heartbeat to heartbeat, we touched something larger than ourselves.

When I closed my eyes, I kept seeing that white light, which may have been the sun rising, though I felt sure I was on my way, on a long brain wave, rolling back inside my mind, to a place I could almost remember, erupting into a new primordial landscape which we were dreaming together in living color.

The next day I woke earlier than I would have liked, because Harvey, my half-coyote, had his own needs to be met. I rolled out and left Meditation-Music from Outer Space with a light kiss on his sleeping eyebrow. I thought of leaving a note, but the mutt couldn't wait. The sun was on its morning ascent and I could tell already, it was going to be another hot one.

I went over to his place off and on the rest of the month, while Isadora was away. We worked on the piece as often as not and made love as much as possible. We both knew it would be over, in this way, between us, the moment she got back. We had an agreement to keep this just between ourselves and spare her unnecessary pain. He assured me she would know nothing but happiness upon her return.

We picked her up at the airport and she fluttered up the off-ramp in a swirl of exotic colors and light-weight cloth. We'd driven out in "Old Betsy," her older-model, navy blue Rover. Meditation-Music had washed and waxed and shined her up bright as wet pavement. I brought her roses and sat in the back seat while they glued onto each other in the way that reunited lovers do. She gurgled and gasped about Costa Rica where the National Ballet was mounting one of her dance pieces. Her eyes sparkled with the bliss of one whose dreams may still come true. They dropped me at my place and went on to hers where, I was sure, she would be seeing blue-white lights all night.

The very next day after her return, the two of them came over to my house. Isadora was radiant and pretty, with the dayglo pink cheeks of happiness lighting her face.

They held hands and smiled beatifically before she said, "He asked me and I said, 'Yes, of course!'"

"Asked you?" I asked.

"Asked her to marry me," he said, and looked her in the eyes when he said it.

She smiled and nodded fast up and down, "Yes, I said, yes, I will, yes!"

I'd heard that line before. I said, "Wow! Great! That's really great!" I *think* I meant it.

And it was great, for a while, until the night the other shoe dropped and the world as we knew it ended with us, naked, on top of Mt. Pinos.

THAT NIGHT ON MOUNT PINOS

Isadora called. We'd been missing each other for days, trying to get together to exchange borrowed books, costume pieces, props, and other evidence of our collaboration. I was going to miss her. She put me in touch with certain deeper feelings which remain mostly submerged in the soup of my unconscious.

Real terror is a terrifying thing. I know. I've been there. That sudden twist in the solar plexus when you think, "My God! What might have happened!" usually the moment *after* the danger has passed. I say after, because, at the time of the terrifying terror itself, a person is usually pre-occupied with survival factors, if not actual survival.

I think of my friends who flew, accidentally, over a cliff and landed at the bottom of a canyon, 150 feet below where they had been driving only a moment before, on a beautiful clear desert spring day in Arizona. They survived the fall with one broken neck, a few chipped teeth, and some serious scrapes. The neck got fixed, the teeth got capped, the flesh healed, and, basically, they walked away from it, a couple of lucky ducks.

But I have the feeling that the sensation of plummeting down that cliff is going to stay right next to them for a considerable time to come, maybe even a lifetime. They both say it's not something to forget, it's something to remember. They both say, if they could do the whole thing over again and have the same outcome, they *would* do it again. It has caused a heightened awareness in their lives which has changed them forever. I believe them.

That night, out on Mt. Pinos, when I really expected the world as we knew it was going to end by morning, I learned just how powerful an aphrodisiac such sheer terror can be! People who ride rollercoasters say the same thing—it's hot stuff for your sex life. For me, it was earth-shaking.

I was over at Isadora's apartment. She was working on a new giant-sized performance piece and I was marking movements for her in a calligraphy of arrows and sparse word descriptions like: "Alert Heron stands tall" and "sleepy sea kelp waves legs" which all meant something particular to remind her of each movement and the emphasis to put on it.

We did this kind of creative work with each other sometimes; I danced with her, she wrote with me, I tracked her as she charted her many meanings with movement, feeling, and design. Sometimes I just sat around with her while she was hot-gluing feathers on a mask and we'd talk; she'd tell me of other times and places and people in her life which were so vividly described, I felt I knew them, intimately. Later on, some of them, I did.

Whenever I went over to her place I felt myself leave the country, if not the world. Her apartment lent itself easily to that kind of magically real transfiguration. It was situated in an older complex of buildings, on a side street off of Vermont, just south of the freeway. It felt exotic because it had an authenticity in its Spanish-influenced architecture which most of the newer apartment buildings in Los Angeles sadly lack. This one was different. We could have been in Portugal, or certain parts of Rio, or maybe some place else I've never been, like Cuba or Trinidad, Tobago, or Tortuga or even the Isle of Capri. From the looks of things, you could have been any of those places. The fact that the place was in L.A. on a street off lower Vermont, is a reminder that it was built to look like other places—like all cities of dreams are built, to be anywhere but there.

The limestone and stucco buildings with their terra-cotta roofs faced each other in a gentle horse-shoe shape around a flagstone courtyard with fruit trees embedded in it. Hibiscus and huge, old bougainvillea vines lined the sides. At the street entrance to the buildings, the stairs diverged into two pairs around a large, poured-concrete, hexagonal planter which spilled a multitude of succulents surrounding short, pointy palms and sharp, star-shaped cacti. Red and orange and pink geraniums filled in the rest and ran wild on the small hills on either side of the stairs, which met again at the bottom of the planter and became one wide stair-case to the sidewalk. It was exotic, slightly shabby, and charming. It suited her perfectly.

A door from her kitchen opened onto another staircase, which ran down to the alley street behind the building, where garbage cans lived and grocer-ies were unloaded. Her stairs dripped with clay pots of aloe and ice plants and herbs of all kinds—rose-mary and mint and chives, as well as the more ex-otic varieties—pau d'arco and horehound.

We often sat out there and drank strong black coffee which she brewed in a slightly obscene cot-ton windsock hanging from a fold-down drainer tacked on a nail to the wall. Her Costa Rican coffee making was like a secret alchemical recipe—she boiled the water in this one certain kind of pot and then just as it was boiling, she removed it from the heat and sprinkled finely, finely, freshly ground beans of a very special variety across the pot, put the lid on it, and let it sit until all the grounds soaked through and sank to the bottom. She then poured this thick dark liquid through the sock to a warmed earthen-ware mug, waiting below the sock-holder. With or without cream, a spoon could stand up in it.

We sat in the sun amidst her staircase garden and drank this Costa Rican rocket fuel and dreamed up huge elaborate productions and then tried to think of ways to get paid to accomplish them. That was the trick—to get paid to do what you love, to get paid to be an artist. If you could just do that, it would prove to yourself and anyone else that in fact you are *that* at least—a *real* artist.

"Just think," she said, with her Eloise smile and her Sendak hair tied back with a gypsy scarf, "when they are writing our cross-referenced biographies, these will be the *early years*, and how fondly we will look back at them!"

She lived life at such a scale, in her imagining of it, that nothing in reality managed to daunt her vision of what was meant to be for her in this lifetime. I warmed myself by the flame of her intense conviction that her day would come and she would enter the annals of the greats with Sarah Bernhardt, or the real Isadora Duncan, or Eleonora Duse, or Martha Graham. I believed that dream with her and I still do. I believe she is out there somewhere becoming a legend, *beyond* her own mind.

That particular day we were working together, she was headed in the general direction of interpreting her personal mythopoiesis through the articulations of her body. Or that's what she said she was doing. I took it down in the notes I was keeping, documenting her choreography and our collaboration, trying to remember it all for future reference, though a combination of words and drawings that, to an outsider, would look like chicken scratches and verbal grunts. She was choreographing a set of gestures and motions, which entailed swinging around with a shiny, sharp, silver-handled ceremonial knife. It was beautifully dangerous. She moved like a Balinese shadow puppet with it as she recit-

98

ed a story, a poem of her own, about all the knives she'd ever known and how at last she'd seized this one for her own. It was her kind of thing all the way. Even when she worked small and solo, it was with some larger Jungian or Freudian or otherwise universally recognized large scale archetype firmly in mind. It was her visionary aspect, conjunct with her inner shamaness transiting Pisces at the new moon—or something.

The phone rang in the middle of a movement and she swooped down to pick it up with a breathy "*hellloooo?*"

I could tell by how she warmed up immediately, that it must have been him, Meditation-Music, her *fiancé*—a word she used with great relish. She bubbled and effused about what she'd been working on, until suddenly, she stopped cold in her mental tracks. I could see that whatever he'd just told her had shocked her to the bottoms of her feet and was now wending up to the center of her soul where a heavy tempest was brewing.

When I heard her say, in response to something he said to her, while looking at me with a dense combination of pain and anger moistening her eyes, "She would and did but I never would and couldn't!" I knew I was in trouble. When she grabbed her knife, and began doing wildly gymnastic whirlings around me making guttural keening noises of pain, I thought "Uh-oh."

I picked up the phone which she had thrown down in disgust and fury, with heavy emphasis punched into the gestural movement. "Hello?" I said, tentatively, hoping I was wrong, hoping that it wasn't who I thought it was, telling a tale that was better off left buried.

But it was him, Meditation-Music from Outer Space. "Well," I said, holding the phone up for him to hear the sound of emotional agony in the ambient room, "These results just in. Was that *really* necessary?"

"Yes it was, I thought it was," he said not a little defensively. "After all, we're going to get married! We can't start a marriage with a secret buried in it! It's a very unhealthy start! It's the sort of thing that starts a time-bomb ticking that's bound to go off down the road."

"I would have thought of that before, but I don't think I knew you were going to propose the night she got back. If I knew she was going to be your *fiancée*, instantaneously upon arrival, do you think I would have crossed *that* line?"

"Yes, given the feeling, given the circumstance, I believe you would have anyway."

"That's beside the point, isn't it? The question is, where do you suggest we go from here?"

Isadora circled by me and took the phone and in a very matter-of-fact voice said, "You better come over here right away. I'm having a very powerful feeling that something terrible is about to happen. Bring your sleeping bag and a full water canteen. Don't take the freeways. It might not be safe." And she hung up the phone.

I tried to talk to her a little about the situation. "Really, it wasn't anything against you, no ill will or *anything*. In fact, we both just missed you so much, we..."

I stopped. She was paying me absolutely no mind. Instead, she was packing a knapsack with survival gear. A flashlight, a flare, a can opener, a plastic water bottle, a package of hardtack, some tins of liver pâté, a chocolate bar, and a can of mandarin oranges. "Think how cheery these canned oranges will be, when we've had nothing but hardtack for a week," she glowed.

"And why would we be eating hard-tack for a week?" I was curious if this was going to be my retribution for having made love with her boyfriend—forced consumption of nothing but hardtack and water for a week.

"It's going to happen," she said, distractedly. "I knew it would and now it is, and we just have to get to a safe place before it actually does."

With more gentle prodding and careful questions, I determined she was having a presentiment about a seismic upheaval she was feeling in the bottoms of her feet.

"I had that dream, and now this has happened, just like in my other dream which led into the one where the walls shook and fell down around me, and then suddenly there I was, on the top of Mt. Pinos, and I knew I'd be safe there. So that's where we're going, until we know it's safe to come back."

I could see she meant what she was saying and this was no joking matter for her. It worried me. But what worried me more was the dream which I had had, recently, of a giant tidal wave crashing against the torn-up cliff where California used to be. I had dreamed it only the night before last. I was someplace high up and watched it from afar. I gulped. I thought, could this be it? The end of the world? Or the night that California finally drops off into the Pacific Ocean! A little panic-fear raced like a scared mouse around my chest cavity, before nuzzling into the solar plexus.

"I think if we can just get to this safe place, we might be able to shift its course. If we can just take the energy into us and move it around." She did a swerving melting thing with undulating hips and arching back. I could see by her now total obsession with the idea of impending doom, she had utterly abandoned, or at least set aside, the anger and pain

she must have been feeling, with the recent install-
ment of True Life Confessions from her *affianced*.

I began to think over the possibility that some
huge natural disaster might in fact be about to
happen. It had been a hell of a hot summer and
now the last days of it were sweltering up to a final
meltdown. Could it be a sign?

I myself come from a long line of psychics and
religious visionaries dating back to rune readers of
the Ancient Celts. I know better than to outright
ignore premonitions. The times I *have* taught me
stern lessons.

I didn't call a friend when I knew I should have.
I had a bad feeling about it, but just overlooked
it. I was deadlining on some pointless academic
paper and said to myself, "I'll call her, just after I
get through this stretch. I'll call her when I have
a break."

Instead, a mutual friend called me to say that
she'd killed herself.

So, when I have a feeling about something, a
strong feeling about something, I try to pay attention
to what it is and do right by it. When Meditation-
Music got there and heard her tell her dream of
earthquakes and upheaval, I followed with my tidal
wave and cliff—a wall of water heading towards us,
standing on the cliff above what used to be the beach.

"That's scary," he said, "because, in fact, I had
a similar dream—but it was a giant explosion, a
fireball of some kind, sweeping across the desert."

Oh my gosh! The skittering little panic-fear had
become a parrot pecking at my rib cage, trying to
get out. The three of us looked at each other and
hugged tightly, all together. "Well, if this is it, this
is it," Meditation-Music said.

Ever notice how ordinary language fails us, when
up against the giant, catastrophic events of real life?

"I feel we should all stay together tonight." Isadora was calm and controlled and clearly having the lead vision. Who were we to dispute the resident shamaness?

We made a plan for an alternate escape route using the surface streets in case the disasters started before we got to Mt. Pinos, and we had to get off the freeway. We were taking the Rover, Betsy, because Isadora felt the spirit of the car would never let us down. As for my fast Little Green Car, I decided that my roommate and my visiting cousin should have a fast getaway car, in case they had to outdrive a tidal wave or ball of fire. I believed it, I really, really did. The scent of inevitable destiny was in the air with the heady fumes of jacaranda and a cloud of crazy mixed up ions. The world as we knew it was going to end tonight.

The two of them followed me in her Rover over to my place in Silver Lake where I changed my clothes and picked up my toothbrush. I never went anyplace, including to the end of the world, without a toothbrush. I gave my visiting cousin—all of eighteen—the keys, with the stern stipulation, "Only use this car in case of an emergency of major proportions—like an earthquake, a tidal wave, that sort of thing."

He'd recently had a run-in with the LAPD when they picked him up for riding a bicycle under the influence. I don't know why I trusted him to handle an expensive sports car in a natural disaster.

"Skinny," I said, turning to my roommate who'd been my closest friend from college, "if anything happens, and for some reason I can't get back here tomorrow, Harvey will be here to protect you."

Harvey the half-coyote was still a big puppy. He specialized in chewing anything leather and rummaging through garbage bags.

103

She looked at me with wide eyes and raised eyebrows and asked, "Are you sure you're doing the right thing?"

She meant about the car. I thought she meant about the apocalyptic vision.

"Trust me," I said, in all seriousness. "I'm sure it's what has to be done."

I hugged her hard, hoping I'd see her again, pointed a teacherly finger at my ne'er-do-well cousin and said, "Be better than you know how!" and ran down the flight of stairs to the waiting getaway vehicle.

We drove down the street and then up and over the huge hill which landed on the other side, on Alvarado Street. We were going to make a quick stop at Safeway, in order to inconspicuously buy some bottled water and canned food. We didn't want to start a riot by making a lot of noise about water shortages in a disaster. After that, we sailed to the freeway only pausing just before the onramp, where I opened the car door to deposit my cigarettes on the sidewalk. I thought now was as good a time as any to quit smoking.

We took I-5 north out of Glendale until we got off at a seemingly deserted exit outside of Gorman and began driving and driving and driving into a pitch black night, up and up a winding road somewhere into the Sierra Madre Mountains. Isadora wasn't fazed. She'd been here before and knew the exact spot we were headed.

We turned up a road marked with a little camping sign and followed a snaky road to a parking lot.

"Where are we?" I asked, wondering that such a long and arduous journey should arrive at such an innocuous place as a blacktop parking lot.

"It's the end of the road," she said, with pluck, in the spirit of one who knows the worst and is bravely going on.

By flashlight, with knapsacks of provisions and blankets rolled in with sleeping bags, we made our way in the inky black beneath the canopy of giant tall pines whose resinous smell permeated the still night air. "Here," she said, leading us off and up a smaller path which ended in a clearing. Patches of star-speckled sky could be seen above, between the interlacing fingers of the trees.

"This is it," she said. "This is the spot in my dreams." She pointed vaguely to a nearby opening between the pines, to a place invisible to the eye from where we stood but from where, she said, you could see for miles.

We'd been very serious throughout the drive, listening to the radio for any hints that these premonitions were coming true. Now, here we were, over 8,000 feet above sea level, on a moonless night among the trees. Isadora had brought a storm lamp, which she lit. We unrolled our sleeping gear and made a beautiful bed in that pine-scented arbor, just above a little barbecue pit which came with the campsite. We gathered kindling from dead scrub which we scouted from around the site and into that small blaze we lay down a few logs which Isadora kept in the trunk of her car for occasions like this—the end of the world or something like it.

Very quickly, we had a comforting fire. Twigs and pine cones made a menthol smoke pour from the flames, over which we warmed a couple of cans of vegetarian beans and boiled a pot of water to brew thick Mexican chocolate made with dry milk and a whole slab of the dense cocoa, cinnamon, and sugar combination.

Meditation-Music brought out from his knapsack a wooden flute of Peruvian origin. He played it like an alto sax, its sweet half-flat tones ricocheting off the timber surrounding us. Very slowly, and imperceptibly, at first, Isadora began to undulate her middle body and ululate her voice which erupted low and animal-like from the middle of her chest and then stampeded out at the top of her lungs. Myself, I had a large gourd rattle which I shook in and out of rhythms I heard and felt between each of us and the certain fears and dreams we brought to Mt. Pinos that night.

There was such a stillness in that night—no wind, just the hot, dry trees settling their scented souls down among us. The dancer, swaying where a windy stillness came to life, asked them through the bottoms of her feet, "Who will speak for the trees? Who will come forth and speak for the trees and all the elementals?"

She paused and listened, in a crouch where her feet were flat upon the ground, and her pelvis pointed straight down to the earth like a woman giving birth on the forest floor. But instead of giving birth, she listened intently to the very quiet voices of deep roots talking to deep roots; to which she responded in syllabic tonal chants. Things like "*Ayyyyyyyyyyyy-yaaaaaaaaaaaaaaaaaa*," and "*Hooooooooooo-soooooooooooo*," and "*weeeeeeeeeeeeee-threeeeeeeeeeeeeeeeee*" were intoned first by her, in a great burst of tonal clarity, followed by me in a choral antiphon of some kind of outer space harmony. All the while, the wooden flute sang its sad earthly pleas to the ground.

And it went on for a while like that, a sort of call-and-response communion between ourselves and the emanations from the earth, from the pine needle floor under our feet to the very tops of the trees which surely brushed the stars when the wind blew; perhaps up there you could probably catch a falling star if you had a basket as big as the Little Dipper.

At last Isadora got up from the crouch and moved in a wider and wider circle around the fire, humming from her solar plexus and then leaping with each giant burst of "HA!" as though it were coming up from the pit of her stomach. "HA!" She belted, and then leapt like a gazelle into the air.

I stood and stretched my body tall up to the sky and exhaled full round tones, starting high and sliding down to the bottom note of my range, which vibrated warmly from my gut up to the middle of my chest. The wooden flute wove a basket of repeating melody which contained all our mutual sounds in a kind of polyphonic unity. When at last Isadora leapt and "HA!"-ed her last and threw herself into pod shape on the ground, the Meditation-Music and I came to a conclusive silence as well.

The only sounds were the dry voices of insects in the undergrowth and the hissing sound of the wood fire dying. When Isadora finally stirred, she did so with a long sigh. "I feel much better about things now. We may have turned the tide. There's only one thing left to do," she said with a vague quiet distance in her voice.

She poured a circle of water around the glowing embers and said a few quiet words to herself. When she looked back at us, it was with a fierce, almost angry yearning, a stricken face like a mask in a Noh play, as she held her arms out to us in that eternal gesture of longing, poignant as any Grecian urn. Of course, we followed her where she led us.

She drew us with her to the bed we'd made on the soft pine-needled forest floor; above us, the stars trickled through the branches; they appeared closer and brighter than I had ever seen them before. She opened her warm strong arms to both of us and we each went in under one of her arms, seduced by her thickly sensual, animal aura. Smiling and rubbing the precise key sensitive spot on my back and his neck, she whispered, "We have to meld our energies now, we have to make three separate nightmares into one sweet dream."

Six separate hands became the hands of Shiva and undid buttons, pulled down zippers, lifted up skirts, and began to touch and ignite exposed patches of skin in a musical rhythm of an otherworldly nature. We seemed just to know, intuitively, what to do to and for each other. With hands and nose and tongues and toes, we sought and found each other out.

He kissed her neck and licked and sucked at her ear. I pulled her leotard down off her shoulders and exposed her breasts which were small girlish handfuls with nipples that pointed out like ski runs. We knelt on the double sleeping bag which had been zipped together and padded with blankets. I continued to suck and lick the one nipple, while he stroked and pinched and teased the other. Between her breasts, at the nape of her neck, the scent of Mysore sandalwood lured me closer.

I vaguely became aware of a primal humming sound which emanated from Isadora's deep-throated middle. Meditation-Music chimed in, at a harmonic fifth below while I joined in a third above.

It was truly a beautiful, sonorous sound we made together, a corporeal rendering of some Music of the Spheres. Together, we shed layer after layer of clothing and coverings until we were just us, naked and cloaked only in that dense night air. We clutched each other then, aching to feel the hot bead of an orgasm start at the tail bone and shoot straight up the spine. We hadn't gotten there yet, though. With three, there's a lot more territory to cover and quite a bit more to do, to get everyone there on the same wave length and then riding the long, rolling curl of it into shore.

We made an isosceles triangle while she sucked him, he sucked me, and I sucked her. All the while, we each took in the building ions and felt the hot red molten stuff bubbling from the first chakra, the base of the spine from where the lava floods up like the mercury in the bulb of a thermometer on a hot day. All the while we hummed and made the deep animal noises which the release of so much sexuality in the aftermath of so much pent-up guilt, anxiety, and fear conjured from a wilder, deeper nature. Wetness poured out of her into me, out of me into him, and he held onto his hard-on until she couldn't stand it anymore and broke from my lips, climbing onto him as he lay on his back, and she faced him.

She took him in and held him squeezed tight by her tight pelvic muscles. I turned, braced on my knees. He licked me and fingered me, all the while I faced Isadora and we held each other forearm by forearm, and kissed, mouth to mouth. I started to come and held even tighter onto her, while she lifted her buttocks and sat down hard. With each groaning gasp, we got closer and closer to something so hot among us, we might have flown apart in opposite directions. Instead, the heat went round and round like a Catherine wheel.

Then we were a flesh-formed fountain bubbling into a three-tiered cascade of love stuff. His innate heat lit her womb room, searing up and through to her solar plexus and beyond the gonging chakras of heart and mind, opening her throat with a long wailing siren of a sigh, surging past the port of her third eye, and straight out the top of her head with a flare of oohs and ahs.

She let loose a cry and I held her, naked breast to breast. The wetness dropped down from inside me, the force of the orgasm throwing me forward as he came—he into her, she into me, me into him.

When it happened, there was no mistaking it. Just as we built up and up and up to the jagged edge before the best feeling ever finally broke loose and flooded the territory with its intoxicating exhalations, a flash of heat lightning lit up the sky. We screamed when it happened, and then again when the thunder cracked, like the crack of a baseball bat. The after-shocks of the orgasm rolled and rolled like big stormy rows of breakers, breaking and rolling one onto another on top of another. Again, the dry, waterless lightning flashed and the thunder cracked—this time more distant—as though the discharge of the three-way circuit had scattered the force of the electrical field.

As it passed, a gentle, cooler wind stirred in the branches of the trees. From the deep sleepy place of utter release and relief, we rearranged our sweating limbs and dripping parts and slid under the layers of blanket and sleeping bags. We slept with Isadora between us, interlocked our lazy limp noodling tentacles in and 'round about each other and drifted off in a spent wet-noodle soup. I heard only the eerie hoot of a predatory owl and Isadora's voice which sighed, "I knew, if we melded, we could move the energy around. I knew we could stop it, just had to focus where the pain was."

She spoke this like a person speaking out of a dream, which Meditation-Music and I melted into, like butter on a warm muffin.

In the morning, the sun rose and made beautiful golden shadows against the trees and out over beyond them I saw to what place Isadora had lead us in the pitch black night, by her instincts and inner vision.

It was a beautiful view, in a frightening sort of way. I had gotten up to go pee in the woods away from where we were sleeping. That's when I saw that we were no more than three, three and a half feet from a cliff's edge and I jumped out of my skin to think of what might have happened if one of us had thrown ourselves, in the throes of passion, a little too forcefully, and found himself or herself taking the shortcut down the mountain. We were pitched on a high incline, near a promontory which jutted out over a valley between mountains which fell endlessly below where we were. I almost wet myself.

Instead, I moved back from that edge and walked naked as a cavewoman up an incline away from the campsite and found a fallen tree which I braced one leg upon. This position, I found, allowed me to force the water out of myself without squirting on my feet or dripping down my leg. I went back to the sleeping bag and crawled into the captured body heat that glowed within it.

The fear that the world was going to end reached closure, but the fear that we might have died, in a simple passionate rolling over, lingered on. I put it aside in favor of Meditation-Music, who also woke, gasped at the near-death view, and went and peed over the edge. When he came back in under the covers, he came over to my side and without asking or saying a word, he put himself, rigid with a morning hard-on, right into me and got me excited all over again. Isadora woke and found us that way, and looked somewhat alarmed, until he pulled out of me and went into her. I was glad he did that. After everything we'd been through that night, I didn't want to start the new day, The First Day of the Rest of my Life, with pain or anger, on top of the fear. I wanted to wake gently and have my own dreams to myself. But there he was, doing me and then her and then me and then her until she just held him tight in her own strong arms and made him finish hard, in her.

I wanted to go back to sleep then and would have, but big black clouds rolled in out of nowhere and broke open as suddenly as they had appeared. In a matter of minutes, we were drenched in a hard, cold rain. We scrambled to find our clothes and get them on, then grabbed up the forest-floor bedclothes. We made a dash for the car and sat in it, then took turns running back to the campsite, bringing down the knapsacks and bean pots and chocolate mugs. We realized the rain meant business and lost our enthusiasm for waiting it out when so much water fell we could barely see out the windows, even while the wipers clicked at top speed.

Slowly, slowly, we worked our way down the same snaky road we'd driven up, which now ran with a small river of water. In all our dreams and nightmares and presentiments, there had been no mention of rain. Earthquakes, tidal waves, fire balls, yes, but rain? Big rain? No. A real surprise, just like in real life!

It took five hours to get down the mountain and back to town. Once, I thought we were going to be marooned at the side of the road just before Hungryville, as we crept along towards Tejon Pass. As we made it to the center of the little town, we noticed a rippling tide of water cascading down the street. We stuck to the high side of town and found a greasy spoon for breakfast.

A couple of plates of buttermilk pancakes and a few strips of bacon later, we were back out there, trying to make our way through the deluge. No one said much except things like "Wow! It sure is raining hard!"

When at last they dropped me at my house in Silver Lake, my roommate informed me that my cousin had called from Disneyland where he had driven in my car. Someone had slashed my tires

112

in the parking lot, he claimed, and told me that he had to have the car towed from Anaheim to my house. How did I want to pay for it, cash on arrival or with a credit card?

Meanwhile, the rain fell and fell and eventually filled our roof up to the brim. The water found every crack beneath the deteriorating stucco and tile trim, and then proceeded to run, like a water-fall, down the living room wall, flooding the floor and heading for the front door.

I looked at that and saw my dream, my prophecy come true, a wall of water facing me, racing past me, and roaring down our front porch to steps down to the street. I threw towels everywhere and pulled myself up onto the living room couch, contemplating the last remark Isadora made, before we parted company that day. I had asked her, "What do you think? Would the world have ended if we hadn't gone away?"

She answered, the shamaness of her own religion, "Who's to say that the one correct thought, the one perfect individual gesture can't change the course of even apocalyptic disasters? It may be raining now just *because* we took that huge ball of energy into ourselves and moved it from where it was to some-place else. If this deluge came instead of the fires, the earthquakes, and the tidal waves that are going to take California down to the bottom of the sea one of these days, then I, for one, am glad for the rain."

She smiled, her hair in wet Medusa ringlets round her face, and then disappeared down the steps to take her soggy lemon-honey lover home to hot tea and a long, long nap.

It rained for five days, just that hard. Lakes which were reduced to bare muddy bottoms filled up and came alive again. Part of the Coast Highway did sort of slide into the beach, but not enough to

113

really frighten the cliff dwellers into moving, not quite yet.

When it stopped, all the lawns were green again and the dichondra went madly lush wherever it was planted. The three of us separated back into the two of them and the one of me. We finished our collaboration and witnessed the performance during a special literary week for undergraduates at the university where I was still a graduate student. Life normalized.

But at the back of my mind, that feeling of terror lingered. Not the terror that the world was coming to an end, which it may yet, but the terror of waking and realizing how close we were to falling off, into the pitch-black hole of night, down the face of Mt. Pinos, without knowing where or how we would land. That was the unsettling part, which even now will emerge from my unconscious from time to time and give me a full-blown case of cold nightmare sweats.

BLUE MOVIE AT DODGER STADIUM

There were still an awful lot of papers to sort—first, second, and third drafts of several lengthy graduate school documents, and all my notes for the doctoral dissertation I was living instead of writing: *The Rhetoric of Sex in the Post-Modern* Imagination—for that heap, I had a special plan. First, second, third or more drafts of poems, stories, and plays from the first ten years of my more-or-less first grab at grown-up life, ages sixteen to twenty-six. There were letters I was saving and letters I was tossing. A collection of confetti-bright origami papers I had been collecting since age twelve. Scraps of paper with scrawls of ideas, phone numbers with no names, and words for my word collection which I kept in notebooks and date books, and on heaps of foolscap pads filled with words like "sesquipedalian" and "boustrophedon."

And then there were the drawings and art pieces and all the supplies that went with them and heaps of scrolls of brushed works made with my friend, Isadora-the-Dancer, who convinced me I had to keep even our rough outlines of projects because someday they would be used to document our collaboration. These remnants would give the critics something to write about.

She was very convincing on the subject, and so for a long time I did carry around a file box of things labeled with our two last names and then the title "A Working Relationship." This bit of young, archival hubris on our parts was born of my literary scholarship into the ars dictaminis—the art of letter writing—wherein vast collections of letters revealed huge untold stories—mostly the stories of the women left out of history: Her-story vs. His-story. Anyway, I came to regard even scraps of paper we made notes on—the backs of paper place mats in restaurants, that sort of thing— even they were in the box, saved for posterity. Isadora believed, really believed, that her fate was sealed with the sign of the Artist, and that history would record it—her story would matter, because it was the life of the artist that mattered above all. That's what she thought, and I guess I shared that suspension of disbelief, at least while we were there and then, when we were young and doing everything for the first time, with big, blinking eyes.

And maybe being an artist did matter more back then. It was the '70s, and Art was valued as something special and apart from mass culture, rather than being condemned on trumped-up charges of elitism. Art stood in for a lot in those days—icons for peace, political dissent, and Freedom—just to name a few crucial areas of discourse where Art had a place at the table. Whether it was Judy's Chicago's Dinner Party, or a monument to 50,000 dead soldiers, Art had a hand in it all.

For me, the very word "Art" seeded in my heart of hearts a little wish-hope for the kind of magic that comes when one has held true to the course, sustained belief, walked on water, and gotten there—wherever there might be. In *that* place, at *that* time, it was all about Art and becoming the Artist I wanted to be, and the intellectual busy body I was abandoning to do so.

In mid-June '79, I believed anything could happen because just about anything was already happening, and it didn't look like it was going to let up any time soon. So, I sorted and packed, and the disparate points of my life continued to unravel around me into brightly colored spiraletic heaps all over the floor of the living room, the dining room, the kitchen, and my bedroom. A second set of sorting, stacking and spiraling was taking place in my studio out back. It was overwhelmingly everywhere. My roommate clung close to his room, ate meals out, and avoided kicking my heaps as best he could.

Harvey the half-coyote didn't care for it much either; he got up from time to time, picked his way through the discrete messes, wagged his tail, whined, and then wobbled into the foot space under my desk, flopping down with a groan and a high squeal and looking at me with sad eyes.

"Don't worry, Harv," I said, reassuring him. "When I head out of this pop stand, you'll be right beside me as we speed up the Coast Highway to finally begin *Our Real Life: A Woman and Her Dog on the Road*. We'll eat hot dogs and burgers all the way! You'll love it!"

He looked at me with those shiny dog eyes and a big coyote grin and wagged his tail hard against the wall. I knew he got the point.

Gem-Man came and picked me up in the early evening and I was ready for an escape. He was taking me to Dodger Stadium for a baseball game. It was another place I hadn't been and something else I hadn't done. He made a list which included it and other such places, checking them off as we went along, counting down the days to the last.

In point of fact, I *had* been there before, but not for a game. I didn't mention it because it was a little complicated. Besides, we were there with an old friend of his whom I didn't know at all and wasn't about to include in my intimate sex secrets.

We pulled into the huge lots and parked behind the stadium, then became part of the cheerful leagues of baseball fans moving in waves toward the stadium stairwells. We had our tickets already, so we could go directly in and find our seats, which were on the first-base line. As soon as we got settled, Gem-Man and his friend went to hunt and gather a box of beer and hot dogs from the nearest stand and (I later surmised) trade trips to the bathroom for little silver spoons of something pharmaceutical.

I was left to examine the players warming up on the field through the binoculars we'd brought along. I also scanned the crowd for anyone interesting to look at. There were skinny girls in halter tops with thick red lips and Farrah Fawcett hair, demure in baseball caps; guys with long hair tied back with bandana browbands, rakish under baseball hats; guys with short hair and skinny tees, macho-n-fuckin' 'A' in baseball hats; big women in butterfly-print Ban-Lon shells and flowered pants, bosomy in baseball hats—all of them, came in all colors: black, white, brown, pink, you name it. A lot of America was out there that night.

The boys of summer in all their finery, trim-calved and beautiful, threw long fast hard balls, ninety miles an hour, from one end of the field to the other. Base to base, base to pitcher, pitcher to outfield, outfield to first, first to home, catcher back to pitcher. Thwap! Balls hit leather mitts. Everyone is awake with the sound, anticipating the game. I liked to watch the concentration in their faces as they threw. They were beautiful in their precision, their utter focus on one single thing—the ball. I admired their arms and studied their crotches. I contemplated pinching their buns.

I looked at them, I looked at the crowd, and cast a quick fast eye on the dark glass enclosing the Stadium Club. I looked at it through the binoculars and wondered, was *he* there now? I could see nothing. The stadium faded and all I could see were the pictures in my head, a few strong recol-

118

lections of the whole brief affair. I could roll the reels at any time and review them, in there, where the best movies are. Reel I: *The Seduction*, Reel II: *The Consummation*, Reel III: *The Brush Off.*

Reel I: The Seduction—I can see his cheeks dimple and his red car shine. He engages me in conversation at H. G. Daniels where I buy my art supplies. He is looking at the India Inks and I am lusting over a complete set of technical pens, while I am supposed to be buying props for a project with Isadora-the-Dancer. He asks me, "Have you ever used this stuff before?" pointing to the rack of various colored inks.

"Only black. With pens. Sometimes with a paint brush. They're permanent and you can water color over them."

"That's what I really like to do," he says, nodding, smiling, his Clark Gable ridges making their first impression on me, "watercolors."

"Oh yes, they are nice," I go on, continuing the conversation, knowing the guy was turning on to me, not caring, because he is handsome and has a familiar texture about him.

"Are you a painter?" I ask, expecting anyone who buys art supplies to be striving in that direction, to be an artist, which is what I thought everyone wanted to be and only became other things, like doctors or lawyers or insurance salesmen because they couldn't make art.

"No, no," he says, a little embarrassed, "it's a hobby. I took as many art classes in college as I could, but I was in the School of Business for the most part. We didn't have much time for extracurriculars like that. But I made do."

Then, in one of those enough-about-me-let's-talk-about-you romantic comedy switches, he manages to shift the focus onto me and of course I spill all over the floor. I'm there buying vivid red paint and the perfect brush for a poem/dance/mixed-media piece I'm doing with my friend, Isadora, at A Woman's Place, an experimental gallery in the industrial section of downtown L.A.

"It is a poem," I explain, "which is choreographed with exact painting gestures in red, on long scrolls of white paper hanging from the gallery ceiling."

I describe the piece enthusiastically and the dark stranger appears to be equally interested. I tell him, "I have to find the perfect clay bowl to hold the red paint."

"I know just the place to go," he says, elated for the opening to wedge his way into my day.

"Really?" I say, with wide eyes and girlish wonder. "What a coincidence!"

We ride in his fast red sports car, glide onto and off the Pasadena Freeway, to a large open-air market of articles made of clay. I find the perfect pot, an archetypal one which could hold red paint playing the part of menstrual blood, in fine, highly symbolic fashion. We smile and drive off again—fade to black.

I came back to Dodger Stadium when Gem-Man and his friend returned from the lavatory or wherever they went to snort up. The friend sat on the aisle so he could stretch out his six-foot-something length and settle his two-hundred-and-fifty-pound bulk as comfortably as possible in the usual stadium seat. His nickname was Tiny Tim and I hated it—that dumb cliché forced upon extra-large people to be called Tiny or Teeny or Little Something-or-Other. I put the animosity aside and stood up to allow Gem-Man to take the seat on the other side of me, sandwiching me between them, which they seemed to want to do. They had brought back several very tall and wide-mouthed cups of foaming beer and more than several feet of hot dogs rolled up in paper and dripping with onions and mustard and relish. We all stood for the National Anthem and then cheered when the announcer barked over the loud-speaker, "Play Ball!"

I can't remember the team the Dodgers were playing because that's how I am about baseball games. I am literally, "Who's on first?" My knowledge of the rules is limited to "Three strikes, you're out." Also, "if you get hit by the pitcher on the pitch, you walk, if you are able, to first base." I do understand that every time a player crosses home plate, the batting team gets a point. Other than that, I am an innocent and I don't care who knows it.

But I didn't labor the point to Gem-Man. I knew he was really looking forward to the "Take Me Out to The Ball Game" expedition and I felt the least I could do was eat my hot dogs and drink my beer uncomplainingly. We stood, we cheered, whenever *Our Team* made a hit. It was part of the choral dance of this large, mythically proportioned National pastime. We acted out its antiphony and it didn't matter that I didn't know who the Dodgers were playing or how many balls make a strike.

Reel I of my Inner Blue Movie was still going off in my head. The handsome, dark-haired stranger with a Clark Gable smile takes me to lunch at one of those places you hope you'll find but don't because only the really cool insiders know about them. This place makes the best hamburgers in L.A., and serves them with homemade potato salad and tall icy glasses of fresh-squeezed lemonade. They have sumptuous pie. He takes great pride in bringing me to this place and I am far more impressed than I would have been if he had started out in some Scandia-type joint. I've always been a sucker for plain good food in an unpretentious atmosphere.

At the end of our outing, he asks if he can see me again. "Of course," I say, "call anytime," unconvinced somehow that he will. He is more or less

121

self-impressed and very interested in the sound of his own voice. But I'm not paying much attention to that or what he's saying. I'm busy admiring the combination of his Hollywood smile and that deep California tan.

It was the end of the third inning and Gem-Man and his big Tiny friend went to get more beer and do more of whatever they were doing. Gem-Man offered me a miniature bottle to take to the girl's room with a little silver spoon. I said no, I didn't feel like biting my cheek and clenching my jaw for the next couple of hours.

It was more than that, though. People I knew and loved were dying of the stuff. Myself, I didn't want to go that way. I had enough vices to take me down that cul-de-sac on my own scenic route. I was smoking Russian Sobranies, English Cut Ovals, and a variety of French cigarettes. I didn't need to take the fast track on something I was already chipping away at, bit by bit, puff by puff, persistently over time, in my own private love/hate relationship with Lady Death.

When they were gone, I floated out there again, where *He* was waiting for me, for dinner, at the top of Reel II. *He comes by the house in Silver Lake which I imagine he'll really like. Instead, he makes some remark like, "Oh yes, when I was in school, I might have had a place like this." Only I don't think that way about it. I love it as a great place to live and be an artist in. I'm writing and drawing in tandem, and I have my art work in process all over the house. He says, "You leave your stuff out like this?"*

"When I'm right in the middle of it, why would I put it away? It's an ongoing process. It's art."

"It's just different from how I do things," he says. "I like to take out my paints, paint a while, do a picture, then put it all away, until I want to paint again."

"The point is," I go on in a tone slightly testier

than I mean to project so early in the encounter, "I want to do it every day, like it's my real life, not just on the weekends or some late night I can't sleep and so I think, 'Oh I'll make a little art tonight and feel better, if you see what I mean."

He raises his eyebrows slightly and looks me up and down, "Are you ready to go? We have a reservation at Genevieve's. Let's not be late."

He says it like he knows me well and is prepared for me to dawdle. Somehow, he's already made up his mind about what kind of person I am and how I will behave in such and such a circumstance. I don't like it very much. But he has something about him I am getting drawn into, an annoying magnetism, or the confidence that comes with a hugeness of material wealth behind it.

And he does have that. His family, it unfolds, owns some several hundred movie theatres nationwide and a number of multi-star restaurants. That's what he's doing just now, managing one of the restaurant/bar combinations. It's just temporary, until he decides what part of the family business he really wants to tackle. I want to be interested, except every time he starts to talk about what he's doing and why, I can't help myself from stifling a yawn.

He takes me to a very exquisite, undoubtedly fantastically expensive restaurant, where movie stars come and go, and nobody bats an eye and neither do I. I try to find some shared, ordinary territory where we can speak and be stimulated by each other. He's busy in another direction, explaining just how all women in their mid-twenties go through the same thing; they all go through the marriage crisis—either they decide to get married or they decide not to, and the ones that decide not to don't think about it again until their mid-thirties or else don't think about it at all.

123

"Oh," I say, not wanting to let on that I am going back and forth on that very subject. He seems to know it already and I also find that very annoying. Still, he keeps smiling and ordering the most delicious food on the menu, which comes with extraordinary panache and bottles of possibly great, but definitely audaciously over-priced, wine. I keep my cards close to my chest and keep him on the track of himself, which is easy since he's a natural born "talking man."

After dinner that night, I say I would just like to go home, that I have things to do and think about the rest of the night, and I let on that these things don't include him at this time. I think to myself, that'll be it. I won't hear from this hard-on again. I think to myself how perverse I am, letting this one get away like that. A handsome, rich, single man in a fast red car? Most girls would just tuck and roll for him and apparently, a lot of them already had.

But he surprises me when he calls a week later and asks me to have Sunday brunch with him at a cozy little spot near where I live.

The crack of a bat caught my attention, and everyone jumped to their feet and brayed and hooted like crazy birds. Someone on our team had just hit a home run. The crowd went wild. The guys on either side of me brayed with the rest and sat down again.

It was the top of the sixth inning and I wanted another hot dog to balance out the beers, which were making me cross-eyed. But Gem-Man insisted I wait it out. "We're going to have a really terrific meal at "Machu Picchu" afterwards. I promise, you won't be sorry you waited."

In the meantime, I thought, what's going to get me through to the bottom of the sixth and the top of the seventh? "Peanuts," I insisted. "Just get me a bag of peanuts and I'll be happy."

Reel II kicked back in and the *Dark Stranger* comes into view.

It's a gray rainy day and not at all like a day in May, which it is. He picks me up at my place. I'm wearing one of many vintage dresses I've collected over the years, a deco pattern of Lily of the Valley on a sheer, see-through late '30s rayon. I wear a pink silk and lace slip underneath and a well-cut gabardine jacket over it. It's my own particular style and that's how I want it.

He drives us east on Sunset and makes a quick left turn into a slightly hidden drive which arrives at a rear door to Dodger Stadium. "Oh, are we going to eat at the ball game?" I ask, amazed that there's a game on such a crummy day and that we're going to it.

"No, no," he laughs, his teeth glinting, even in the gray of that day. "We're just going to the Stadium Club."

We take a private elevator which he operates with a key and up we go, arriving in the sparkling stainless steel kitchen of the Club.

"Listen," I say, "this place doesn't even look open, are you sure we should be here?"

"Don't worry about it," he says. "I know the people who own it. I've got the keys to the place."

Then he proceeds to make a beautiful breakfast of little tender steaks and Eggs Benedict with hollandaise. I sit on a stool and watch him work, drinking a bottomless mimosa—freshly squeezed oranges mixed with a decent champagne which he imperceptibly attends to, between watching the eggs and toasting the muffins, flipping the steaks, and whisking the sauce. He cooks gracefully and cleanly, and I really admire his proficiency.

I have always found men who cook sexier than those who merely eat, however well they do it. Men who cook often have a good woman buried deep inside of them, a secret nurturer. Except for when it doesn't mean that, but means instead that the he in question went to school in the restaurant trade and knows how to do it all for show. At that moment, it doesn't matter which it is, because I'm entranced by it and him and the big empty restaurant in which he's preparing an intimate breakfast for two.

We sit at the bar, in the high, leather-backed seats. The food is professionally delicious, and I eat it with gusto, swilling cups of steaming hot coffee between mouthfuls.

Then he begins to pull out the liquors and make fluffy sweet espresso drinks for dessert and that's when we start to get hot and sticky with each other. We had already gotten a little warmly gooey in the course of the meal and now are sitting knees within interlocking knees, facing each other on the bar stools.

He grins at me with those Clark Gable trenches again and says, "I'm trying to decide whether we should go slow for a long haul, or go fast and free with the thrill of the moment."

"That's easy," I say. "Ontologically speaking, I am born of the thrill, I drive a fast car, and "free" rhymes with me. I think it's pretty obvious where we're going from here, don't you?" I am playing my hand boldly.

"That's interesting you should say that. I was in fact hoping you'd say that. What are you doing for dinner tonight?"

"Whoa, wait a minute, didn't we just eat breakfast? Do we have to make a plan for dinner before we've even digested?"

"Well, you may not have to, but I do, because it's Mother's Day, and I'm booked for dinner with my mother, so I was just wondering if you would consider having dinner with us."

"Dinner," I say, "with your mother?" He nods. "On Mother's Day?" I ask again, incredulous. He nods.

"No, I can't do that. That's way too personal for me."

"It doesn't have to be. All you have to do is be yourself, be the pleasant company you already are, and enjoy the dinner."

"And meet your Mother? No, I really can't do that right now. I just did that only too recently and it makes a lot of things a lot harder because, in the end, I liked his mother more than him. And that just made everything that much harder when I was trying to not get married to him. But that was before I began to think that I probably should get married, particularly to him."

"And where are you on it now?" he asks, pouring another small snifter of Kahlua into my Coffee Nudge, with which I guess he's planning to nudge me over.

"Not," I say, matter-of-factly. "Maybe never."

"Not?" His eyebrows arch high over his Tia Maria-colored eyes.

"Not getting married. No Mother's Day. No thank you."

"I see," he hums, and bends his face into mine and dives for my mouth with his lips. Our knees open to each other and our limbs interlock. He pushes the skirt of my dress and my pink slip up and back and looks for the way into my panties. My knee presses against, rubbing rhythmically against, his crotch and I know he is on, instantly, as it happens, play by play.

We make out like that for a while and then he's pulling my panties off, down my legs from underneath my garter belt, which I like wearing with dark silk stockings. He peels them down and then picks me up and moves me down the bar, to where it was standing room only. With no chairs to block us from the counter he puts my bottom down on the glossy mahogany; he spreads my legs. "That's

127

very pretty," he says, stroking my electric fur.

My cheeks flush and I know I am dripping.

"Hmmm" he says, *"oysters on a half shell."* And he tips me back and sucks me on the hot spot.

I'm squirming but he keeps his wits about him. He picks me up and puts me down again, facing the bar, with my feet on the foot rest. He opens my dress and lifts my breasts out of the cups of my bra and fondles them, one and then the other, with one hand while the boys of summer cracked another one out of the ball park and the crowd went insane again. The announcer belted in that weird hyper-amplified way, "He's done it again, another home run for the Dodgers!" And the organ went *"doodle-lee-doo-dee-doo!"* And everyone screamed and jumped up and down and screamed some more and Gem-Man slapped me on the back and congratulated all of us, "How about that! Wow! We're in for extra innings tonight! I'd better call the restaurant and move our reservation! Do you want that hot dog after all, just to tide you over?"

"Yes!" I shouted "Yes! I want a hot dog! I *need* a hot dog! *Please,* get me a hot dog!"

He left and his friend stayed and smiled broadly at me, as he toasted me with another cup of foaming golden possibilities.

I used the binoculars again and studied the crotch of the pitcher one more time, wondering about the size of his guard, in relation to the size of what it guarded. The sun had gone down and now the cool desert night was dampening my enthusiasm for Dodger Stadium altogether. Still, I ate my footlong hot dog and didn't complain. I went back to my X-rated recollection and caught up with the footage at the point where *he* was unzipping his pants with his *other*, unbusy hand.

I'm stretched forwards, over the mahogany bar,

layers of dress and pink slip up around my waist. My black lace garter belt holds up my silk stockings, legs spread, black heels braced on the footrest of the bar. I hold myself in place, holding the edge of the opposite side of the counter top. His unzipped pants are held in place with his buckled belt. He pulls his hard-on cock out of his red silk briefs and he's just the right height to push into me, from where he stands behind me. He pushes in and stirs it round and round and rubs my swelling pink wetness with fingers that like what they feel.

I come before he does and he holds himself still while I rattle the coffee cups with jiggling hips and threaten the wine glasses hanging upside down over the bar mirror with high-pitched happy She-noodle noises.

He likes it but he doesn't let go. Instead, he scoops me up and lays me out on a long banquet table covered over with a triple layer of white table cloths. My dress fans out all around me. Now he drops his pants for real, right down to the ankles and steps out of them altogether. He keeps his argyle socks and yellow oxford shirt on. It isn't warm in that room, even with the body heat full on. He opens my legs and comes back in where he was, but asks, as he is doing it, "How 'bout it, are we safe?"

And by that I take him to mean birth control, which I assure him I am, with copper-seven in place. We are thinking of issues of life, not death. I am glad he asks, because not all do nor care to think of consequences. I want him to know that I appreciate his thought so I grab him inside with my pelvic muscles, which he likes and says with hot breath in my ear, "Yes, do that, do that again, squeeze hard."

I hold it like a tight fist while he gets a rhythm going. I know when he's going to come, he goes fast and I can feel it in his skin, the warmth pouring off

129

him. I grab his ass and squeeze with inner pulses just as he goes off in his own shiver of spine and thrust. And then we are quiet except for the sound of my own heart sounding a pulse in my own inner ear.

It's the top of the ninth and the Dodgers have managed to trade a seven-point lead for a seven-point lag. People were beginning to leave. Gem-Man was inclined to do likewise. Tiny Tim was inclined to agree. I said, "Sure, why not! Let's beat the traffic." I was less than a hundred percent present regardless of the beer factor, which was not inconsiderable. I said vaguely, as though from the back of my mind, "If I'm one of forty thousand people here tonight and if they all feel the way I do, and see as many simultaneous balls as I do, I don't want to be in the same parking lot with them, never mind let loose on a freeway in any direction!"

I sat in the back seat of the yellow Mercedes as we sped into the purple-ink night. I rolled the window down and Gem-Man rolled back the sunroof. The wind blew in and around and shook up our brain cells. We were listening to the end of the game on the radio until it was just too bleak for the guys to take. Then it was an old tape of the Rolling Stones singing the way they did, the way no one will ever sing it again, *"I can't gehett no-oh, sa-tis-fack-shunnnn...I can't get no... satisfaction, but I try, and I try, and I try and I TRYYYYYYY..."*

The boys sang along, while I ran Reel III.

I pull myself together in the ladies' room, while he picks up the dishes and changes the tablecloth. He piles plates in the big stainless sink and squirts them with water from the tall, overhanging professional kitchen spigot. "Should I dry or anything?" I ask, hoping he'll say no.

"I'm just rinsing them," he assures me. "Someone will get them in the morning."

130

"Don't you think it might annoy the people whose keys you have, if you use the place and don't clean up after yourself?"

"Not to worry." Teeth gleam and eyes twinkle in the steamy water he sprays in the sink. "The manager is a very close associate."

He drives me home on slow, clever streets in the old neighborhoods between the Stadium and Silver Lake. We don't talk much. We percolate on the afterglow of hot sex and a good breakfast. When he pulls up to the steep front steps to my white stucco bungalow, I turn to him and am just going to say, "Goodbye. Thanks for brunch and blablabla," when I'm overcome with a sudden urge to speak exactly what I am thinking at that exact moment.

I say, "That was a terrific date. I'll never forget it. If I'd just known you a little sooner in my life or met you sometime later from now, we might have had a chance. As it is, I'm a woman on my way someplace else." I kiss him fast on the cheek and say, fast, "I'm sorry I won't meet your mother."

"I am too," he says. "She's a redhead like you. I think you would have liked her."

"Oh!" I say, a catch of regret in my voice, which catches even me by surprise. Still, driven by some sort of species instinct, something akin to flight over fight, I get out of the car and run fast up the steps to the porch. From that safe distance, I watch the fast red car slide away, turn the corner, and disappear down the street lined with tall Egyptian palms from another era. Fade to black.

TALKING MEN

Over the years, I have noticed a characteristic shared commonly among men as a group. Apart from a single-minded interest in their own penises, men share the trait of being chiefly interested in talking about themselves.

I believe I noticed this early on in my teens, when I saw how it went with the popular people— the girls who knew intuitively that the way to get boyfriends was to dote and cluck, while fanning those burgeoning boy-man egos. And, of course, the other way to get them was to have sex with them, which was problematic then in a different way than it is now, but problematic none the less. We were worried about getting pregnant from having sex, not dying from it.

Then as now, "Talking Men" turn up everywhere. I've met them on planes and in lobbies of hotels. I've met them at cocktail parties at faculty clubs and in smoky back corners of blues bars. I've met them in coffee shops and movie theaters, gallery openings and theatrical closings. Once they get a hold of your ear, they can't let it go. They've just got to tell you everything they know and everything they think they know, whether they really know it or not is irrelevant, because they are going to tell you anyway. There's no stopping them. And if you try to tell them something they don't know, they just interrupt you, shush you, or rapidly topic shift to something more about themselves.

I once tried to hang up on one Talking Man's tirade and at first, he forbade me to do so. When I did anyway, he called me back. When I wouldn't answer the phone, he wrote me a letter which picked up where he'd left off on the phone. He was an aggressive and self-impressed little man who took ex-

treme umbrage that I did not find him interesting, that I did not regard him as a mentor, and that I did not care about his very important work. I believe he is still plotting his revenge against me.

That was an extreme case. Not all Talking Men are busy boring the tea cups over Chinese food or hammering a point while sawing a T-bone. Some Talking Men I have had to draw out and I wasn't the least bit sorry. The ones with the real stories to tell— like the painter who spoke his life in Faulknerian fragments or the genius son of Russian immigrants who survived his childhood in Bedford-Stuyvesant by running fast and talking faster. Those were the ones for me, the ones who had lived life largely and had learned something from it; survived great pain or grief and lived to tell their stories. I count myself lucky to have known a few like that, a few good Talking Men.

And of course, because absolutes are so absolutely wrong-headed, I do want to point out that there have been some excellent men of few words, who know when less is more and who actually might ask a woman for her opinion, outright and then listen when she tells it to him. Those men exist! I have met them!

As for the rest, it makes dining out with those hungry talking ghosts a tad more bearable if you can remember to apply this simple formula: the exchange of endless yammer for the price of dinner should amount to roughly the equivalent of going rates for therapy--a minimum of sixty dollars per hour, but more like ninety. Otherwise, home alone with Lean Cuisine just might be the better option.

TAPAS DANCING

When the yellow Mercedes came to a rest, it was under the overhang of the restaurant we'd been saving ourselves for all evening. Though we really hadn't been, because I couldn't even remember how many hot dogs we'd ended up stuffing down and who knows how many humongous cups of beer to follow them. Still, Gem-Man and his Big-Tiny-friend-who-wasn't-very-small were just thrilled to have a table at Machu Picchu in West L.A. To me it was a very nondescript building behind a tall hedge which was supposed to barricade the large-surface street noise that roared by out there on some boulevard like Olympic or Wilshire. I think I was supposed to be impressed that we got a reservation there, but I didn't care one way or the other about it. I was strictly along for the ride.

I ordered a hot cognac and black coffee to get my feet and fingers warmed up after the cool car ride. They ordered an obscure Peruvian specialty of the house, something called a pisco sour. It was a frosty whipped lime affair which they drank several of, rapidly, and became very jolly, very quickly.

It was ten o'clock and we were finally sitting down for a late-night tapas dinner, at this top-of-the-line, very private place. We sat in a curved leather-seated booth which allowed us to look out together at the rest of the room of other booths built into and against the curving walls of the building. From our booth, we could see just part of another booth across the way, where a party of four or five were arranged on the curved banquette so that from where we were, we saw only one of the people at the table. Albeit, she was the only good one to look at—a high-class natural blonde, Bel Air bred and fed. Hair waved down to a strapless evening gown held up under some gossamer wings over her shoulders by something heavily underwired and hooked into place.

We all noticed her at once, and then Gem-Man and Big-Tiny, *especially* Big-Tiny, latched onto her as a topic of conversation.

"Nice emeralds," Gem-Man remarked. She was wearing an astonishing choker, like a dog collar, made of huge green jewels set in circles of discreet little diamonds.

"Do you think it's got a little grommet on the back? For the leash, I mean?" I asked with mischievous candor. I didn't know what effect it would have.

"Oh boy!" said Big-Tiny. "A leash! You could use it when she sits on your face, you could pull her down, make her heel, and suck you off."

He started like that and went on from there. I thought, "Oh boy! This guy is going to jack off with his mouth for our dining pleasure!"

I asked Gem-Man, "What's the food of the house?" moving to step around Big-Tiny's opening gambit, like a pile of dog doo.

"Tapas," he said.

"Stop us?" I asked

"No, no tapas, it's a Spanish thing, little dishes of food for a late supper, but this place does it with a South American touch. Exotic, with a kick."

"I get it. Menu of the conquistadors meets sweet South American produce. They have a hot Latin affair and tryst late at night in dark places like this, hold hands under the table, and make delicious dishes together."

The raver stopped slurping for a minute to wipe pisco foam from his mouth and repeat the phrase, "delicious dishes, delicious dishes, delicious dishes" and then said "Now *that's* a mouthful!"

"One can only hope!" I threw out, craning my

neck to see if there was a waiter on the horizon.

"Don't worry, they'll bring us one of everything and then if we need more, we can order whatever we like the best," said Gem-Man, meaning nothing more than "Sit tight! Dinner's coming!"

His friend jumped in the deep end of suggestive meanings. "That says it perfectly!" He lurched toward profundity. "My exact theory and practice at whorehouses nationwide: one of everything and more of the best."

"Whorehouses?" I asked, not without interest.

Gem-Man filled in, "Oh yeah, our boy here is quite the patron of first-class brothels."

Big-Tiny suddenly interjected, perhaps trying to derail the topic or perhaps genuinely distracted, "Look at her!" He pointed over to the Dinner Blonde. "She's leaning forward so we can see her cleavage. Look at it! That crack between those bubbies, don't you just want to stick your tongue in there and drive her insane?"

The food started to arrive on big round trays covered with bowls of beautifully dressed tidbits— plantains with a pineapple chili salsa, fried sweet banana with sour cream, grilled steak with peppercorn sauce, chicken with papaya relish, and about thirty other things.

I ate ravenously and prodded between lascivious bites, "Whorehouses, I want to know all about them."

"The best one's out here. The place is run like a five-star hotel. Very discreet. Very expensive. The room fee starts at $200 an hour and then there are the extras—champagne, oysters, Nova Scotia lox, Russian caviar, chocolate sauce, you name it, you can get it there and the same is true for the rest of it. Oo-ooh, look at her eating! Oh, Baby! Eat me! Eat me too!"

He pointed us back to the Dinner Blonde, as

she ate flan with some kind of wild berry sauce. She was eating it, taste by taste, half spoon by half spoon, starting at the outside edge of the bowl containing the custard and working her way into the center, making it last, making a spiral, showing her true brain waves. We all admired her pursed lips around the spoon and her pink tongue licking off the creamy stuff drenched in the red and purple juices of crushed black and red raspberries.

"When you go to this place, wherever it is, what happens first?" I pushed on. I wanted to know.

"It's a very nice Westwood condominium complex." He confided. "The buildings are all owned by our friendly favorite Madame. When you get there, you have to check in with her. She's got the master booking schedule and knows who's occupied and who's free. She'll show you a photo album and let you pick from the available list. For an additional charge, she'll let you view a selection of the available choices."

"When do you pay?" I wanted to know.

"The initial two hundred you pay up front, plus any little special orders you've got, the champagne, the favorite trick, whatever, it's all extra. The Lady of the House likes you to drop at least five hundred bucks a visit, though she'll never say it. If you fall short of the minimum she has in her mind for you to fork over, the next time you come calling, you may not get what you want. You may not get anything at all. She just won't buzz you in the gate. But I guess that doesn't happen too often. Her best clients expect to pay and expect good, confidential service."

"So, do you pay the Madame or do you pay the Service Provider?"

"Both. You pay your minimums to the Madame, think of it as your guarantees, that you're going to get what you say you want to get, and a specified amount of time in the room. Then, when you're there with the girl, you can turn up the volume with tips for special favors, techniques, that sort of thing. Makes all the difference between your ordinary blowjob and a real blow-*out* one, I can tell you!"

He snapped his fingers with delight and out of the side of his mouth he said, "She knows I want her, she's going to give me something too, wait and see!"

He was referring to the Bel Air Dinner Blonde again. Her table was clearly coming to the end of its after-meal repartee. The bald man whose back was to us picked up the check for the party. We could just glimpse the four crisp one hundred dollar bills as he took them from his billfold and tucked them into the leather check billet. The couple on the outside moved out of the booth and went ahead to leave. The bald man stood and went to help his wife out. She moved slowly, moving ass and legs, legs and ass, *bump, bump, bump* across the banquette. Her breasts quivered in her underwired strapless support. The emeralds caught all the light in the room. She pushed her legs out from beneath the table and for a brief moment both calves and part of one thigh were exposed in the slit up the side of her dress.

None of us said anything. Big-Tiny grabbed my forearm and squeezed it hard and whispered under his breath, "O God there it is, there it is, her ankle! Look at that ankle! Give it to me, yeah!"

A moment later, her high heels were on the floor and her attentive bald husband helped her up from the banquette seat. She whispered something in his ear. He glared at us through thick-lensed, slightly tinted, heavy dark-rimmed glasses for a moment, then followed his wife into the darkened exit.

We were left in a brief, stunned silence.

"She had eyes for me, right? She gave me the leg,

right? I could 'a had her, if *he* hadn't been around."

"So," I persisted, on to our own dessert binges of things with cream and chocolate, sugar, and liquor, "What is it that you *like* about the arrangement? Is it that you get what you want?"

"Yeah, you said it. You get what you want, with the babe of your dreams, and the next day, you walk away from it. Clean. No bills from Rodeo Drive."

"So part of it is that you are in control." I was pushing the documentary interview style, pumping the interviewee for the good sound bite.

"Absolutely. Control. That's it. The nail on the head."

"And the money aspect of the thing was...?" I left the question open-ended, waiting for him to fill in the blank.

"Was very attractive!" He was matter of fact.

"Attractive?" I was surprised.

"Yes, attractive! I like to *pay* for sex. It's a turn-on. That's why I do it in the first place. Also, I don't think that Ms. Right is just waiting around the corner for me, to sweep up in my arms and carry off to a nice little house in the suburbs and even if she was, I don't know if she'd wanna have the kind of sex I like to have."

I'm sure he would have been happy to go into particulars, describing exactly what kind of sex that was, but Gem-Man cut in at this point with one sharp detail they had not shared with me. "If we don't get out of here, you're going to miss your appointment and have one mad Madame on your back."

"I see," I said, and I did.

They paid the bill while I went to the powder room and did the usual dabbing of lipstick, refreshing body and point of view. We left in a sustained jocular mood, if somewhat forced, after too much of everything.

We drove Big-Tiny-friend-who-wasn't-very-small

140

to some obscure area of Westwood and dropped him on a street corner, in a pool of tangerine-color-ed lights. He waved, a big hand near his big head, and then disappeared around a corner and down the courtyard to a spot lit security gate.

We drove our own way to Gem-Man's house, with not much talk. We each had a hand inside each other's pants. Words were finally superfluous.

MIXED DOUBLES AT BLUEBEARD'S CASTLE

I needed some space. Gem-Man was inhaling me like a pipe-full of ganga and I was turning into thin, smoky air. I told him I had to pack some more boxes and set things up for the move out of town, which was true.

What I really needed was time inside my own head and some altered state of consciousness within which to mull things over. Important questions-- where was I going and why--plagued me like a hangover that wouldn't quit.

I threw Harvey the half coyote into the back seat of the Little Green Car and took off up the Pacific Coast Highway toward Malibu. I passed the Chart House on the waterside at the foot of Topanga Canyon and a bit further, the restaurant with the blue-lit bar on the deck built out over the sloshing Pacific surf—Moonshadows—hugged the shore.

It was daytime, so the flood-lights that made crazy shadows on the face of the building were inoperative. The mystique and strange magic the place presented when I saw it the first time at night, vanished under the ordinary sun. But the memory of it, the salty sea spray coming off the waves, the glowing blue lights that became the theme, the emotional thread of the story that unraveled while I drove and drove—I wasn't free and clear of it, by any stretch.

It was summer of 1976. Nadia Comaneci was wowing the world with her sensational seal-like body in the Olympics, getting perfect marks for flip-flapping off bars and slap-dashing across mats. No one could resist her huge eyes, the perfect concentration in her childlike face, the perfect condition of her body.

I was spending a good deal of time with Up-in-the Hills, at her place above the Strip, on Sunset

Plaza Drive, watching the Games, in all its twists and turns and dives and throws and leaps and jumps and serves and volleys. We watched, ogled the athletes, did laps at the pool in her apartment building, and slugged through a mountain of books a piece. We were both studying for our Masters exams. I was taking mine at the end of the fall semester; she'd be sitting for her M.A. exams and TESL certificate in the spring.

We laughed and made margaritas and slathered suntan lotion on each other. We stayed up late and had summer meals and when we went to bed, we had some sweet and gentle moments together; they were so sweet, in fact, that I got that sad premonition they were going to end. I put it out of my mind because, I felt, especially then, why face the end before you have to?

It was a private affair. People we went to school with, partied with, or saw individually in our separate lives didn't know we were lovers. I thought we both wanted it that way, to leave the maximum options open for each other. I was probably wrong.

I put the end out of mind because I wanted her to be one of those people I would always know. In the end, I came to feel I had barely scratched the surface.

There were stories she only hinted at, only the smallest tip of the iceberg revealed, the beginnings of which I still remember, the endings of which I will never hear, and the loss of which I will always mourn.

At the moment of its happening, especially that summer, I thought we had something *real and lasting*, I thought it was *one in a million*—and every other *pre-Post-Modern twentieth century cliché* that applies, when real words, with actual feelings attached, fail to report for duty. Everything I said on the subject sounded like I was speaking in italics, like I was stuck with the dialogue of a dime store romance from the '40s, in a pseudo soap opera of the '60s—but now it was the '70s—so everything that used to be genuine, was now tinged with the sticky flimflam stuff of irony. *I thought there'd be time, plenty of time*, to work out what it was going to be between us. *I took a lot for granted.*

It was after that summer and its succession of visitors that things really began to change, and a fog of misunderstandings crept in on mean cat's feet. I should have noticed—should have paid attention to the symptoms: booze and pills and powder and pot and the dull roar of someone trying to get away from more pain than she knew what to do with. Maybe I just didn't see it because we were oddly reflective of each other—we mirrored one another in a strange, spooky-house, circumstantial kind of way.

Her father had died and left her money. My father had died and left me money. She had spent all her money running around the world. I was in the process of spending all mine, running around the country.

I was driving an Italian sports car then, having traded the noble Maroon Mustang in on Little Green Car, which had been My-Old-Flame's expensive habit. He needed the money and I loved the car. It was a beautiful racing green coupe, and when I drove it, I always felt that particular man somewhere nearby, if only in spirit. He remained an important and effective hungry ghost, lingering vaporously around me for a long time. I really couldn't kick the habit of him and that most likely was the problem between me and Hills, me and, well, *everyone* who wasn't him.

Anyway, I had his car with me then and it was chronically going into the shop to have some work done. I had just taken it in, in fact, and mentioned it to Hills. She was driving an older car, 1965 or so, kind of a beater of a white Dodge Coronet. When she heard me mention the Italian ride, she got a Sphinx-like smile on her face.

"I remember all that business: the shop, the pick-up the drop-off, and all the fussing," she said.

"Remember it?" I asked. "You mean you're having car problems too?"

"*Sports* car problems, specifically" she said, if not a little facetiously, if not a little jealously, at least a little teasingly. "Dropping it off, chatting with the mechanic, always you have to do that, you have to charm your mechanic or they just treat the car like a piece of furniture. But if they know you, *like* you, at least they'll do what they say they're going to do, instead of just sort of *not* doing it, and charging you anyway. Then there are the phone calls: "How's it doing?" "What'll it cost?" "How soon can I pick it up?" When you finally *do* get your car, there's that great excitement, where it feels practically like a holiday. And of course, there's the excitement of the bill. Usually a large one. You write the check and drive around to see your friends, and catch them up on what's new with the car."

I laughed at the perfect cartoon of the sports car owner, though for myself, I believed and told myself and anyone else who'd listen, that the sentimental attachment to the car meant more to me than its material status ever could. I was always glad, however, when I pulled into the driveway of the Bel Air Hotel, that I drove an Alfa. It gave me the confidence to just pull in and park with the celebrities. Still, the *fact* of its being an Alfa Romeo wasn't what I cared for most about it.

"When you *did* drive a sports car, what kind was it?" I wanted to know now, intrigued by another un-heard chapter of her life.

"It was a Jaguar, an XKE," she said, smiling broadly, behind her huge dark glasses, her teeth glinting in the yellow-gold L.A. light that bounced off the still, swimming-pool-blue water. "A sort of metallic putty pink, with pearl gray interior. A gorgeous hunk of metal."

I said, with interest, "That's the only other car I've ever been attracted to, in the sports vein. It's a very lady-like car, with its huge-breasted front and nice rounded ass."

"More like a bitch," she said, laughing. "The more you loved her and took care of her, the more she wanted your time and money."

I laughed too and asked, "Well, what happened to it? Did you sell it?"

"Did I sell it?" she asked herself rhetorically, then answered, "That, my dear, is a story you're not quite ready to hear."

"Come on! Let's hear it!" I protested. "I really want to know what happened to it."

"No," she said, firmly. "I don't think you're ready to hear that story just yet."

"Well, when?" I wanted an answer. "When will I be ready to hear it?"

"Maybe later. Maybe never. Definitely not now."

She was like that with her stories. They were her jewels, her riches, her treasures. They were all she had left of that life which had become invisible, unreachable, except through words and recollection. Her stories were the only wealth left of those years of living high on "free" money; she doled them out, one by one, making me savor each and every one, and I did, I *really* did.

But I never heard what happened to the Jaguar. And it took me a long time, practically the length of our relationship, to hear what became of the real family jewels, the garnets which her father gave her mother when they were married. They'd been in his family for such a long time, that when her mother died, her father gave them back to his mother for safe keeping, until his one and only daughter was old enough to wear them and understand their value. The last I knew of them, they were in a drawer in her grandmother's house in Israel.

"All right," I said, "forget the car, just tell me what finally happened to the garnets."

"The garnets..." she said, as though she couldn't quite remember which garnets.

"Come on, come on," I said, implying, *you know the ones*. "Your mother's."

"But they weren't really my mother's; really, they were my grandmother's, my father's mother's. They'd been handed down in her family for, *Ai yi yi, hundreds* of years. That's why she was so careful with them, kept them so specially so I wouldn't get irresponsible and lose them. But I really *should* have taken them with me, after all, the last time *before* the last time I was there, because after that they were lost for good. You see, my grandmother's house, which my grandfather built for her when Israel became a nation, and which stayed *always* in the family, even *after* my grandfather died, even *after* my grandmother moved back to the States to help raise me, when my mother died, always this house was kept in the family. It was a beautiful stucco house, in an older part of Haifa. It was all hand-plastered, and finely finished with beautiful wood and handmade tiles. And there was an inner courtyard, where an orange tree grew and gave us fresh juice in the morning. Oh," she sighed, "how I loved that place."

She stopped a minute and shifted her sun glasses up to her forehead, and she closed her eyes and turned towards the sun which was moving around the patio, as the afternoon wore on.

"It's gone now, completely eradicated."

I couldn't believe what I was hearing. "What do you mean eradicated?"

"Just that. Bombed out. It got caught in a Palestinian retaliation in the war. The building was leveled, everything lost in the rubble. My grandmother was at a neighbor's having tea when it happened. She came home and found everything, her entire life's collection of everything—books, artifacts, jewelry, clothes, photos—just *everything*—in a steaming heap of rubble. If I could have gotten there sooner, within the first day, I might have saved something, I might have even found the garnets. I knew what to look for—the blue velvet box with the gold snap.

"By the time I got there, afterwards, weeks had gone by—you couldn't get a commercial flight in or out—all the bombed-out buildings had been leveled, all the rubble bulldozed to make room for rebuilding."

"And your grandmother? What happened to her?"

"Well, she lost everything she had in the world. She took it very hard. I moved her to a place, a sort of condominium for the elderly. We bought new furniture, and hung new art work on the wall. But it wasn't home. It wasn't any place. It was just a place to die.

"Her heart went bad on her, then it was her mind, which began to dissolve with senility. My own theory was that after so much loss, the most painless alternative for her was to forget everything and just live, right there, inside each separate moment.

"I went and stayed with her there and looked after her. I knew she would die soon and, after all the years she took care of me, the least I could do was stay with her until she checked out, which

149

is what I did. Every morning, when she woke up, after I fed her breakfast, I wheeled her in her chair out to the balcony which overlooked the Bay of Haifa. Every morning she'd say: "That water. It's so blue, such a beautiful color blue. What water is that? What's its name?"

"And every day, I would take her somewhere else. I'd say, 'It's the Indian Ocean and we're on an island in the middle of it,' or I would say, 'It's the Riviera. We're on a boat, cruising for the day.' And I would bring her drinks and lunch and all day I would tell her things about the water we were looking at. She never remembered where it was or where I said we'd been. I began doing research and really studying up on large bodies of water we could be visiting. For me, it was the perfect way to while away the seconds, minutes, and hours of her final piece of life. She was the last really important person in my life to die."

She was quiet after that. When she spoke again, her voice rasped in that husky timbre of a throat closed with tears and painful emotions, "*Things*," she said, "you can always get *things*, they come, they go, who cares? It's the people, the ones you love and can't get back that..." and she broke off and turned her face away from me. I reached across the lounge chairs and grabbed her hand and held it tight until the phone rang and she got up and went into her apartment to answer it.

I couldn't hear what she was saying, only a tone of enthusiasm and surprise. When she came back out she said with a smile, "An old friend from Cleveland is coming to stay. He's been in L.A. a couple of days, but he's on his way over with his stuff and then he'll take us to dinner!"

"Us?" I asked, doubtfully.

"Sure, 'us', I told him you were here, he's dying to meet you."

"And who exactly is *he*?"

"It's Earl-the-Pearl, Earl of *Earl's, the* best, as well as the only, live fern-bar restaurant in Cleveland. It's a great place. Earl used to feed me when I was flat broke, waiting on the next dividend check. He's a good friend. Trust me."

And I did trust her too, mostly because, after all, she was older than me, she'd been around the world, she knew what she was doing. That's what I assumed, at any rate. I was at the start of my Roaring Twenties; she was at the end of hers. I still believed in the myth of chronology which dictated "She's older, she *must* be wiser!" Now that I am older myself, I can see just how foolhardy an assumption that was!

I wanted to believe that I could trust her, that she would not lead herself or me into a dangerous or unpleasant situation. Still, there it was again, the edge, some edge she was leaning over, going all the way out to that nervous edge and back again, barely back again, to the thin line marking a narrow margin of safety.

Some major part of me was attracted to that dangerous person, attached to her like body to soul, and, I venture to say, in love with her in the only way I knew how to be. She needed the kind of help I couldn't give her. She needed a strong, solid person to pick her up and put her back together. I didn't know it and couldn't have been it, even if I had known. I was just figuring it all out for the first time myself. But while I really didn't understand what I was dealing with, I should have picked up on the clues, that night with Earl-the-Pearl and his old pal Merv-the-Perv.

Earl picked us up for dinner. He dressed in black and white. A black cotton t-shirt tucked tidily in white ducks and a black leather belt were partially visible under a white silk baseball jacket. He had very little hair on his head and what was there was cut close, like Yul Brynner, with a reddish brown Teddy Roosevelt mustache which he often touched and shaped with his fingers while he was thinking or talking. He moved like a fast slick animal: a wolf, a jackal, a coyote. Intense coffee-bean eyes flickered around a room, while he assessed the ambiance at a per square foot price. He carried a black briefcase which he never opened and a small leather-bound pad in his inside pocket on which he made notes with a slim silver automatic pencil.

He'd just gotten in from Cleveland, but he looked like a lifetime of L.A. Earl was going to stay a couple of nights with Hills and work his way west, dining in restaurants of a particular mid-range chic between her place and Doheny. Earl was looking for things to add to his menu, so he was eating his way through Los Angeles. We started at the bottom of Sunset Plaza Drive at a place called Cyrano's. We ate *Hors d'oeuvres* there with a nice cold Pouilly-Fuissé and even went so far as to try the cold soup of mint and melon. Then we moved on to Butterfield's for a main course of rack of lamb with roasted garlic, rainbow trout stuffed with hazel nuts, and breast of duck under a cranberry-orange glaze over puffy, steamed wild rice. The She-noodles smiled and sighed and licked their chops with gustatory glee.

"Such good food," gushed Hills, "reminds me of good sex!"

"Does it!" exclaimed Earl. "I'll want to remind *you* of that later on."

"I hope you do," she smiled and turned up the heat in her eyes. My antennae went up.

We ate Key Lime pie for dessert and headed up the Coast Highway for drinks. We took Earl's rented car, which was a convertible Cadillac, and drove with the top down, the three of us in the front seat with Hills in the middle, the heater blasting hot air up our legs as the chill ocean wind blew two red manes and a handlebar mustache straight back from our heads. We played the radio loud and laughed about who knows what? I had a picture in my head of how things were bound to end up and I was giddy with over anticipation, so I laughed a lot, at anything.

We went to Moonshadows on the southern end of Malibu. As Earl swung the Caddie into a fast, left u-hook, he announced we were going to meet up with a friend of his from school, who lived in the Colony not far from there. This was the first I'd heard of that plan. I nudged Hills and caught her eye, with a raised eyebrow like "What gives?" She ignored me and instead focused her attention on the exterior of the building and said to anyone listening, "Isn't that a great design concept?"

A big Klieg spotlight was planted inside a wooden box and made a huge moon-shaped glow on the side of the restaurant, while plantings of dune grass and blueberry bushes created a flickering intricate pattern inside the circular spot. It was like a poem with no words. It was the last perfect thing about that evening.

We went inside, and it had the feeling of a spooky movie theatre with the lights half on and half off, and the movie already begun—everything blue, including the light from the tropical fish tanks which covered a wall separating the bar from the dining room. It was the kind of place where you really did need a flashlight to eat. We went to the bar, ordered drinks, and then went out to the narrow deck, where you could stand and look out over the crashing surf, spotlit with more floods, blue ones, and yet more blue lights strung overhead. This was not a place to see or be seen. It was a place to hide in plain sight. with floods.

A waitress in a space suit brought us our order of big, blended fruit margaritas, peach and strawberry and watermelon. Earl left to call his friend and I said, looking her straight in the eye, "So, what's it gonna be?"

She said, "I don't know yet. I don't know *who* he's calling."

"Well," I said, "it wasn't exactly what *I* had in mind."

"Let's wait and see," she said with that wicked-fun look she got in her eyes. "Whoever it is has a house up the road, which might be nice to see."

Earl came back and said his friend Merv would be along shortly. "Merv," said Hills, with eyes wide and somewhat surprised.

The three of us huddled together for body warmth and drank our margaritas, shivering while Earl expounded on the finer aspects of alcoholic esoterica: "Now these are *good* margaritas. It's the Cointreau instead of Triple Sec—more alcohol, less sweet, more bitter and sour—fresh lime of course, and the tequila itself. I ordered Herradura in these. They had it hiding behind the Cuervo. Old family recipe--they've been making it the same way since 1870 something. No comparison with that commercial stuff. Don't get me wrong, Cuervo is good, good enough for being that big. I'm just saying big isn't necessarily better. Hand-crafted—that's the next big thing in booze—mark my words!"

I was stunned by the esoterica of bar talk I knew nothing about, but I was shivering in the wind and from the icy drink in my hand and was about to cry "Uncle!" on it all when a door behind us from the bar opened and leaked a big enough blast of hot air from inside to warm my legs. We all turned to look, and Earl barked like a seal. "Merv!

Over here! Merv!" and he whistled, in that way that boys do, with two fingers pushing the tongue back.

A tall, heavy-set guy, late thirties or early forties, with black hair shining with Vitalis, turned and moved through the thin crowd of deck huggers.

"Earl! How 'ya doin' man? How 'ya been?"

"Great, man, really great. How 'bout yourself, Merv? You gone California crazy yet?"

"I love this fuckin' place, man. It is so fuckin' great. You can keep that Ohio shit, man—that humid shit in the summer and that snow shit in the winter, *man,* you can keep it!"

"Yeah, well, someone's got to live there and while they do, I'm makin' some pretty good money feedin' them six nights a week."

"I always knew you would, man, I always knew by the way you picked your threads, man, you were gonna *make* it."

Earl's black-and-white look contrasted with the powder blue and polyester on Merv-the-Perv. The best you could say about it, was that it matched the color of his eyes which were the most striking thing about him—cold blue and bulging out of the sockets. They were an odd pair of friends but, apparently, they went way back.

"So, you two met in school," I asked tentatively, wondering what halls of academe harbored this pair under the same roof.

"Yeah, that's right," Merv said. "The good old Thompson School of Mixology."

"Mixology?" I asked, eyebrows raised.

"Bartender school," Merv elucidated.

"Oh, so that's where you two first shook it up together!" I quipped, pulling out another cigarette. Earl picked up a box of silver-tipped Moonshadow matches, which made a tiny sparkling array when ignited, struck one and cupped his hand around

155

its hot glittering to light my cigarette.

"But say," Merv went on, slapping Earl on the arm, and knocking the match out of his hand, " Arnent'cha gonna innerduce me to yer gurls, Earl? I mean, here I am goin' on 'n on n' I don' even know whos'it is I'm talkin' to..."

"Well, that's nothing new," Earl chided him, like a homeboy from Philly (which he was).

They were both from Philly but had branched out, so to speak, Earl to Cleveland, and Merv to a lot of places too numerous to mention, but all of which led ultimately to where he was now—here. "Well, a little Nort' of here, to tell da trut'," Merv added, tucking into a large dinner he ate while we watched, as we had already eaten. Instead, we drank bottle after bottle of unbelievably expensive wines they took turns pulling off the wine list. We had moved inside to a round table in a square corner. Merv had hold of an enormous lobster with monster claws, which he ripped off and cracked open with large, greasy hands. He tore the meat out with wet fingers and a small silver fork which he manipulated like a Q-tip in an ear canal, pausing only intermittently to dredge the white meat in drawn butter which dribbled down his chin.

He kept offering us all bites, but somehow it had little appeal.

I sat back, sipped wine, and smoked cigarettes, trying to think of a way to get out and get home. I looked at Hills, she didn't look back at me; instead, she appeared to be enjoying herself enormously. I nudged her elbow and said low, with one eyebrow arched, feeling like Judy Holiday in *Born Yesterday*, "My nose needs a powder, how 'bout yours?"

"S'cuse us, boys," Hills said, in a Minnie Mouse voice I'd never heard her use, "the girls have to go tinkle!"

When we got to the bathroom, I extended my hand in a business-like manner and said "Hello, My Name is ———. I don't believe we've met."

She laughed it off, but I went on, "I am serious! Who *is* that guy? Bartender's School? Is that where he got that weird glow-in-the-dark look? A fluorescent light tan, so to speak?"

"Aw come on," she says to me, "give the guy a break. He just got out of jail."

"Jail? Jail? What for jail?" I became a little incoherent.

"Look, all I can tell you is this, Earl has known him for years and years. They literally grew up together. I didn't know he'd turned up here, but I remember hearing about him. Earl said the jail thing was a bum rap. Well, actually they got him on indecent exposure, because they followed him around and waited to catch him doing something they could charge him with, just so they could bring him in and try to get him to name names and numbers— turning evidence for the State, that sort of thing."

"Indecent exposure? You mean, underneath the polyester, there's a secret streaker?"

"No, no raincoats. They caught him masturbating in the back row of a girlie show and booked him. He wouldn't squawk so they sent him to jail for the max which I guess in New York is something like 18 months. I honestly didn't know that was who Earl was calling. Besides, can't you just enjoy him as a character? I bet you never met anyone like him before, back in, where is it, Long Hills, New Jersey?"

"Listen," I said, "maybe not exactly like *him,* but related, but more mainline Mafia. I dated their kids, and hung out with them at CYO dances. But you're right about one thing—Merv is definitely not my type."

"But how 'bout Earl? You like him, don't you?"

157

"Well yeah, he's got something, I don't know, some kind of strange feral virility."

"He moves like a snake, and he's smooth on top. I know, I've thought about it long and hard."

"You mean you didn't have a relationship with him before?"

"No, no. He was just a friend, a really good friend. Like I said, he fed me dinner at the bar and looked after me when I was at the bottom of the blues. That's why I don't mind him staying at my place, when he's in town. It's a payback for previous kindness."

"Does the payback include mixing up a couple of redheads with a couple of mixologists and serving over, what, ice or toast?"

"Come on," she said, "lighten up! We don't like it? We can leave."

"Count on it," I insisted. "He's finished his lobster, we've finished the last bottle of wine I can possibly drink and remain standing. It's 'Thank you very much for the lovely evening' and we're out of here!"

She finally agreed she'd put the squeeze on Earl to leave, so she could study for her summer course finals.

When we got back to the table, the dinner dishes and wine glasses were cleared and in their places were snifters of brandy and cognac and liquor.

"Oh boy," I mumbled under my breath, "We'll be held as hostages for the bar bill alone!"

"Gurls!" called Merv. "Hey, we thought you fell in and drowned in there!" He smiled—a Charley Horse toothful. He was having the time of his life and Earl, we could see, was enjoying every minute of his old friend's gladness.

We were sipping and swapping the snifters of pear and raspberry brandies with those of the cognac and the Grand Marnier. I wondered how it was going to feel tomorrow but I was too far gone to dwell on it. "So," said Merv, "I'll pay the bill, you'll

158

follow me up to my place."

This is it, I thought, Hills will make the excuses and we'll blitz out of here. I was reaching for my coat when I heard her say, "That's a great idea. I can't wait to see your place."

I looked at her with crossed eyes and said, "Hey wait a minute, you've got finals coming up! Don't you think we better head back to town so you can get an early start on it tomorrow?"

"I'm not too worried about it," she said. "I'm all caught up on assignments and I know the stuff cold."

"So, I'll just clear up the bill and we'll clear out." Merv pulled out a wallet stuffed with hundred-dollar bills and threw a large wad of them down on the table. A waiter flew down like a carrion bird and picked them up. "Keep the change," Merv called with a toothy grin, as he stood up from the table.

We left and in the parking lot, Merv grabbed Hills by the hand and called back, "*I gotta have one of deese wit' me so I don' get lonely on da way!* "

He laughed a sort of inhaled, gasping honk and drove off with her in the front seat of his baby blue Lincoln Continental. But what? Me, worry? I was terrified. I jumped in the front of the rented Cadillac and said a classic to a guy named Earl, "Follow that car!"

He said, "Relax. Everything's great. Merv is having the time of his life. It's good. He deserves it."

"I wasn't thinking about Merv. I don't know him and so far, I don't know why I *should* know him. I did just notice that he drove off with my friend and I was wondering, how *good* a drunk driver *is* he?"

"Merv?" Earl looked at me with disbelief and irony. "Merv could walk a straight line down the middle of the highway. I mean it! It's the way of all bartenders. We don't get drunk. It's bad for business. But if you're worried about her, don't be. She's a big girl. She knows what she's into."

159

"You're sure of that, are you, Earl?" I smiled at him, Sphinx-like, and wondered how much he really knew about his friend.

"As sure as I need to be. Besides, this gives me a chance to have a little one-on-one with you. Which I would like to have, now that we've been hanging around together a whole, what? Ten hours?"

"Uh-huh," I said, with little intonation.

"And for about the last nine hours, fifty-nine minutes and forty-five seconds, I have been very attracted to you."

"Really!" I said non-committally. "That's nice."

Fortunately, I didn't have to say much more than that because the Lincoln Continental made a hard left, across the highway, through an electric gate into a driveway on the beach-side. We followed, making a mad cut through southbound traffic. The gate closed behind us. It was a Friday night and people were on their way to summer weekend destinations. I guess we were on our way to ours, only we didn't know it then, or at least didn't recognize it formally, as such. It just ended up that way.

We parked behind the Continental and went in through a series of locked chain link gates. The walk was paved with crushed white rock which was lit with blue floodlights. Every few feet a flower box held small, square-pruned trees. The floods were hidden behind the boxes.

"Hey Merv, nice effect with the crushed rock and blue lights," said Earl.

"Yeah, I got some Beverly Hills babe comin' out here to help me wit' my "environment." I told her, the only missin' ingredient from my "environment" was *her*. But I dunno, she didn't believe me. But yeah, the crushed rock works like a dream. I got the whole thing wired, so anyone steps foot on that path, I'm gonna know about it. I got sirens like a nine-alarm

160

fire goin' off and TV camera security, the works! But you'd never know it to look at it, would'ja?"

We passed a little outbuilding and through a thick window I could see a private security guard staring at a TV monitor. We passed by it without stopping, just a token nod between Merv and the guy with the pistol.

The path ended at a recessed front door, the same powder blue which matched everything else in this guy's life, starting with those weird eyes. He took out his remote and clicked it with his wide, fat thumb. It opened like a trick door. We all went up a few steps to a large open room which reminded me of a beach house from the '50s, a big open floor plan with doors off to both sides. Dead ahead, picture windows faced the ocean. You could hear the reassuring sound of waves pounding sand close at hand. The powder blue theme was prevalent, including a shag rug, a circular leather couch facing a built-in slate fireplace, over which hung a huge abstract painting in harmonic tones of blue and gray and black.

"I don't click wit' tha pit-cha, myself," said Merv. "But the babe said it would pull the room together. told her, 'Send me the bill, better yet, bring it in person,' which she does, but she brings a couple of furniture movers with her to hang the thing. Protection," he said, shrugging his Mister Munster shoulders up to his long ear lobes. "Around me, can you believe it?" and he laughed with an inhaled hooting sound, kind of like a backwards, hiccupped cough.

"Now, gurls, I wantcha to make yourselves comfortable. Earl and me, we got a little biz to finish. So's in the meanwhile, why doncha take yer buns into the Ladies' bedroom and help yerselves to what you need for the hot tub on the deck."

161

Hills oohed at that suggestion and dragged me along with her, as I was starting to say something like, "No thanks, that's OK, I'll just sit here and stare into the gas-log flames."

The large room to the right of the living room was also a mottle of blues and grays, with some lavender thrown in for contrast. He showed us the closet where the towels and robes were and then threw in, "Anything ya gurls want, you just ask, I got it stashed—reefer, sniff, Quaaludes, you name it, Merv's got it."

"I think I'd like a glass of ice water and an aspirin," I said in all seriousness.

"Har! Har!" he hiccupped backwards again, "A glass of water and an aspirin, you're a card, doll, a regular card." He pulled the door closed behind him and left us alone with each other.

I looked at her like "So, now what?"

She smiled something gleeful; she smiled in that "Isn't this a great adventure" way she had, which always made me melt and give way, to whatever she had her mind or heart set on, and she said, "Great house, huh! I told you you'd love it."

I thought, "If this is what she wants to make her happy, for this instant or some other, so what? Give it to her." So I did. I looked around the room which had a California king-sized bed in it, with gray satin sheets covered with dozens of satin-covered pillows and said, "If this is the guest room, I wonder what the master bedroom looks like?"

"We might find out," she said, as we stripped to nothing in a stranger's house, put on thick terry cloth robes and slipped through a sliding glass door to the hot tub built into the deck. We hung our robes on a rack, which warmed them, and then slipped into the Jacuzzi tub, which had different kinds of jets in every corner. We left the light in the tub off and moved from jet to jet, massaging this

162

and that of one another and each other.

By the time we She-noodles were close to a boil, Earl-the-Pearl and Merv-the-Perv had finished whatever transaction they were engaged in and didn't discuss with us. I kept trying to find out what Merv did, to get a place like this, but Up-in-the-Hills headed me off in the tub and said in a very soft whisper next to a jet, "Don't ask Merv about his business. He doesn't like to talk about it and I guess it's better all the way around. If you know nothing, you tell nothing."

"Fine, I said, "no questions. But I am just telling you now, I am not, repeat *not*, going to do him. If you want to, you're on your own."

"Fine," she said. "Don't do anything you don't want to. Just relax, enjoy the hot tub, forget about it!"

The guys came out just then in big robes which they took off in the dark and then slipped nude into the invisibility of the foaming black water. I saw only that Earl was lean with good muscle and that Merv was a doughy white all over. This became even clearer when Merv flicked a switch and the underwater lights went on, and we were all exposed in a dreamy, dark, sapphire light.

"Look at d'ease nubbies, Earl, look at d'ease *bee-you-tee-ful girls*! I'm a very happy man tonight. We're going to have some fun."

Under the water, I found Hills with my foot and poked her a little with my big toe. "I'm going in to change," I said, "I'm par-boiled verging on soggy."

"Hey," said Merv, "use the bathroom in the Master. It's got a great shower and heat lamps in the ceiling and it's real comfy. There's fresh robes, everything you need, in the changin' room next to it. Help yerselfs."

"OK." I said, looking back at Hills, hard, in the dark, knowing she was looking past my shoulder. I slipped in through the sliding door on the far side of the deck, which I presumed was the master suite. A

163

super king-sized waterbed was dressed in black satin. The closet wall next to the right of it was double, sliding-door mirrors. A door to the left led into the bathroom which was large and tiled in black marble and powder blue tiles. With a turn of a dial, the whole room went red with heat lamps. I turned on the shower which was slightly sunken behind a see-through tempered glass curve. Six shower heads at different heights, on three sides of the shower, spurted water at me. Each was adjustable for the intensity of the pulsing water. I indulged myself wherever it felt good.

Hills came in and called, "*Caught cha!*"

I said, "Water therapy for sex maniacs."

She came in and we washed each other's hair, back, and muff.

The guys left us alone until we came out wrapped in big fresh towels and Merv said, "In the closet, there's some things to put on. Feel good, gurls, relax."

He was sitting on a black leather director's chair, arranged around a glass coffee table. On his lap, he had a small glass-bottomed tray on which he was chopping, with a razor blade, a mound of white powder. Earl was sitting across from him, smoking a joint the size of a cigar. We retreated to the walk-in closet where cedar walls held racks of clothes—cashmere leisure suits next to polyester, next to Italian silk jackets, next to black gabardine business suits. At the end of the wall, there was a selection of women's evening lounge wear—everything from skimpy see-through nighty things to silk kimonos of various lengths and thicknesses.

Hills put on a deep rose silk kimono over a matching G-string and chemise. For me, she chose a frilly see-through green lace teddy with stockings that attached to elastic garters. Over it, she put me in a dark green, velvety robe lined with pale, mint-green silk.

164

"Wow!" I said. "That's some texture against the nearly naked flesh! You really want to do this?" I asked her, staring steadily into those tortoiseshell pools of light.

"Don't you?" she asked, challenging me every step of the way.

When we re-emerged from the closet, wrapped in silk and glowing, Earl and Merv smiled appreciatively. They were both wearing black silk kimonos, which looked ceremonial in nature. "Come on, gurls," said Merv. "Siddown. Whaddaya want? What will make you happy? We got it all here."

Hills helped herself to the powder. "Colombian," said Merv. "The best. Uncut. Help yourself."

I took the big joint from Earl and puffed on it for a bit, thinking how much better it tasted than cigarettes, remembering and recounting a story I'd heard in college from a friend-of-a-friend of one of the big tobacco families. He knew for a fact that his family's company had patented the "trade names" as brand names for future cannabis products, in the event of legalization. The company owned names like "Panama Red" and "Acapulco Gold."

"Legalize dope?" said Merv with scorn. "It'll never happen. It's just worth too fuckin' much money to let it go loose."

I believed him. I'd been hovering around Earl's chair, sharing the boo, which went around to everyone but lingered around us. The other two were more interested in the powder. I took some in both nostrils and felt the nose go dead and then my teeth hummed. There it was, in long lines of a seemingly endless supply. I didn't care too much about it. It numbed me out in more ways than one. Hills went head long into it though. She took as much as he laid out and more when he offered it to her. She got giddy and laughed a lot and Merv said, "Hey, how

165

'bout some champagne?" and he popped the cork on some Veuve Cliquot and pretty soon we were all giggling with the bubbles. Earl pulled me back onto his lap and wrapped cobra arms around me. Merv just looked at Hills sitting across from him and opened her robe enough to see one breast pressing against the silk cup of her chemise. He put his hand inside his own robe and touched himself.

"Looks good," he said. "You should leave it like that." And she did, while he filled her glass again with his other hand.

Pretty soon Earl had his hand inside my lacy thing and was squeezing the tit hard between his fingers, while with the other hand, he was rubbing my clit with his knuckles. Merv was on the floor in front of Hills, then, and was very slowly opening her robe, rubbing the silk against her inner thighs. When he finally opened her legs all the way and saw her little G-stringed pussy, he said, "Oh you beauty, I'm gonna get that juicy spot of yours real wet."

We were in the chairs and he had her legs pushed up and pinned back to the chrome arm rests while he licked and jammed his fingers in her. I could see all this from where I was sitting and it made me wetter and hotter than I had expected. When we started to make those love noises together, the men got hip and picked us up, one and then the other, and laid us side by side on the black satin-covered water bed. Our bodies giggled in the watery bounce of action and reaction of the bed. We turned our faces towards each other and did what we did then, for each other.

She opened her robe and touched her breasts, squeezed nipples between her long-nailed finger tips. With her other hand, she touched her clit, opened the labia with her two fingers and showed Merv what she looked like under the lace and silk

166

G-string. All the while, she looked at me, I looked at her, an odd mirror image of one another.

Earl was all over me. He was working his way down my front, touching and pinching and rubbing what he found along the way. It was wetness. I reached out for Hills and we touched and interlocked fingers.

The two of them, Merv and Earl, caught on fast and crawled up and onto the watery world of the bed. It was big, with plenty of room to roll around in all directions, which we did. They kept their black robes on while we stretched out and lost our silk wrappings. Earl said, "You girls like each other, don't you. Huh? Don't you?" He asked this while he was touching himself, and pointing his hard penis towards my shiny opening.

"Yeah," I said, "we do."

"That's beautiful." said Merv, "I love that. I want to see you do it to each other. Come on, gurls, show us, we want to see it, right Earl, don't we want to see it?"

"Yeah, I want to see it, I've had it on my mind all day."

Wet noodles that we were, we wrapped and writhed around each other's buttery limbs. We kissed and rocked and rolled from side to side while those guys watched and touched themselves, cooed encouragement. We were kissing each other and holding on tight still, when I felt Earl pull my legs away from Hill's and felt him stick himself in my sticky slit.

Merv came at Hill from behind as she knelt down and kissed me while Earl fucked me from the front and Merv banged her from the rear. They worked hard, moving their cocks in and around us and came within moments of each other while the bed rolled and rolled in waves that moved our hips in synchronous rhythms. I kissed her hard and sucked her tongue inside of my mouth as I felt us coming in our own places beside each other.

What a steamy pile of He- and She-noodling appendages we were then! Hills and I held onto each other with girl things while the bottom halves held onto the boy things. The final release was a lot for the guys. They crumpled over in their way and fell, snoring, to sleep. Hills and I looked deep eye to deep eye, kissed a gentle small kiss and dozed off into our own delirious directions.

In the morning, I woke up with that strange panicked feeling of not knowing where I was, the sound of ocean out the window, the feel of satin sheets and a hot unfamiliar body next to me. Earl was still deep in dreams with eyes flickering in REM beneath veined lids. The room smelled of stale cigarettes while a headache from too much booze wiggled behind my eyes. I was waking up with a bad, shaky feeling.

I slipped out of bed from between Hills and Earl. She was still deep in sleep, as well. She had the waxy patina of someone completely unconscious. I went to the bathroom and peed and looked around for some painkiller which I found in the medicine cabinet hidden behind a spring-loaded mirror panel next to the sink.

It looked like a pharmaceutical sample case. All I wanted was some aspirin. I settled for some Tylenol with codeine.

I found the terry cloth robe I had been wearing the night before and threw it on while I went looking for my clothes in the guest bedroom we'd changed in. Merv was on the phone, drinking coffee, sitting on a stool at the counter which separated the living area with its powder-blue-everything from the kitchen. He faced the picture windows where the sunny bright California light illuminated the large rolling cerulean blue waves of the Pacific. Tufts of morning fog, still clinging low to the water, were burning off one by one, a disappearing cloak of invisibility which I wished I was wearing at that very moment. If I had had one, I would have put it on, headed down the steps to the Beach and started walking south. If I got to the Charthouse, I could probably call my roommate to pick me up.

I almost made it to the door of the guest room, where my clothes and an escape route awaited me, when I heard Merv speaking low into the phone, in street talk I'd only heard hints of—"*Shuah, Lou. Fuck dat shit, man, I'm wit choo one hunderd pahcent on dis and you kin tell da boys I sez so. Wait a minute, would-cha Lou, hold da phone, I got someone here...* Honey, cawfee's on the stove and whatever ya need is in the ladies' room, down the hall on the right—clothes, unda-wear, toot-brush, you name it. In closets, spare clothes. Help yourself. Relax. I'll be wit-cha in a minute."

"Uh huh," I mumbled and continued my bleary trajectory. I locked myself in the bathroom attached to the guest room, which I guessed then that Merv kept for whatever female companionship he rounded up for himself, which is why he called it the Ladies Room. It was stocked with little packaged bars of soap and complimentary shampoos, conditioners, bath gelée, etc. from every hotel the guy had ever stayed at. There was a preponderance of shampoo from Vegas and Reno, quite a few from Florida and an emerging collection from Maui. In the medicine cabinet, there was a toothbrush and little sealed units of toothpaste, with the airline logos on them: Mexicana, PanAm, TWA. The guy traveled quite a bit; that was clear.

In another drawer were heaps of body lotions— suntan oils and aloe gels, and massage combos of

169

coconut and pine. In among the selections, which also included lubricants and spermicide, I did find a bottle of baby oil. I used it to take my makeup off and show the bare truth of my face. The mascara had melted down my cheeks in the hot tub and then left little raccoon eyes behind, which I was happy to get rid of. Without it on, I looked somewhat less than my actual age of twenty-three. I took a plain shower with a small bar of Ivory soap from the New York Marriott, washed my hair with shampoo from the Virgin Islands, and conditioned with goop from the Fairmount in Chicago.

I combed and brushed and anointed myself with oils and balms and sun protection. Then I went looking for my clothes, which were not where I remembered leaving them. In the state I was in, this did not surprise me. So, I began looking for them in all the logical places. I started with the closet.

In the closet, I found bathing suits in several sizes, which still had the labels attached, also a whole array of clothes—shorts, skirts, tops, evening wear, a couple of this and a couple of that—all with the labels and price tags sill dangling from them. All designer. None of these things bore any resemblance to my clothes.

I checked the drawers. Nothing in there but pure silk underwear, a couple of garter belts, lace, net and black-seamed stockings, a choice of full length bras, and a can-can skirt. I put the terrycloth robe back on and opened the door and cleared my throat and said, as nonchalantly as possible, "Say, has anyone seen my clothes? I'm sure I left them somewhere in sight."

Earl was up by then and dressed in silk boxers and a t-shirt he had stashed in his car along with his running shoes. He looked neat and clean and ready for a few rounds in the featherweight division. He smiled and toasted me with a glass of fresh orange juice that I longed to down in one gulp.

Merv responded to my question, as he was whipping up eggs in a bowl with a wire whisk. "I sent 'em out to the cleaners. Don't worry. They won't fuck it up. They know better! They fuck up with me, and they're dead! Ha! Ha! Ha! No, seriously, they'll do a good job. They'll be back first thing Monday morning."

"Monday morning." I repeated this as a person trying to absorb new information in a foreign language. I asked a follow-up question: "What *is* today? Does anyone happen to know offhand? The last *I* remember it was Friday night!"

Merv beamed, "You got that fuckin' right! It certainly fuckin' was. You fuckin' gurls! mmm-mmmm, no shit," and he made more boylike yum-yum noises.

"So Merv, as for clothes for right this minute, what am I supposed to do?" I said this with as little aggravation in my voice as possible, sensing, somehow that aggravation would get me nowhere.

"You don't like what's in the fuckin' closet? What's a matter wit' it, don't it fit?"

"I didn't try anything on. I thought maybe they were somebody's clothes."

"Yeah honey, they're somebody's clothes. Take your pick, they're yours. Yours and your girlfriend's. What a babe *she* is. Earl's been tellin' me about her for years. Earl man, I'm glad we finally connected man. All these fuckin' years man and then the lock-up. Shit man, we owe ourselves this, man, am I right, man? Am I right, man?"

Earl smiled that Teddy Roosevelt smile with dimples, tweaking his mustache and I knew he was thinking about the sex the night before. He beamed a cloud of wild loose pheromones at me and I blushed, literally.

171

"Um, so, I'll just find something to put on, then." I was trying to edge my way back into the Ladies' Room.

Merv called after me: "So, just relax, babe. You're at the beach. Take your clothes off, get a little sun and fun. You know, *relax*." All this time he had been whipping eggs, melting butter in a pan, chopping a variety of vegetables into tidy little chef-like piles; he turned his attention to his other guest, "So, Earl, what'll it be in the omelet, the works? Or, somethin' custom. You call it. So fuckin' great to see you, man!"

Back in the Ladies' Room, I picked a bathing suit—a French-made black string bikini—and a white cover-up which was made of the simplest white, draping cotton gauze. It had a hood and when I tied its wide folds around and in front of me, it looked like a toga. I tied my hair up in a knot on top of my head and in this Touch-of-Venus get-up, I re-emerged for coffee and a gallon of orange juice.

I asked Earl about Hills as I gulped. He said she was still asleep. I said, "I guess she needs some sleep. Best to let her catch up on it."

We all agreed. Later, I would remember this moment as a signal one of our collective unconsciousness burying the facts.

By the time Merv had made us all individual omelets to order and served them up with toasted bagels and cream cheese, we were moving into the kind of Bloody Mary that only a professional can make. When Hills still hadn't shown her face, I thought I should go in and check on her.

Lavalier blinds on the south side windows made a shadow of prison-like lines across the bed. She lay still in the middle of the bed where she'd been the night before. Her face was unlined, waxy like orchids, and so still it frightened me. I looked under her eyelids and found dilated pupils rolled

172

back in her head. "Oh shit," I said quietly and then a little louder to get anyone's attention, "Oh! Shit!"

"What's that, babe? You talkin' to us, babe?" Merv clucked and puttered like a matronly hostess.

"Would you guys get the fuck in here, please?" I was feeling on the verge of hysteria. They could tell and hurried right into the room. I told them, "She's unconscious. We'd better call an ambulance."

"Fuck no! No ambulance," said Merv, all niceties aside. "That's all the Feds want is one tiny scrap like this, a fuckin' drug overdose, and they'd be all over me, all over again. No fuckin' way."

"So, what are you going to do, let her die here instead? I'm not going to let you do that. I'm calling 911." I got up to do it too.

Merv said, "You touch that phone and I'll have to hurt you. I don't want to hurt you, so don't touch the fuckin' phone. Earl, go get Jimmy. He's knows CPR and all that crap. Tell him to bring the first aid kit, the big one, with the stomach pump."

Jimmy, it turned out, was not only one big hunk of a bodybuilder with Olympic pectorals, he was also a paramedic. He took her pulse and peeled back her eyes and then threw her over his shoulder and carried her into the bathroom where he leaned her up against the wall in a sitting position and turned the cold water on her body. This had a rousing effect on her and she very vaguely came awake and sputtered some. Jimmy then picked her up and sat her on the bathroom counter next to the sink and near the toilet. He called her by her name as she stared through crossed eyes at us and her surroundings, not really registering anything. It was scaring the hell out of me.

When she did begin responding to questions like "What's your name, where do you live, what's your address," Jimmy asked her, "What did you take last night?"

I heard her say, "Valium, I took some Valium."

"How many?" asked the Hunk.

"I dunno," she answered. "I lost count."

I found the bottle rolling around under the sink. I showed it to Merv and asked, "You remember how much was in here?"

"Oh shit, probably half a bottle," he said.

"Now we're getting somewhere," said Jimmy. "OK I'm going to put this tube down your throat and pump the stuff out of you."

She didn't like that at all and fought it with considerable vigor. Jimmy won. The tube went down, the stuff came up, pills and booze and duck in cranberry orange glaze. The guys left the room. I felt pretty sick myself, just a reflex reaction to the sound of someone gagging and puking their guts out. I stuck it out, though, with a cold washcloth against her face, helping to hold her over the toilet bowl for the outgoing contents.

When it was over, she was weak but semi-awake and aware.

Merv propped her up in his black satin sheets and brought her breakfast in bed. He looked sad and puppy-doggish in his bulging blue eyes when he brought it in. "You're some nut, babe. What kinda dumb-fuck thing was that to do. Best fuckin' night I've had in years and you're eatin' a bottle of valium on me when I'm not lookin'. Fuckin 'A. Don't do it again. Scared the fuckin' shit out me. You got problems? I wanna know about 'em. Earl, you and the girl take a walk on the beach. We're gonna have a private talk, while the babe eats her breakfast."

I started to say something, but Hills waved me out. She was bleary-faced and the corners of her mouth were turned down. She looked sick, unhappy, and suddenly slightly shopworn. I had a pang of sadness, right in the middle of my solar plexus.

174

I left the room with Earl.

I wanted to walk on the beach by myself for a minute, to process the events of the previous eighteen hours, but Earl stuck right with me. I grabbed some towels from the rack near the hot tub and went down a long tier of steps which arrived at another chain link fence and an electric gate, which Jimmy snapped open from the video monitor room.

I was saying to Earl, in utter disbelief, "How could we have missed it? When did she do it, for God's sake? How could I have missed it?"

Earl said, "Listen, honey, where there's a will, there's a way," quoting yet another age-old adage. He had a million of them.

When we got out of range of the house, I stopped him and looked at him, into those coffee beans behind the Raybans, and I asked him, "What does he do for a living, Earl, what's his *real* story?"

"Same thing I do, only different. I run a restaurant, I buy and sell commodities. Buy low, sell high. Same thing he does. That's all you want to know about it. Don't push it. It won't get you where you want to go."

"How 'bout home, do I get to go home soon? Or am I going to be prisoner of a designer wardrobe and chained to a hot tub in a blue house in Malibu for the rest of my life?"

He laughed and slapped his leg and said, "No, no, I'll take you home whenever you want, I'll take you *any* place you want to go. You wanna go someplace now? Let's split. Merv's happy. He's got a broken bird to nurse. He loves it, in fact."

"Actually, I wasn't thinking about Merv at this exact moment. I was thinking about my girlfriend. And I was thinking it would probably be a good idea to get her back to her own place, sooner rather than later."

"Back to *her* place! You're fuckin' nuts. That's the *last* place she needs to be. She's in the right place, right now. Trust me, she's where she needs to be. Merv fixes everything. He'll fix it for her."

"You really think he's her *solution*? You've got to be joking! You don't know her at all. Not at all!" I was indignant.

He raised his eyebrows and looked at me, eye to eye over the rim of his dark lenses and said, "You don't believe me? Ask her. When we get back. Ask her if she wants to leave."

"I will!" I said. "I very definitely will. And when she says 'yes,' which I know she's going to, I know you'll be a gentleman and take us both home, *no problemo*, no questions asked. Right?"

"Right," he said, "and if she wants to stay, what'll you do for me?"

"Is this a wager or a dare?"

"Both. Neither. It's an idea. Something to imagine or make up along the way. A fantasy you always wanted but were afraid to have. It's here, for the asking. Just ask me."

"That's what you want me to do, if she wants to stay with Merv instead of go with me, you want *me* to tell *you* my favorite secret sex fantasy?"

"That's right," he said, "so I know what I should do, to surprise you."

We were lying on hot sand, while waves broke and rolled and sprayed our feet with a cool gasp of sea mist. Small sensual trickles of perspiration rolled down my face. I lay on my stomach with my suit untied and I drifted into a mid-morning half-doze, half-dream, thinking about the answer to his question. I tried to imagine some unthinkable thing that I might secretly want, that I wouldn't tell him or anyone.

I opened my eyes and saw him looking at me in that certain way, animal to animal, and said, steady,

"OK, it's a deal."

When we got back inside, Hills was up, but lying down, in the sun, with a perfectly cut, metallic gold, Italian two-piece. She had giant sunglasses on and looked like a person I'd never met. I sat down near her and put my hand on hers. "Hey, Sweetie, how are you doing?"

"Eh, I'm OK. It really was an accident. I swear I didn't do it on purpose. I was just taking a couple of Valium to take the nip off the edge of the coke and we'd had all that brandy and liquor and cognac and then the champagne and everything we'd had before, I guess I just sort of lost track of how much of anything I was into. It was just a dumb mistake. I'm sorry it fucked the party up."

"Come on," I said. "I was only in this whole trip for you, you know that."

"Oh yeah?" she said, looking at me with raised eyebrows, doubt creasing her forehead.

"My thought was to split at the restaurant. Your idea was to get in a baby blue Lincoln Continental and lead the way here. I did what I thought you wanted me to do."

"And you didn't enjoy it?" She said this resentfully, almost angrily.

I stared at her in disbelief. "I did it, and got into it, because I thought that was what you wanted from me, a lover to push the limits with. I'm on *your* side."

"My side," she repeated. "I wonder what that is, *my side.*"

I said, "Come on, let's get ourselves together and get out of here. Earl will take us to your place. Let's go dry out and relax by the pool."

"Hmm, I don't think so. I'm happy to relax right here, right now, no questions asked. Don't you love this suit?" She sat up so I could see how it form-fit her round places and flat spots.

My solar plexus twisted a little tighter, something cold punched inside my stomach. "So, you're going to stay on, then, for the weekend?"

"Mmmm, the weekend, the week, whatever, I'll let you know, when I get back. Meantime, would you mind looking after Earl? I'll give him the keys to the place and you know, just make sure he's *happy*. You don't mind, do you?"

I was surprised. I would have banked on things going the other way, on her leaving with me, two She-noodles giggling all the way back to her place a long way up, up into the hills.

Earl had gone into the house while I stayed with her and talked. Now he came out with his small black attaché case and his clothes on a hanger. He said, "Merv says, leave an address and he'll have your clothes delivered to you. He's on the phone, otherwise he'd say goodbye in person. He gave me this to give you." He gave me a white envelope. I didn't think much about it, just stuffed it in my pocket book, unable to pay attention to anything besides the roar in my ears which was either the sound of the ocean or the sound of my heart pounding and breaking, pounding and breaking, as I left her there, stretched out and glinting fake gold in the sun.

"OK, then, call me when you get back to town."

"Right," she said, half asleep, half yawning. "I'll do that."

Earl and I got in the Caddie and instead of heading back to town, we kept on the Coast Highway and went on to Santa Barbara. We spent the night in a cottage at the Biltmore. Earl paid the tab and collected in full on my lost wager.

178

GINGER NOODLE WITH WILD MUSHROOMS

I was almost to Zuma Beach by the time I came out of the spooky house trance of blue dreams and came to my senses. I had to double-back on Westward Beach Road to the enclave where the Ginger-Noodle lived, after he moved out of the apartment complex his ex-girlfriend still lived in. He got a good break for a grad student. It was a one-room not-quite-apartment in a substantial beach house built in the '50s. It had a tiny refrigerator, a hot plate and a toaster oven, a reading chair, a desk, and a single, built-in bed. Though it wasn't much, it was all he needed. He did have a stereo with large speakers which he dragged outside through his French doors facing the back yard and garden—when the landlady was away, that is.

It was bachelor's quarters for one, and when Mrs. McWilliams was gone visiting her son in San Diego, or taking a cruise to the Hawaiian Islands, it was a love nest for Noodles of the She- and He-persuasion.

I had called him earlier from the gas station at the western foot of Sunset, and told him how it was for me, and that I was on my way.

"I need to get some psychic distance, I need the sound of the ocean, I need the smell of your soap."

I told him that and he laughed in that specific way he had which most closely resembled that of a giraffe, if a giraffe *could* laugh.

It was a hidden place, down a long driveway of tall eucalyptus. When I pulled in, he already had the speakers outside and he was listening to Springsteen's "Born in the USA." It was loud. I gathered the landlady was away and I relaxed into the leotard I wore as an all-purpose undergarment, part-time bathing suit, and occasional yoga tog. I liked being prepared at all times to swim, dance, or relax and put my feet up over my head.

It wasn't even noon and the air was hot enough to make me break out in a sweat, lying flat in the sun as I was, slugging down fresh orange juice and club soda. I told him all about everything, the way I always did when we got naked and laid aside the crap. We were insiders standing side by side behind the curtain, watching and enjoying the theatre of each other's private lives. This was a place called safe—it wasn't exactly "home" but it wasn't a war zone, either. It was something else. It was a reprieve from doubts or recriminations.

I told him I was flabbergasted by it all. "The guy has got a hold on me. It's driving me crazy. He's consuming me for breakfast, lunch, and dinner, and between-meal snacks besides. I haven't even picked up my mail in over a week. I say, 'Look, I've gotta go home and get clean underwear.' He says, 'Forget it. We'll buy some at Fredericks. I say, 'I've got to get some estimates from a couple of movers for my things,' he says 'You can phone from here. In fact, I'll call into the office and have my secretary take care of the preliminaries.' It goes on and on from there. He is so unbelievably nice to me, at the same time I'm making my plans to leave him and you and the whole game show of Los Angeles in a matter of days. I've got to get clear about what I'm doing next! I can't just go around eating three meals a day and shopping at Fredericks!"

Ginger-Noodle asked, Zen-like, "Why not? Don't you need the underwear?"

I dismissed it with a wave and said, "Crotchless panties in assorted colors, a purple lace camisole and matching teddy, a black satin full-torso strapless bra with garters and black lace stockings with seams."

"That's impressive! I hope you're going to model

some for me."

He said it with smile, but I knew he meant it. "I'd like to, but he keeps the underwear there, at his house, in a *special* place. He likes to pick out what I'll be wearing, so he can think about it all day."

"You mean, between meals?"

"I mean *all the time*, on our expeditions consisting of his hit list for me. I call it: *Sights I Almost Missed in the Greater L.A. Area*. We went to a baseball game at Dodger Stadium last night and we're going to the Chandler Pavilion to see *Evita* tomorrow night. He's got everything planned, down to the last detail. Except the exact positions for sex. He leaves room there for imaginative surprises and believe me, I *have been* surprised!"

We laughed together and I began to feel like my old self again and less like a love toy for a man with time and money on his hands.

My Ginger-Noodle and I walked to the ocean and hiked down the high-banked cliffs. We swam hard with waves that carried us on strong tides to the shore. Afterwards, we lay on hot towels in a high sandy spot in the dunes.

While I'd been sputtering and raving in mostly incoherent and over-wrought dithyrambs upon arrival, he worked a kind of calming magic on me. There was no particular way I had to be and so could just be myself and talk saucy if I wanted to or turkey if I needed to.

He was a real He-noodle, that Ginger Boy. He-noodles are specifically not Yum-Yum boys on the one hand or He-Men, on the other. Yum-Yums are only in it for the yum aspect of things. He-Men are the ones with a big point to prove. But He-noodles look at it like the She-noodles do—they fall in love with the spirit of adventure and sometimes they fall in love with love. We were all of us looking for

181

true love like buried treasure, but in the meantime, back then, we seldom refused a chance to sail behind a pair of shining eyes. Nor were we hesitant to *let it be*, in the nick of time, just before anyone was compelled to sign on a dotted line.

He-noodles are notorious lovers of life, liberty, and the pursuit of good sex, without the mean-spirited, crotch-grabbing He-Man brouhaha or the single-minded, one-time, good-time philosophy of most Yum-Yums.

A He-noodle is an equal player on the field. And that's what this Ginger Boy was; he was smart and funny and athletic and handsome—the whole ball of wax. But for some reason, which I can only identify as his He-noodleness, I never was afraid he'd break my heart. Of course, I wasn't in love with him and that made it easier. I don't know why I wasn't.

There was every reason to be, except I guess in my heart of hearts, I identified him as a brother with whom I was having quiet incest. I thought of us as *Fellow Travelers* becoming *Persons with Real Character*. We stood on the same side of the line and looked out at the fray from the same vantage point. Nothing came between us, because we had no stake in the outcome, which sounds brutal, but is actually very freeing. There's no compulsion to rearrange a mutual noodler's mental furniture or censure his or her living habits, or read the mail noodlers keeps stuffed in their underwear drawer, or any of the other million little digging motions one employs while on the trail to true love.

"Ginger Boy," I sighed in the hot sun, "my mind's a clutter with if/then clauses and an abundance of dangling participles. I need to clear the junk out and see what it is I *really* want to be when I grow up."

"I happen to have something that has been useful throughout history, when individual tribal members needed a ritual for formalizing their inner quest."

"Oh yeah?" I said. "What have you got, a bag of coca leaves to chew? *Nooooo* thanks, I'll save my brain cells for the last three days of packing."

"Well, in fact, I have a small stash of high-grade hallucinogenic mushrooms. The breakfast of shamans!"

It was still early in the day and neither of us had had much to eat, which was preferable, and no one had to drive any place soon, which was good, and it was going to be a beautiful sunset, which was highly favorable. He pulled some ghostly looking fungi out of a baggie and split them with me. We each had swigs of water from the Girl Scout canteen I carried with me almost everyplace I went, to wash down the bitter aftertaste. Then we lay back on our towels, laced fingers, and slipped into a sun-baked afternoon doze.

I woke when I felt my muscles tingling and my skin cool off. I sat up and looked at the ocean which had become a swirling mass of Van Gogh brush strokes swirling in a variety of turquoise greens. The clouds were fluffy faces smiling down at us; I knew we were coming on. Ginger rolled up into a sitting position as well, with a big grin across his face. We entered that gooey place of melting minds and shifting consciousness. It can be a frightening place to be, if you're in the wrong place.

I had friends who dropped acid and rode around in the subways in New York. I don't know how they did it. One look at the teeming masses yearning to breathe free packed into underground tubes made of metal and glass, lit fluorescently the color of urinals with walls scrawled in angry words, and I would have lost it. Visions of Hades and Dante's Seventh Circle of Hell would have danced in my head and I'd have had to go home and hide under the bed.

But mushrooms are not the same as acid and we were far, far away from the public transit system of Manhattan. The Pacific Ocean shimmered like a jewel—like that big blue sapphire that had burned a hole in my hand the day Gem-Man showed me his trade.

Jewels and gems and all that glitters shimmered back at me from the surface of the water. Inside my eyes, everyone's dreams of Hollywood erupted and washed down the side of the day. I saw faded starlets waiting tables and beach boys wearing beer bellies. I saw the sad dreams of service people drive away in someone else's Maserati, waxed and shining like onyx. I saw the endless wait for the big break leaking light away from the illusion of endless sunny days of May which stretch across the years. I saw the fruit trees drop their leaves in late October light, like aging actors losing hair by someone else's pool. A pit of aching wishes welled up inside of me and mirrored the sound of the ocean in my ears. I listened and tried to hear the sound of my own voice as distinct from the roar of the Other, that amalgam of personalities forged out of the assemblage of everyone else's we've ever known—

Motherfathersisterbrotherauntsunclesgrampsgrannies—followed by a cast of changing characters chasing through the years from nursery school to college and beyond. Chance acquaintances, bosom buddies, old friends, new friends, enemies and lovers, they are all there jitterbugging behind my eyes.

I heard their voices in the white noise of waves the wind brings to shore. I listened to the din until I could just make out the sound of my own voice coming back to me, the one that knows and speaks out loud the will, *my* will, to make my own way, off the path and out of the tracks that do not fit my footprint.

These are the thoughts I am thinking, while I am hiking up the dune cliff with the Ginger-Noodle in the lead. Finally, the metaphor crystallizes and I break out on my own and pick out an imagined path between scrub brush pines and scotch broom copses.

"Hey!" Ginger called, "where are you going?"

"My own way," I called back, definitively if not defiantly, "I'll meet you up top!"

I cut across the hillside and began a series of serpentine traverses, the way a snake might wend its way up a steep incline. When I ran out of path in one direction, I switched back the other way, always looking for the animal path, up and up the steepening hillside. Each time I thought I'd lost my way, but in a moment saw the opening, the way up and further into the still wild side of the hill.

I came to another place which switched directions and saw the sandy opening just as before and I had just taken my first step into the brush, towards the sandy patch which was my next path, when I heard something I had only heard in movie theatres or on public TV nature shows. I heard that unmistakable sound of the rattler on a rattle snake. I stopped exactly where I was and waited and listened. I was absolutely petrified.

This was good, because it helped me keep absolutely still while my mouth went dry and my heart pounded blood madly into my ears. Then I saw it slither its gorgeous diamond skin across the red-brown dirt which the sand had become as the ascent continued. It was headed in the opposite direction which was at first a relief until I contemplated the possibility that there might be more coming from the same direction I was going which was the direction it had just come from. Perhaps it had a nest up there with a few new hatchlings.

Hooboy. I stood still as stone, stuck in a mushroom cloud of my own making, with death ahead of me and death behind me and perhaps on either side as well. Either I was going to have to stand here until someone came and got me or move ahead on my course up the hill. I examined every bush and patch of sand like a tracker after that. I found a stick and used it to poke about, before I put my feet in unseeable places in the brush. My adrenaline hit an all-time high after the brush with that rattler and it gave a new clarity and focus to my inner ramblings on identity.

I thought to myself: *if I could just make it the rest of the way up the hill without getting bitten by a rattlesnake, I would pack my boxes and leave town. I would move to a new city and a new life and I would not look back; no, I would not look back and turn to salt.*

So up the hill I went, still following the animal path where deer and coyotes wrangled their ways into the tall grass at the top of the hill and then into the undergrowth, which interfaced with residences built up next to the park boundary. When I finally pulled myself up the last embankment of my "alternate route" I didn't recognize where I had come up. I had somehow moved myself further south on the bluff than the usual path and so I came up closer to the road than I had expected. I followed it back to where the other path emerged and found my Ginger-Noodle, pacing first one way and then the other, stopping and moving out over a promontory where he tried to see the path below leading up from the beach.

"Don't jump!" I called from behind. "It isn't worth it! Tomorrow's another day! The world is waiting for a sunrise! Go singing in the rain, not gentle into that good night, Sweet Prince, but above all, rage! rage! rage! against the dying of the light!"

The crazy medley took him by surprise and he guffawed at me, "I was about to call the Rangers when I looked at my watch and noticed it was sooner than I thought it was and so I decided to wait a little longer to see if it got to be as late I'd imagined it had been."

"You're melting time again," I admonished. "Keep a grip or it will be the day after tomorrow before you know it!"

We laughed at that and linked our giddy bodies together while we walked the longest half mile since Zeno tried to cross the room by halves. Behind us, the sun went the way of raspberry sherbet that someone had left out on a hot day.

When we got back to the bachelor's quarters, we both drank long, cool glasses of grapefruit juice and soda. We weren't hungry for food. I wanted just to feel my naked skin wrapped round his naked skin and I was shivering from too much sun and the late afternoon wave of adrenaline. I told him about the snake and the bargain I'd made. I felt I'd looked death straight in the face and come away with a sign. The Sphinx which rattled the riddle's answer in my ear said, clear as day: *Get out of town while the getting's good.*

I told him how I knew now I had to leave and then I held him tight against me, like a person who has to let go.

We made love carefully, going over each square inch of each other's epidermal layer. He shimmered around me and shimmered inside of me and I thought I saw a circle of blue flame about him, where I envisioned his spirit and mine expanded into adjoining circles like ripples from a stone skipped on smooth glassy water make interlocking rings. He pushed inside of me and I felt every wet cell of my vaginal wall rub against his stiff pink pego, I felt it paint my insides with the same shimmering light of the sunset and I grabbed at him with my inside muscles and we both arched up and held on tight. He went through the roof and I followed.

Stars cut through the California sky where their light is often dimmed by headlights or street-lights or power stations for all of L.A. Here, near the ocean, you could see the stars in their true strength in a sky that smelled of eucalyptus. I felt the little beads of sweat he made across his fore-head shake loose and drip onto my breasts and then trickle down my stomach. He pushed in and around; I held him tight and wouldn't let go. We became one crazed bird crashing against that ber-ry-black heaven. When the rose inside of me went red and opened, he did too and sighed and shook his last drops of consciousness into my eyes and then we both whirled off to another planet where dreams had their own lives.

In the morning, I was slow to wake up and as I did, I reached out and found an empty place where a body might have been. Ginger-Noodle was up al-ready and back to reading in the sun with a cup of coffee from a one-cup automatic maker.

I began in the shower and let the water pound down on my head and stimulate thought. I knew now what I had to do and nothing would sway my course. I threw a cup of coffee down to chase a dry piece of toast and drove, with a clear conscience and crisp intention, back to my place in Silver Lake.

It was time to pack. For real

SMOKE AND MIRRORS

The end of the affair. What can you say about it? It hurts here, it hurts there, it hurts more than you thought it would, or it hurts less than the hole in your soul where all the light got sucked away. When it's bad, it's as if it never happened. You say to yourself: *I was never there. You were never it. We were never in love.*

Bent as the wind bends small trees to test them, broken lovers feel the pull of gravity against dry limbs that might (and sometimes do) crack under the weight of frozen water in an ice storm.

How sad it seems to me now, to lose so much in a moment's hasty rush to forget every sweet word, to count every gentle gesture as a part of a final betrayal.

I wasn't going to have that when I left L.A. this time, for good. I was leaving with clean breaks all around.

When it went smashing to pieces and sharp shards between me and Hills, I was surprised. Years of thinking about it have come and gone and I am still puzzled by the enigma she turned out to be. I think, maybe she was in deeper with me than she knew how to handle. Maybe she had to push me away in order to push herself away from a whole set of feelings she could not speak out loud to me or anyone. So, she got rid of the whole problematic area which started with her relationship with me. Decades later, I can still feel the pain of it.

I knew how *men* were. I'd known the worst since I was fifteen and a guy in his late twenties who should have been prosecuted for statutory rape walked away from me, a victor in denial. It's what I came to expect of most men, having their little pleasures and moving on—Odysseus, a fugitive, a desperado, just trying to get home. Poor Penelope, at home, weaving and unweaving her days away, waiting, hoping. "Will he come back to me? Will he come back?"

Men, they like to leave you hanging, they like to leave, period. Or so it seemed to me then.

But a woman who rips and reads you like news copy off a wire and then tosses you in the recycle—a woman like that always takes you by surprise. A woman like that can *really* hurt you.

In the end, she reduced her history with me to a simple lie, which she "proved" to herself on a number of occasions: the overdose at Merv's, the bad timing of the Swiss-Wristwatch affair, and a little nightmare dinner party with her "new friends" in yet another new life.

The Swiss-Wristwatch was my mistake; I freely admit it. I misconstrued everything about the situation and did absolutely the wrong thing at the wrong time with the wrong person, right in front of her. I can't explain what compelled me to do it, only that ours was a sexuality of taboo testing, of pushing the limits. I guess I thought we were going to take it another step. I practiced the philosophy that anything could be fixed with good sex. I learned, more or less the hard way, how the flip side of that goes: anything can be wrecked by bad sex.

Bad Sex? What's *that?* Everyone has their own idea about it. For some it's too much, for others it's too little. For guys, there's the spectre of impotence always looming. For girls, it's the fear of rejection, the pain of loss, hidden beneath the covers. It's always something particular to the person or persons involved, something that sticks in your mind as the pivotal twist before the bomb explodes and the crime scene that was your heart is exposed.

For me, the bad sex has been the stuff that happened when I was desperate in one way or another—desperate because someone broke my heart again, or I'd lost a job and had no money, or was frightened of something huge and unnameable which lurked darkly down the side streets of any city I lived in, just as the sun was going down and the lights went on, glowing warmly and remotely, in *other* people's houses, in *other* people's lives. That quiet desperation of looking in at unattainable golden lights has driven me from time to time to grab at someone— anyone—late at night. When the drab, thin morning comes, no one's the gladder; I've often been the sadder and, I know, it was the bad sex.

With Hills, it was some of the best I'd ever had, until the moment it went bad and I lost her in the rubble with her heirloom garnets, lost her to that place of irretrievable things—the one missing glove, a favorite pair of earrings, my great-grandmother's hairpins. I lost *her* because I missed the obvious signs of strangeness and miscommunication.

I should have known better, but I was just too green and stuck on an unattainable vision of the perfect relationship—the one in which you could have and be had utterly; totally; yet remain completely free to come and go as you pleased, like white ideas of swans moving across the flat, black, metaphorical pond.

The Swiss-Wristwatch was just some guy like so many other mystery men who showed up at her apartment, camped out for a week to ten days, and then moved on or went back to where ever they came from. This one was certainly Swiss. Was he a banker? A financier? A futures dealer? A spy? I never figured it out. There were lots of them like that. They were there in her life; you didn't know what they did or how. At most, you'd know what city they'd come from. That was it. Like other people I'd met through her, he was a friend of a friend and she did not want him to stay with her. She was irate, in fact, because she just wanted to be in her own apartment, by herself, living on her own. The visitors, the drop-ins, were leftovers from some other part of her life when a place to crash was the coin of the realm.

She wanted him to leave and I don't know why she didn't just draw the line and throw him out. I realize now that drawing the line, any kind of line, except maybe a coke line, was very hard for her. And that's where I went wrong. I should have considered what it meant to her, to be on her own and making her own way. I should have remembered that every action has an opposite and equal reaction. But I didn't understand then what I understand now—that chronological age as a measure of maturity or wisdom or even experience is a false god, not to be followed. I didn't know it then. I was just figuring it all out for the first time and busy making a catalogue of mistakes—perhaps not mistakes—perhaps just experiences, some good, some rotten, some painfully true. Whatever it was, it was the first time through it for me. Still, I might have known better. I wish I had *done* better.

I am sure because it was "bad sex" for me, I can't remember much of it. And I don't care to re-imagine it into anything better than it was, which was a mistake. I went there for her; I was only ever there for her. But the Swiss-Wristwatch was a time bomb that was bound to go off. It was one of those late-nights-into-early-mornings that she and I specialized in. The moon had set, the sun was rising, and the sky was that empty grey color of nothing which early morning L.A. delivers with the newspaper.

I had been saying to her, "Why don't you just make him your lover and make him take you out to dinner every night and enjoy it? That way you'd get some value out of his being here which so far, I am not seeing. I am seeing you angry and annoyed."

"I am angry and annoyed because he's *here*. I don't want him as my lover, I don't want him at all. I just want him to leave."

"I understand. But since he *is* here, and you haven't asked him to leave, perhaps if you just incorporated him into your life—made him pay *rent*, even—and help out with the dishes, I just think it might help you get through it."

She was silent for a minute and then she said, "What, so you want to do him?" We were in her room, in her bed. The Swiss-Wristwatch was on the mattress in the living room. I didn't know what he thought we were doing and I didn't care. He was just there with the sparse furniture and he wasn't important.

"No, I don't want to *do* him. I'm here with you. I want to be here with you."

"Come on," she said, egging me on, smiling in that way she had, to lead me on, make me admit my fantasies to her, a game we had learned to play so well that we did it without thinking about it. "Come on, I know you want him. You should do him, then. You should do him now. I'm sure he'd like it. You should get in his bed right now and surprise him."

I sat up and looked at her, to see what she was doing. "Are you razzing me?" I asked, trying to see into her eyes, even in that weird puce pre-dawn light.

"I think you should do what you want to do, and I think what you want to do is do him. So, I *want* you to do him, if that's the case."

"Honeylove," I said, "it's five o'clock in the morning. I just want to go to sleep with *you*."

"No you don't, you just want to go fuck him. So

you should. Now."

I sat up and repeated somnambulantly, "Fuck him. Now. Don't you think he ought to have a say in the matter?"

"Oh, I know what he'd say, all right. He'd say *'Danke schön!'* He started hitting on me the moment he got here. I had to growl at him quite a bit to get him to lie down where he belonged."

"And why exactly do you think I should go *do* him?"

"Because I know you want to you. So, I want you to."

"You want me to?" I asked, still trying to wrap my mind around what she might mean *behind* those words. I thought, she really wants me to, or else she really *doesn't* want me to, or else she's running a completely separate number on me.

"Go on," she said. "Go wake him up!"

I can't imagine why I did, but I did what she told me. I got up out of the bed we were sharing in a confusion of She-noodle limbs and loose parts and went into the living room where the Swiss-Wrist-watch was snoring. I wanted to be asleep. I did not want to be waking anyone up, let alone a guy I spoke with in limited, if not downright broken German, English, and French. In the ten days he'd been there, he had not communicated a single idea in any one language.

I got into the bed next to him and felt his body heat radiate out from the soft center of deep sleep. Hills came out of her room and sat nearby in a chair and watched me and I watched her watching me while I made the Swiss-Wristwatch tick louder and louder until his alarm went off and then he inhaled me like a box of chewy cough drops. She was right. He was thrilled and counterattacked by fucking me thoroughly. She watched. I watched her watching me, and so I faked it for her benefit.

He finished with me and I peeled myself away

194

and found her back in her room, with the covers pulled up over her shoulder with her shoulder stiff and turned away from me.

I said, "Hey," tentatively.

She said nothing.

Then, very quietly, I heard her whisper, "I can't believe you did it. I can't believe you fucked him right in front of me."

I was horrified. "You told me to! I thought you wanted me to, and so I did!"

"I just thought," she said, her voice thick with emotion and her nose and eyes filling with water, "you'd say 'No.' to me, you'd say 'No, I want to be with you.'"

The invisible knife that lives in the solar plexus opened its switchblade. Everything was suddenly different. Nothing I said could change the bare fact that I had not done or said or been the right thing at the right place at the right time for her, at the most crucial of moments.

We didn't talk about it much, but we never got over it. And, as I said before, I believe it was part of her overall effort to accumulate evidence against me, in order to put me and this whole can of worms of her sexuality behind her.

We didn't see each other for a while. When the semester started up, I thought we'd straighten things out and get together again. She had another plan.

She invited me over, presumably to meet her new boyfriend whom she'd started dating when I was out of town, on one of my usual long, L.A.-to-Minnesota-to-New York junkets to see family, friends, and lovers. It didn't bother me that she'd met a man she liked. In fact, I was sort of relieved. I always felt it would be better if she had a steady man in her life—it would even things out between us. I didn't really think about its effect on our relationship. I just assumed that we were separate from all that.

The dinner was at her boyfriend's place. Gerhardt from Stuttgart—he was very handsome, with a German accent and perfect teeth. Here in L.A., he was a photographic fashion model which let him pursue his real vocation of writing and illustrating children's books. He had a few of his colored pencil works framed and hanging on his walls and I oohed and cooed over them. I was a little stunned, too. Here was this guy, my girlfriend's boyfriend, who was doing the one thing in the world I *wanted* to be doing. Had I told her my secret ambition, to write and illustrate children's books? Is that why she was doing this? Presenting me with my own replacement who had somehow captured my dream and my girlfriend at the same time?

I tried to be friendly and natural, just myself under unusual circumstances, and since I had studied German in College and then in Berlin, I spoke to Gerhardt excitedly in baby Deutch with English add-ons—a hybrid I called Deutchlish. Phrases like Ab-gefucked and aus-geflipped come to mind. I spoke to him like an old friend, using the familiar "Bist du? Weiss du?" I was neither jealous of him nor attracted to him, though he was handsome in an ordinary, dark prince sort of way. I just thought we'd be friends because of her. We both liked *her*, and so I assumed we'd like each other.

The other friends invited were some new people in Hill's circle. I don't know where she met them. None of them were grad students. A woman named Marianne, someone else—a friend of Gerhardt's—who was a transplanted New Yorker, and a newly fanatic Californian. His name, like his person, was utterly forgettable.

I thought we were all getting along famously until I noticed that, except for the brief, enthusiastic conversation I had had with Gerhardt, a certain icy coldness emanated from Hills and her new gal pal, toward me. I would say something to Gerhardt in German, just trying to use a language I used to know, saying things like, "Nice weather we've been having!" and "I wish it would rain" and "The speed limit is fifty-five miles per hour in California." Directly afterwards, the women would look at each other, knowingly. Then they would both glare at me.

The forgettable friend from New York was trying to engage me in conversation and was coming on to me in some way or another. He seemed to want my attention but if I did give him my attention, he'd drop the conversation and start talking to anyone else within earshot. This happened several times over the course of the evening.

It began to feel even odder when, throughout the dinner conversation, anytime I suggested or floated by an idea, thought, or opinion, everyone else at the table would take an opposite and contrary point of view. I began to feel very much like a cow in a closet-sized gift shop. Wherever I turned, I heard the psychic crash of a fine piece of Dresden china, a Steuben crystal glass, a perfect Royal Doulton tea cup. The night wore on and it didn't improve.

Whatever I did, whatever I said, I was completely wrong, as far as anyone there was concerned. When I said something about my Little Green Car, Marianne said, "I hate sports cars. They're too low to the ground."

No-name from New York said, "I hate 'em because you have to drive the suckers. I like to have my arm up on the seat-back and the cruise control on and forget about it!"

Gerhardt said, "*Zay are just too small. You can't do anysing vis sem besides indulge yourself.*" Then the room went silent and they all stared at me.

When it wore down to the end of the evening, I began to feel that these four people had gathered together to indict me, try me, find me guilty, and sentence me to something like death.

All night I tried to get Hills to look at me, to talk to me, to tell me what was going on here, at this dinner in the Twilight Zone. But she wouldn't. She held herself frostily apart from me, and clung to these brand new people as though they were her oldest and closest friends.

I finally left, because it just hurt too much to be there. On the way home, I tried to understand why she needed *all* those people with her to reject me. I wondered why she couldn't just have told me herself, privately, why she needed this backup band of people she hardly knew to prove the point that our relationship was over.

It was so weird, it left me with the feeling of reality caving in. It was *so weird*, I thought I must have hallucinated the whole thing and so I called her, like I always did, the next day. She was brusque and to the point.

"As far as I'm concerned, you've done nothing but *use* me to hit on men. You've slept with every one of my friends and Pierre (the Swiss-Wristwatch) which was the *worst*. Right in front of me, in my own living room, with me right there."

"I thought it was what you wanted me to do. You set it up, you set it *all* up, and I was doing what I thought you wanted."

"What I wanted," she said this like a dead person, "what I wanted was for you to love me, just me."

I said, "So the whole time you were testing me, waiting for me to say, 'No, let's go.' What about the rest of it? What about just us?"

She was silent. Then said, "The rest was just scenes that went down. That's all."

198

"Well, I guess I failed the test because I misread the question."

"I guess you did," she said. "Don't call me anymore," and she hung up.

There were a lot of things I wanted to say or explain or argue for or against, but she never gave me the chance. I thought I would know her forever. Instead, we were reduced to a *scene*, some *place* we just happened to pass through at the same time, sort of together and sort of not, like strangers sharing a moment of intimacy before getting off the bus and going separate directions with utterly different luggage.

The magic, the real love stuff I knew was there, she hid. She made it all go away with a wave of her hand and the usual smoke and mirrors.

MOVING DAY

The big burly men came up the steps with their hand trucks and their hats pushed back on their heads. The one who owned the rig, which was taking up half a block on the street below, assured me, "No truckers' strike is going to stop me from makin' a livin', No Ma'am! I'm takin' a full load up the Coast and expect to deliver to your destination by the day after the Fourth of July. I hope that suits your timetable, Ma'am."

He was chewing tobacco. I was frightened he was going to spit.

"Sure," I said, "that was how I was planning on it myself."

I was in a daze. I had stayed up the whole night before, engaged in my last momentous twenty-four-hour binge of packing and sorting and discarding and packing some more. There were still boxes unsealed and small heaps unpacked, but in a matter of minutes the burly men had scooped it all up and taped it up tight. They'd hauled the only bits of furniture I'd chosen to take—my mattress, my desk, a straight-backed chair—down the long flight of stairs from the porch to the street. They'd whisked away the stereo, the vacuum cleaner, and the one brass lamp, a box or two of kitchen stuff, a wardrobe full of California clothes, a wood-framed mirror, and fifteen boxes of books. That was it. The sum total of my worldly possessions.

I signed the papers which the widest of the burly men handed me. I took out a dog-eared white envelope a guy named Merv had given me a couple of years back and which I'd accepted, thinking it held some dry-cleaning receipts. In it, in fact, were ten unmarked, unused one hundred dollar bills. I'd kept them in the same envelope at the bottom of my desk drawer, as the last remnant of the ruined loved affair with *her*, with Up-in-the-Hills. Now I pulled two of the C-notes out and handed them to the movers, a partial payment on the paltry load of my stuff.

Then they drove away to the nearest weigh station, where I should have followed them. The last thing they hauled off, ostensibly doing me a favor, were the stacks and stacks of newspapers which my roommate and I had accumulated over the years. I had always thought I was going to clip them—what for now escapes me. In any case, the movers moved them for me and it turned out they used them to boost the weight of my own haul. But what did I know? I'd arrived in L.A. with nothing and now was departing with a little more than nothing and had no idea how much that little more might weigh. All I cared about was the fact that now I could be on my way, me and my half-coyote, onto our new life up the road some 1,500 miles or so via the scenic route.

After the movers left, I was moved to sweep out the house and the studio where I'd had all my best ideas for the last four years. It was the late afternoon and the sun poured in through the windows of my room, and through the branches of the orange tree outside, making a shadow play on my wall.

Perhaps it was the lack of sleep combined with too much nicotine and the invisible psychochemistry of the smog, but I saw things in those shadows that now, close to twenty years later, I still see flickering in the fire of my sense memory.

I saw the end of the world. I saw earthquakes and floods and catastrophes. I saw miles and miles of cars stalled on the freeways and angry men raising their fists to one another and fires burning and lands sliding down and down to the sea. It scared the hell out of me. I thought to myself, "That's it, the end of California, maybe, even, the end of the world."

I realized then how glad I was to be on my way to a place where, if the sky did fall, at least it would be clean and mixed with shades of evergreen. I saw it all unfold before my tired, delirious eyes, myself alone on the road and the welcoming fireworks of the Fourth of July burst up and over my head. The last ray of sun struck the center of the lavender glass doorknob of my closet, next to the wall of the shadow play. It made a sudden hundred rainbows on the walls around it, just before the room went rosy in the after light of setting sun.

My last tidying done, I roamed the place, empty except for the couch which wasn't mine and the this-and-that of my roommate. It wasn't much— he lived sparsely too. Instead, the place teemed with ghosts, "lovers and friends I still could recall." Pacing the backyard, I gathered little treasures to remember that place which had a magic all its own—a snippet of coral hibiscus to press in the book I was reading just then—Edith Wharton's autobiography, *A Backward Glance.* I stopped and smelled the faded pink roses the last time I ever would in that yard, in that city, at that time. I hugged the fig tree which looked like a boy with his arms outstretched. I made a picture in my mind of what the whole place looked like, inside and out, and put it in my inner album, next to Fire Island and the house where I grew up.

On the porch, the moon was just beginning to rise into that particular color of sky I think of as metallic purple. It was huge and shiny, the epitome of a prop silver dollar, bigger than life, pasted onto the sky. The street lights went on, distracting from the stars, and the houses up the hill opposed to us went, one by one, that glowing gold of lamps turned on—that color which always kicked me in the gut with loneliness.

I said, "So long!" to that old fake moon, kissed my roommate, my old friend Green Eyes, and acknowledged Philosopher King, "Goodbye, goodbye!"

He waved from the porch as the half-coyote and I dashed down to the street and took off in the Little Green Car and left bottle-washer palms, twinkling hills, and night-blooming jasmine behind.

I drove the Hollywood to the Harbor to the Santa Monica Freeway and got off at the exit for Gem-Man's place, as we had planned. I was spending the night with him and then, at 4:00 a.m., we were driving east to Perris, California, where we were going for a last gasp of adventure—a hot air balloon ride at dawn. It was something I had always wanted to do and this Gem of a Man was giving it to me as the perfect *bon voyage* gift.

I was thrilled. Who wouldn't be?

When I got there at around half-past eight, he had a beautiful little spread of take-out gourmet Szechuan food warming in the oven and a couple of bottles of good champagne cold in the fridge. I'd been awake for over thirty-six hours, and at first the hot food and the cold bubbly made me feel ready to fold. Not him. He began to nuzzle and snuzzle my ear and I swear there was something in that food, something hot and peppery, and so sexually arousing, it might have been the mythic Spanish fly or powdered rhinoceros horn. Whatever it was, I felt myself topple over into something wildish which I had to pull myself away from.

"Wait, "I said, "I want to shower and get sweet." I was feeling sour, after the last long wave of packing and clean-up.

"I thought you would. There's a hot bath ready for entry when you are."

And there was, too—a bath scented with bath oil and sprinkled with rose petals. Candles lit the room. *"Dahling!"* I said, feeling suddenly like Zsa Zsa Gabor, "You are perfection itself!"

I tied my hair up in a bun, shed clothes down to skin, and slipped into a tub of water that had only recently cooled down from a scald. He put the lid down on the toilet and sat there, sipping the remains of the bubbly we opened. I breathed deeply and let go in all directions, scattering my elbows and hips and thighs and shoulders and toes to the hot dense atmosphere of the water, letting it go, letting it all go—feeling like Molly unraveling her thoughts and Penelope unweaving her rug.

He said, "I want to watch you in the tub. Show me what you do when you're alone."

"Generally, I try to avoid falling asleep in the water, though sometimes it is tempting—very tempting."

"Don't you think breathing the water would wake you up?"

"Not really, because it's like going back to the womb, breathing in the warm waters which run together with your own warm waters."

"You sound like you speak from experience?"

"I've almost drowned, more than once, most recently, in someone's overheated swimming pool. But the unseen hand of Fate pulled me out of the deep end just in the nick of time. Lucky for me—what a dumb way to die! Even so, I can see the natural attraction, waters joining waters."

As I spoke I had lifted one leg up onto the side of the tub and with my fingers opened the airlocked labia to let the warm water fill me up. I expelled it again, like a tidal flow, with muscular contractions within me. He rested his chin on his hand and leaned onto the edge of the tub. He was watching me wash myself, so I began to do it for his benefit.

205

I foamed up a large natural sponge with a bar of rosewater glycerine soap and stood up to lather every crevice of my body—between my toes, behind my knees, under arms and under breasts, front to back and side to side. When I came to my crotch I stopped and handed him the sponge and said, "I need your help with the hard-to-get places."

At first, he scrubbed me up and down but then I showed him how to do it, round and round, charging the nerve endings with the unwinding heat of a moving spiral, gyrating out from a liquid jewel center. I was purring like a Jaguar just tinkered under the hood, while I stood in a crouched second position, mimicking a ballet dancer doing a thigh stretch before plunging into a plié. He lathered me up and rinsed me off, front and back and back to bottom, inside and out.

I pulled the plug and while the water drained out, sat on the side of the bath while he licked and sucked my clitoris to a dark ruby. Slippery wetness poured out of me.

He was out of his clothes by then and we pulled the curtain round the tub and turned the shower on. I washed him with a loofa, scrubbed his back and bottom and legs, like a careful groom tends a good horse. He just stood there, facing and braced against the wall which shot hot water from the shower spigot. He let it happen to him, like a man tied up for pleasure. I used the oversized natural sponge to wash his balls and the thick baton which was already sticking out and looking for an orchestra to conduct.

The water went cold but we didn't. We turned it off and wrapped each other in towels warmed by the shower steam. He rubbed my bottom and said "I love your hips and that tight little ass."

"My ass?" I asked, a little surprised, "It's a boy's

ass, narrow hips with small butt. I've got the hands to go with it."

I showed him my hands—blunt-fingered and freckled, glowing with pale blonde fuzz on the backs of their knuckles. He was still grabbing my behind, pinching the cheeks hard.

"I noticed," he said. "It's what I like the best about them. The boy-like part."

It was a surprise. I hadn't really thought of him in that regard, as a boy-girl attracted to a girl-boy. Other deeper, longer loves of my life, yeah, sure, they knew my double nature, the boy of me that loves those certain girl-girls or girl-boys and the girl of me that fell into the deepest end of boy-men and *their* boy-girls. People who really knew me knew how that was for me.

So far, with Gem-Man, our sex had been obsessively lustful, but detached in the way that intimate strangers engage each other. We presumed some things. We assumed other things. It was the sex, we knew it. I had no expectations. I found it very uncomplicated. If we got personal now, I thought, things could get dicey. I was leaving town the day after tomorrow. I wanted to know more, but I thought twice about asking. I didn't have to. He began to whisper his secrets in my ear.

We moved to the bedroom. I lay on my stomach. He started to give me a massage. Coconut butter mixed with a drop of rose oil, he warmed it in his hands and then applied it to my back with hands and palms and thumbs serious about untying the knots that tied me up and down my spine.

"Some nights I have to do it, that one certain way."

"How is that?" I asked. I really *did* want to know.

"With boys," he whispered.

"How old?" I asked.

"Old enough, eighteen was the youngest. He

207

approached me. I liked it and took him to a hotel. In the end, he wanted money and, what the hell, I gave it to him."

He sat on my rump and rolled his wide-open hands up and down my back, unleashing electricity stored inside each muscle. When he spoke to me, each time, he bent forward, very close to my ear and whispered it with hot breath against the lobe, against the neck. He was hitting hot spots and I squirmed. Still, he rubbed me with oil. He held me tight. He leaned forward and whispered, "I want to make love to you *that way*."

"I want you to," I said. "I want you to show me how you fuck your boyfriends."

It was the boy-boyness of myself he touched first here and then there. It was that deep part of me no one went near. A dangerous and vulnerable place I didn't go to by myself unless I had to or because someone made me. *Because someone made me.* There it is. The secret is out. There is that about the letting go which is the giving up and the giving over of control which is *deeply sexual.* It stirs me up if I think too long about it. It stops me in my tracks if I try to describe it. I lose words, force, momentum, if I dwell on it. I want to resist. I want to give it up. I want to choose and not choose.

His hands held down my upper arms. He leaned over and whispered in my ear, "I want you to *submit*. I want you to do exactly what I tell you."

"Push up onto your knees and hands. Show me your ass." He was on his knees too and helped me into a position that was first awkward then natural, animal-to-animal, without resistance.

He put a pillow bolster under me so that he could sit back for a moment and pleasure himself with the picture before him, the various shades of She-noodle pink and rosy plum.

"That's it. I want to see your openings, your tight hidden places, your secrets." The man-man of him lifted up the boy-boy of me and with the wide flat of his hand he flushed my bottom with light taps, bringing sensation to my surfaces inside and out.

He reached into my hot redness with fingers and pushed in his thumb and rubbed the inside back of my pubic bone, while I dripped on his hand and his forefinger went round and round my center. With his other hand, he scooped up coconut oil and anointed himself, his cock.

"Show me your secrets," he said again. Again, I pushed up to him, knees spread. He massaged the place between my ass and my cunt, "Relax," he said. You're too tight."

I was so relaxed, I was almost out of my body, was almost dreaming. He slathered me again with oil, up and down my crack, then he took his thumb which had been massaging my low hot spot and pushed it in my ass. I tensed and contracted.

"Don't do that, "he said. "I'll hurt you. Push out when I push in. He pushed his thumb in and pushed down, on the sphincter muscle wall. I instinctively tried to pull away from him but he held me tight. "Let go," he said. "Let go of it." He pushed down and I gave, relaxed and he said, "Good. That's right."

Giving up control, giving it up completely to the other, not me—I resisted and gave in, resisted and gave in, until he finally just couldn't wait any more. He anointed the tall, dark, one-eyed milk man. He put it right there, in the center of my boy-boy place and he pushed until he made entry.

Something cracked in me like wood cracks, felled by axe or gale force winds. There was no sound but summer thunder rolling inside my head.

He was halfway inside me and I tried to pull away now, though I was falling deep into a dream place, as every cell of my body let go of the pain, let go of it, moved past it, became a detached bystander.

"Let me in," he said, "all the way in." He pushed the rest of the way in me and was still for the moment, held fast in my most secret place. Then he rocked, gently, rocked and swayed without pulling out, and with his other hand, he kept me excited, just this side of coming. Then I could tell he was going and I had to, just had to finally let go with it, that bolt of lightning shooting up my spine. I sucked everything out of him with it, until my insides were wet and my outsides were dripping, and he became Peter Pan's missing shadow, now lost within me.

OUT OF BODY

After a while, I was aware of him pulling away from me. He went to the bathroom and washed himself and then brought me a hot washcloth, to wipe me sweet and clean.

We rolled over and put our faces on soft pillows and before the last candle was blown out, I was gone, up out the top of my head, with a foreknowledge that this was going to be a dream of dreams. My spirit body rose up over the lump of clay my flesh had become and moved beyond the vanishing ceiling.

Then it was just me, flying through a starry sky filled with faces by Chagall. I wanted to soar and dip and fly loop-the-loop but I couldn't quite manage. I had weights attached between my toes, holding me upright in proper flying position like training wheels on a bicycle. My arms outstretched, I flew flat, like my own magic carpet.

When I land, it is in a winter place where I visit a woman who seems to know me very well, or she speaks to me as if she does, while I am quite certain I do not know her at all. She is older than I am; she knows things she wants to tell me; but instead she says, "Lie down. Close your eyes. You need some sleep."

I knew she was right, and so I did. No sooner were my eyes closed than my light airy body rose and left the weight behind. I went flying; this time I land at a house which was familiar to me, though it was unlike any I had known in my life. Still, it is uncannily familiar, and physically very real. I am walking towards it as though I belong there, or even live there. In my mind, I am thinking to myself, "How wonderful it is to be a writer, to be able to live so many lives inside of one life, to be able to create any life out of whole cloth and live it as your

211

own, in the moment of writing it."

As I head for this strangely familiar subur-
ban contemporary, I imagine that in there lives a
young woman in her early twenties who has just
finished her degree in architecture at Yale. I think,
"If I write her, it is like being her, like having gone
to Yale which I didn't, having studied and gotten a
degree I never could have in my own life." It gives
me great pleasure, in this dream, to think about
my writing in this way, as a door to other lives I
might have lived.

I enter the house as though it is mine. I am in the
basement, where the laundry room is. Up a short
flight of stairs, I hear footsteps and an older woman
calls, "Is that you, dear? Are you home so soon?"

This frightens me. I realize suddenly that this
is not a story I am writing, I am in fact this person
I thought I was writing; this is her home; that is
her mother coming down the stairs towards her. I
feel certain that if I see her, I will be trapped here,
in this point of a parallel universe—in this place
of my invention which now really exists—at this
instant on this point of a time/space continuum
unwinding as a seashell unfurls from its center—
unwinding like the spiral which connects all the
points of my life, real or imagined, without chronology, but with some hierarchical order unper-
ceived by my body's eyes but seen and known by
the eyes of my soul.

As the mother of this person who I both am and
am not comes towards me, something triggered by
the fear of being named and called and recognized
as this person I am not erupts in my brain as an
epileptic seizure. I feel myself losing consciousness
very quickly now and instead of lifting up with my
ethereal body, I sink down and down and down
into a place I can't move in, the weight of my flesh

a mountain upon me. I cannot open my eyes or see where I lie, but feel only a light wind upon my face. Caught in this dark place, with no eyesight, I feel arms of light and tender love enfold me. The Lost Angels of Los Angeles found me and lifted me up, carried me... lift me up and carry me for some timeless moment and then gently, like a sleeping baby laid to rest, I am laid down there in that room, where my sleep-filled body already rests.

LIFT OFF

4:00 a.m. is the last silent hour of the night in Santa Monica. If you listen, there is only the very distant roar of Pacific rollers breaking and the occasional semi getting on or off the Coast Highway. I wasn't listening. I heard nothing.

The alarm went off and I felt my airy body fall with a thud back into its heavy landing pad of flesh. The last dream I had was still with me so vividly that, when I woke, I could not tell for a moment where I was. I was left with just the feeling of having something rent from my arms, and the wash of grief that followed.

Gem-Man sat up and turned the buzzing thing off and then, before he was tempted to lie back down, he got all the way up and went into the bathroom. I lay in bed and gathered the fragments of my dreams to think about. Like shards of ancient pottery, they stood as parts of whole vessels I could only vaguely piece together.

I heard the shower go on and that motivated me to sit up and fall into the warm fog and drenching cascade of hot water, full force, with the massage head on a hard pulse setting.

He got out as I got in and said, "Enjoy yourself. I'll make some coffee."

I knew what he was saying, and after I massaged the place between my eyes where the pineal gland was buried and took care of my bottom, which was a little sore from the evening's play, I did turn my attention to the other hot spot. Pounding water in just the right place can be as effective a stimulant as a triple latté grande, with none of the caffeine-induced side effects.

I emerged rosy-faced and cheerful and threw on the clothes I'd picked out for the event—a long

215

khaki skirt, a '40s jacket and a long yellow Isadora scarf. I had a vision of myself going straight up into the sky, my scarf capturing the movement of the winds. I didn't know about the big gas flame that could have ignited any and all things fool enough to blow into it. I was thinking only of style and some comic image I had in my head of people sailing around in a hot-air balloon with goggles and helmets and aerial scarves.

We were out the door by 4:35 a.m. I settled Harvey the half-coyote in the fenced backyard with food and water and a beat-up quilt to sleep on under a tree. He looked worried as I left him there. "Don't worry, Harv! What goes up must come down. I'll be back with a burger and fries before you know it."

We drove east towards Riverside where the bottom of the sky cracked its blue armor plating and something shiny, passion flower-red and glowing hibiscus pink began to leak out and fill the straight line of the horizon, way out in the desert flats and farming plains. The pink gash emitted a half circle of ecstatic fire, which we drove toward and watched through squinting eyes and Polaroid lenses. We were off the freeways now, driving the utterly empty surface roads connecting great stretches of nothing with great stretches of nothing. The ground was covered with a foggy violet mist which was the nighttime dew becoming a coat of many colors across the pink and yellow flats.

Finally, we turned down a road which dead-ended at an open, empty field. The violet mist dissolved and turned a tawny yellow. Splotches of cars and trucks intermingled around giant lakes of fabric which looked like enormous wilted flowers. Attached to each was a sturdy wicker basket, a Brobdingnagian nut cup. One by one, the wilted flowers were inflated with dragon's breath as propane gas ignited and heated air which was forced inside the balloon's tent body by fans running on battery power.

One by one they assumed shape, with a graceful roundness tapering to a funnel tip. They came in all the colors of the sun and sky; some were decorated with a certain whimsy from another time, others were from Oz. Taken as a group, they looked to be a merry species from another planet about to have a gabfest in the sky. Seeing them like this, rising in the post-dawn haze, I thought how like a wish each one was—at first flat, without dimension, until the fiery breath of imagination ignites the air within it, expanding the depth, the breadth of possibilities, as the bright and unimagined thing becomes shape and color and begs for release into a wild blue yonder of lightening sky.

When our balloon was ready to lift off, Gem-Man and I put on crash helmets in case of rough landings and, as assistants helped hold the gondola down, we climbed in and the pilot followed. The ropes which tethered us to the ground were untied. The pilot pulled the valve on his propane tank and a small constant flame ignited a long blue tongue that shot up inside the funnel to the body of the balloon. This fire-breathing dragon was taking us aloft to where we could watch the world go by from the perspective of low-flying clouds or high-flying birds.

It was, I thought, the exact right distance from the ground to simulate the effect of flying in dreams. Once we were up to traveling height, we caught wind currents and went with them up and over low hills and rising plains toward distant mountains we never got to. Everywhere was yellow ground marked with dry green brush, clusters of scrawny sprawling cottonwoods or dusty oaks. The dragon was silent except for the rhythmic "*hisst*" and intermittent burst of flame. In the distance, androgynous balloon-beings drifted at staggered heights and distances.

I looked up into the colorful cavern of the balloon over us and a little fragment of poetry blew by. Like a small bird twittering in my mind, I heard Shelley's haunting line: "Life, like a dome of many-colored glass, stains the white radiance of Eternity." Here, soaring a hundred yards off the ground, I felt that radiance enfold me like angels' wings, like love that knows no boundaries, like imagination set loose on big blank canvas with wild bright color. In this unfettered state, we flew and flew, ecstatic. I could think of nothing but glad, bright thoughts and felt our laughter lift us up and up. Not one sad, murky reminiscence crossed my mind.

Instead, I found it wonderfully easy to let it go, let it all go. Broken hearts and racked souls, unexplained endings or consciously bittersweet turns and tropes—each and every one seemed like treasure to me now—a story worth telling, with meaning worth freeing, like jewels and precious artifacts separated from the midden over time. *Over time,* beach glass is worn by waves and becomes smooth and beautiful. *Over time,* scars invisible to the naked eye become pictures drawn by a master hand; where and how the scar was made names me, contains the truth of my Self, and no other. How glad I was to feel in just this way, at just this moment, untethered, released, and truly free.

We went through two tanks of propane before we finally drifted down below low clouds and high birds. As we went, the balloon pilot instructed us to bend our knees in a certain way and lean in a certain direction so as not to break legs upon impact or be thrown out of the basket altogether. For a brief

218

instant, adrenaline-driven fear caught me up, but I breathed deeply and did as I was told and we landed with a *bump clump thump* and then it was over. The assistant crew had been chasing us in their van and they found us in time to help pull down the balloon, squeeze the air out of it, and roll it up before it became lost in a tangle of color and rope.

Afterwards, a honey blonde, who looked more like a pirate than a balloon chaser, opened a bottle of champagne and poured it over our heads. It was the custom of the sport, she said, to initiate first-timers with bubbly shower.

She opened another bottle, which was quickly guzzled. Myself, I didn't need it. It was eight-thirty in the morning and I had touched s*atori*.

THE GETAWAY

The drive back to Santa Monica was vague, like a daydream I was having instead of a drive I was taking. I remember a meal along the way—huge Mexican omelets with bright red, fresh tomato salsa. That image—the red flesh of the tomatoes—sticks in my mind like the symbolic food of my dream life.

Then we were home with the burger and fries combo I'd promised to bring Harv. It was early afternoon. I was going to take a nap before dinner; instead, I fell into bed and slept eighteen hours, one long, blank slate.

I woke very slowly, like a person being defrosted from cryogenic freezing. The smell of coffee, slightly burnt toast, and cigarette smoke finally got to me.

Harvey was at the foot of the bed. When he heard me stir, he began his morning whine and wagfest: *"Please Please Please, lemme out! How 'bout a walk, how 'bout some food, how 'bout it? Huhhuhhuh?"* Wag wag wag. Thump thump thump.

"I know how you feel, Harv. What was it Skinny used to say? 'I have to piss like a race horse.' Me, too. I'm getting up."

I wrapped up in Gem-Man's candy-colored Polo shirt and let the half-coyote out the back door. I hit the can, brushed my teeth, and got a cold washcloth to put on sleep-swollen eyelids. I was thinking to myself, "How do I leave this guy? He's just given me the ride of my life, completely off the record. *Why* leave this guy? Maybe in some odd, unbelievable way, *this* one is it?"

I looked around the house and tried to imagine where I'd put my books and where I'd put my desk and I realized pretty quickly there was no place for either.

Instead, I thought of that stuff in a truck on its way to an address in Seattle and tried to imagine my good friend's face, when the furniture is delivered and I am not there to receive it and I thought, "Well, leave him smiling, then."

He was in the living room smoking some lousy cigarette and brooding over black coffee.

I said, "You're up early for a Sunday."

He said, "You're up late for a nap."

"I'm pretty sure I was abducted by aliens in my sleep. They performed strange experiments on me and programmed me to have alien sex with the first person I see upon return. The proof is that I remember nothing of what transpired but am left only with this urge from outer space to make love to you in a bathtub of black cherry Jell-O."

He half-laughed now, "Yes, we have no black cherry Jell-O"

"Cool Whip?" I asked with concern.

"No Cool Whip."

"That's a blow!"

"Below the belt." He threw it back.

"Ouchy!" I exclaimed. "I better kiss it and make it better."

"I wish you would...and stop teasing!"

"Teasing is the fun part, isn't it?" I was pushing him over and onto the floor. I was molesting him, undoing his pants, unbuttoning his shirt. He started to reach for my breast and I said, "Don't touch me. Lie still. This is how they *really do it* in Venutian counterculture."

I pulled his pants inside out and down to his feet. With his shoes on, they were stuck there and then I moved a chair onto the pants, trapping his legs. I buttoned his cuffs over his wrists and pulled his shirt inside out and back, trapping his arms. I moved an ottoman onto the shirt, restraining the movement of his torso.

"Now, I'll have my way with you," I said with stern irony.

He just smiled and let it happen.

I went in the kitchen and rummaged. I came back with a jar of raw honey and a container of vanilla yogurt.

"I need a healthy breakfast for the road, you know." I opened the yogurt, scooped it out with my hand and smeared it on his stiffening zubrick and all over his balls.

He jumped but didn't get too far, constrained as he was. "Cold," he belted. "Really fucking cold!"

"It's part of the treatment," I said. "First the cold pack, to help with the stiffness problem, then the application of body heat to stimulate the circulation."

I kneeled by his side and sucked him into my mouth. I licked and sucked like a dog licks a paw, but it was balls and cock. I licked until I licked him clean.

"And now for the medication." I took out the honey.

"Did you know that raw honey has some antibiotic properties? I knew a poet who took a teaspoon a day and swore it kept him from dying. He weighed three hundred and fifty pounds or so and had to discover ways to circumnavigate the problem of heart failure in obesity. He didn't die. I guess it worked."

I took the top off the jar and poured it in a fine thread, round and round his sex, until he was drenched and sticky.

"Try to lie still," I said. "It will all be over in a moment."

I mounted him now and pushed my dry vagina down on his works. The friction was virginal. He was thrashing. I said, "Lie still. Don't move. Take it. It's bad for your condition to move."

When he did, I forced open his legs with my

223

knees and fixed myself on top of him, so that his cock felt like it was mine, erect and stiff between my legs. And when I moved up and down on it, I felt and saw in my mind that I was fucking *him* and my vagina was his. The stiff, sweet friction between us was where we converged, girl-boy to boy-girl. He didn't last long in that hot spot. When he went, the sticky fingers of my inside glove held tight and then melted down.

I got up and he looked at me with his hands pinned above his head. "Let me finish you," he said.

"I don't want you to," I said. "I want you to watch me."

And I lay where he could see me and couldn't touch. And I showed him with my fingers exactly what I looked like, lying in a broad ray of morning sunlight, like an orange cat seeking a warm puddle of transparent gold to soak up. When I did feel myself coming, I balanced on my knees over his chest and the female ejaculate went on him, he groaned for me as well as for himself.

Meanwhile, Harvey was groaning at the back door and I knew I had to make my getaway fast, now, or I'd never leave.

Harvey came in and waited patiently for fresh food and clean water. I could tell he was ready to hit the road. "Won't be long now Harv, we'll be hugging the curves up the Coast. "

I moved the furniture and let the guy up, but moved rapidly towards tying up my own loose ends. I dressed and packed the few things I had with me for the road, while drinking a last good cup of coffee, before The Fall into the casualties of road food.

It was simple after that. Harvey bounded into the back seat where I had left a spot for him, wagging tail and all. He had a big dog grin spread across his dog face, and I mimicked him, grinning back at

Gem-Man as I blew him a kiss over my shoulder. I had everything I needed, I didn't look back. I folded myself up along with the one thousand clowns of my life in L.A. and tucked us all into my mental portmanteau. I was happy to hear that Little Green Car start up and backfire like a good sports car should. I pulled out of his driveway and headed for the on-ramp of the Pacific Coast Highway.

Just before I pulled onto that downward sloping ramp, beyond the Santa Monica Pier, I pulled over to the side, and with the car still running, leaned over, opened the passenger door, and tossed my half-smoked pack of cigarettes onto the sidewalk. In a matter of seconds, a guy who needed a clean shirt, a shave, and a haircut appeared from under a bush, snatched up the pack from the pavement, waved vaguely at me, and shouted like a carnival barker, "Hey! You have a nice day now!"

"Thunk" went the door as I pulled it shut, and called out to no one in particular, "Goodbye again! Goodbye! Goodbye!

A final time goodbye!"

I honked and waved and left.

ACKNOWLEDGEMENTS

Boundless gratitude to Beeba, Loosh, and Di, my best friends over the long haul, whose gracious generosity and unconditional love infused my heart with the courage to reach completion of this book.

I bow down to my editor, Dale Winslow, who kept faith with me and did not lose patience, even when, suddenly, there were a thousand things more to do. Thank you for your good ear, your good eye, and your good sense of this particular writer's plight.

And for Rox, who opened the box, what can I say? Something ineffable? Or this list of simple wishes: live long, breathe the beauty, and always cook with song. I am certain the angels have your back.

ABOUT THE AUTHOR

Wynn Frolley is the fictitious author of this fictitious memoir. She grew up in a time completely different from what came before and the now which came tumbling after. She survived TV programs named *Leave it to Beaver* and *Father Knows Best*, as well as the sex advice column in her own father's hidden *Playboys*. She saw the best minds of her older sisters' generation start magazines like *Ms.*, write books titled *Our Bodies/Ourselves*, burn bras outside the Miss America Pageant, march on Washington for the Equal Rights Amendment, and, in general, make a ruckus while still enjoying life on their own terms, unfettered by previous conventions or regrets.

Born and educated on the East Coast (she grew up on Fire Island and graduated from Bard), Frolley moved to Los Angeles in the mid-1970s for a brief affair with graduate school. Her life in L.A. was a cacophonous ride through crazy, hazy, sexy days let loose upon the world, by the post-1960s Love-love-love-is-all-there-is zeitgeist.

She confesses to having studied rhetoric in a serious way once. Even now, she dreams in figures of speech. She suggests that the main problems between humans and their incapacity to really understand each other comes down to differences in their rhetorical styles and choices of literary devices. Making love without talking, she says, is one possible tool to overcome both the problems and the differences.

227

ENRICHMENTS

She-noodle. Noun, Victorian slang term of endearment, referring to delectable companions of the female sex who enjoy the carnal delights inherent in *noodling (see below)* around, unabashedly.

Variant: He-noodle. Noun, Archaic and contemporary slang, referring to the male sex organ. Also see above, of the male sex, who likewise enjoy noodling around with pleasure.

Noodle. Transitive and intransitive verb, noun 1. To actively engage in the delights of carnal pleasure, together, alone, or en masse. 2. To improvise music idly alone or with others. 3. To consider from many perspectives, as in "noodling it around before coming to a decision." 4. noun, usually plural, "noodles," a kind of pasta made with eggs, best served hot and well-buttered. 5. variant slang noun and adjunct adjective, refers to the head, as in "that's using the old noodle!" or pejoratively 'noodle head' aka 'silly head,' or 'air head.' 6. –ish, alternate slang adjective, sexy, sensual, and unafraid of a rollicking goodtime, as "She was rather noodlish, in a foxy sort of way."

Gin is a Dangerous Game

From *Bartender's Guide* by Trader Vic, 1948 edition. "Gin is a grain mash distillate redistilled with such aromatics as juniper berries, coriander seed, and angelica root, or a rectified spirit may be flavored with essential oils. While there are many types of gin, the most popular is dry gin for cocktails."

There are all kinds of gin and the British are famous for theirs—Beefeater and Boodles and

Bombay. Lots of people were particular to ask for Tanqueray–it was kind of a fad for a while –Tanqueray and a twist on ice. In Germany, it's called "schnapps," but when ordering in a bar, you simply ask for "Ein Klar" or "a clear," which means gin. Clear? That's the German way.

The word "gin" is derived from the French *genièvre* or the Dutch *jenever,* both of which mean juniper. And juniper is the key ingredient in the alcohol, which is then twice distilled and provides twice the hammer to the head. This makes sense when you know a little about juniper as a drug that's been around since Tutankhamun was found with a stash in his tomb. Used by the Greeks to increase physical stamina in athletes, if ingested off the tree, the berries, which are actually little pine cones, cause immediate agitation, a hypnotic trance, and/or hallucinations. Too much of that— or the distilled gin itself—will lead to liver damage, and also explains waking up someplace you don't recognize, with people you never met, but just vaguely remembering that last Bombay Blue Martini, right before the lights went out.

When a guy gives a gal some kind of gin drink on a hot day, prelude to what is essentially a first date, he has one thing on his mind, and you know what it is. Gin and women and women and gin—stirred, not shaken, with lime and tonic or dirty with extra olives—this is a dangerous mixture that can lead to surprising behavior as the night wears on.

Of course, a G&T sounds harmless enough, but if someone offers to make you a *Bunny Hug* (½ oz. gin, ½ oz. whiskey. ½ oz absinthe, shaken with cracked ice, poured into a chilled glass), call your Mom and/or a taxi before you see the bottom of the glass.

There is something about the juniper berries

which seems to release a hidden person from normal personality parameters and invites out to the forefront of our personas, that crazy person we like to keep locked up in the attic and/or basement of our being. The Id—out on her own, with a drink in her hand, shouts, while flaunting a feather boa about the neck, "Watch out, boys! Lulu's in town! Yee-hah!"

Jean-Luc Godard. A French filmmaker of the 1960s experimental film movement known as Nouvelle Vague (New Wave). If you really want to impress a date with your innate coolness and utter hipster-dom, take him/her to a foreign film revival house to see anything by Godard, then go to a European coffee house, order espresso in a demitasse cup with a twist of lemon, and talk about "film" or *cinéma* for hours.

Moab. Famous for the Arches National Park of astonishing land formations, enormous petroglyphs on the sides of tall canyon walls, and giant deposits of uranium beneath its strange red rocks and sand, looks and feels like an alien life form landed here first, marked its territory, and will be back to reclaim it any day.

Dante. Dante Alighieri (1265-1321), Florence, Italy. Poet who composed *The Divine Comedy*, considered to be the greatest poem of the Middle Ages and the greatest poem in the Italian language. Most of us only get to read it translation, but even at that one-step removed, it is an impressive piece of work. The plot is simple enough—the first-person narrator gets lost in the middle of the woods in the middle of his life. His pal poet, Virgil, finds him and shows him a few things—the seven circles of Hell, the long slow road through Purgatory, and the glimmering lights of heaven. Along the way, he meets everyone he has known personally who has died before him—Popes, politicians, the literati, and demimonde, as well as a lot of people he never met but wished he had—like Odysseus and Thomas Aquinas. He had a terrific sense of place—you could really feel the heat in Hell and see the lights in heaven! Some of it is so real, you begin to think Dante has really been there and done that. Oh course, the whole thing is a metaphor for the soul's journey to "God" and all that archetypical hankering for the part to return to unity with the one, the whole, the big synecdoche in the sky. If you haven't read Dante, you might want to check him out before the end of the world, in case he's right about the afterlife. At least you'll have a map in mind for which road leads where before you get there!

Metonymy & Facing Figures of Speech Head On!

Metonymy. From the Greek, μετωνῠμία, metōnymía, ("a change of name"), is a figure of speech in which a thing or concept is referred to by the name of something closely associated with it. Red Tape stands in for bureaucracy and The Crown stands in for both the U.K. Royal Family and the State. When we think about our relationships, human or otherwise, we can, with the use of metonymy in all its variants, come to terms with what was or is the gist of "it." Here are some general kinds of relationships where varieties of metonymy come into play. Some of these will be familiar to you, while others will seem strange until you get to know them.

1) **Containment.** When one thing contains another as when "dish" refers not to the plate but

to the food it contains as in "that's a tasty dish" and likewise, when "dish" refers to an attractive female, as in "What a dish!" A typical containment relationship is when the identity of the girlfriend and/or wife of the male in question is an adjunct, as in "This is Mr. So-and-so of such and such—and his wife/girlfriend. In other words, one party contains the identity of the other party, historically the male identity containing or defining the female identity. Feminists of all stripes, times, and places have been fighting back on that score *forever*. I am certain, however, a certain amount of containment—of one by another—is inevitable in the course of a lifetime, if only while in our mother's wombs or while holding a baby in ours.

2) **A physical item, place, or body part** which refers to a related concept, as in "a nose for news" or "busy body," or "a head for numbers," or any of a long list of terms used as stand-ins for the genitalia, the sex act in all its complexities ("shagging," "balling," "playing hide the weenie"), as well as out-come, as in "knocked-up," or "bun in the oven" which is also a euphemism. In fact, euphemisms are the more common garden variety of metonyms in your daily life.

3) **Tools or instruments.** Such as the pen that is mightier than the sword, or "he was a real tool," as in "he was the screw driver that screwed me."

4) **Product standing in for process.** As in "nothin' says lovin' like somethin' from the oven," or "bun in the oven," says "baby on board."

233

5) **Punctuation marks** stand in for the meaning of the punctuation mark, i.e. "He was a question mark; she was an exclamation point; end of story. Period."

6) **Synecdoche** is a kind of metonymy where the part is used for the whole. A hundred-dollar bill is a "Ben" or a "Ben Franklin," for he whose face is on it. In my personal lexicon of synecdoches, "Green Eyes" stands in for the boy with green eyes who kissed me for the first time on a summer's night and "Gem-Man" stands in for the jewels in his pocket, as well as, ironically, the trade he is in.

7) **Toponyms** generate metonymic relations through association of location, sense of place, or purpose of place. such as when "the Kremlin" refers to the seat of the Russian Government or "Las Vegas" is a stand-in for its profligate lifestyle and/or glamorous showgirls. Here, "Up-in-the-Hills" is a blend of toponym and synecdoche, as it recalls both the locale of where she lived, but also the suggestion of her body parts.

As for other **figures of speech**, we have the usual **similes**, wholly dependent on one thing being "like" or "as" another thing. This is a familiar kind of relationship in fact, where "one" is very like the "other"—and energizes a kind of mutual like or admiration for one thing and another, which is very like narcissism. Like, it is...

Metaphors are more mysterious. They require a leap of faith from "my love is like a rose," to "my love is a rose." And "a rose is a rose is a rose," like

Mama Gertrude (Stein) said.

Metaphors are the magicians of rhetorical tropes, transforming one thing into another by imagistic conjuring. I shall always be grateful to the many really good metaphors in my life that have helped me see beyond myself staring into a mirror, transcending into a bigger picture, and through the larger looking glass of...life? Alternate realities? Another world? Yes, metaphors are the flying carpets that can take you there, to another planet, just like that!

Litotes, however, are the contrarians of the lot. Figures of speech with oppositional defiance embedded in them, saying no to say yes, yes to say no, understating and using double negatives to assert the positive—which is an accidental nightmare waiting to happen on a not very short road trip. Litotes and its co-dependent Irony prefer to hang out at the back of the bar and trade insults and insights. Writing a good litotes is no mean feat; living with a litotes is no small deed; being a litotes is like having a lead foot, while driving in reverse.

As for **Irony**—a most untrustworthy figure of speech if ever I heard one. Just when you believe one thing about him, her, it—turns out, it is just the opposite of what you thought! Turns out not only the opposite, but terribly, gone-wrong opposite. Remember O. Henry and *The Gift of the Magi*? The combs for her hair? The fob for his watch? That's the classic case of irony which high school English teachers like to teach.

Real irony, the kind that kicks you in the behind when you are bent over—is never as benign as that. Poor Portnoy and his complaint, uneasy Isadora Wing and her incurable fear of flying, and, good grief, what about Candy? Was she ironic, or what? And at the top of the heap of metonymic synecdoches heaped in irony is, who? Lolita, of course, whose name, and its very pronunciation Lo-Lee-ta stands in, part for the whole of a psychopathic sociopath's sexual obsession with a girl, "Lolita, light of my life, fire of my loins."

Naturally, they are all steeped in "attitude" with a 20th Century twist, when everything but everything comes down to the sex.

But is it good sex?

What we need is an anti-inflammatory antidote to irony and all its counter-revolutionary minions, something to remap the mind with something more pleasant to think, write, talk, and experience. One solution would be to think more sex, write more sex, talk more sex, and have more sex, without getting overly pornographic about it. Use better similes! Enjoy the magic of metaphors! Do it often and in the spirit of fun, and for gosh sakes, laugh more in the process.

On that protocol, it's hard to find a place for irony and its manic-depressive cohorts. It could even save your life or the life of someone you love.

Just remember: Sex *is* the opposite of death and that, ironically, is another figure of speech.

Postmodern vs. New

There is an awful lot of junk you have to get through and talk about with a serious face as though you take it seriously, as though you really *care* about how it all turns out, when you are in graduate school. Postmodernism verses New Criticism, being a prime example. If you want to sound smart, talk about Derrida and the French Structuralists; Want to sound old and out of it? Talk about "New" criticism which isn't and I.A. Richards who had the hubris to pen a

236

book called "*The Meaning of Meaning.*"

What do these things mean and why should we care? I came to wonder about that a good deal in graduate seminars dedicated to speech act theory and practical applications of various rhetorical devices. Postmodernism? Deconstructionism? New Criticism? What a plethora of –isms! And what for?

Here it is in a nutshell, in case you were wondering: The Postmodern mind sees reality as a construction of the mind trying to understand its personal reality. It is *post,* or after, *modern,* because unlike the Modern mind which distinguished itself by looking for one unified theory to explain everything, the Postmodern mind has no such optimism that such a theory could possibly exist. The Postmodern mind knows there is no one explanation for everything because everything is a matter of personal experience and interpretation, and possibly, even, chaos and randomness. It all comes down to you, baby, it's you... A literary theory worthy of the Boomer Generation, to be sure!

Deconstructionism is the Bobbsey Twin which comes hand and hand with the Postmodernist rooty-toot-toot because it is not enough to personalize reality down to its metaphorical atomic structure, one must commit to unspeakable acts of exegesis upon the text, to disembowel any notions of "ultimate" truth or "objective" reality because much of human history has been defined by "domination" of one person, place, or thing over another and this idea of one truth to explain it all—is just another example of that. What is "real" is deconstructed down to whose reality we are talking about—the specific, the local area reality. Clearly, the reality outside your door is the only one to trust—the one you already know about because this IS class war fare as exemplified in theories of

"What is Reality?"

So, what's yours is yours, what's mine is mine, and it is unlikely that we will ever agree. That's Postmodernism deconstructed in Deconstructionist terms.

Get it?

New Criticism, on the other hand, was very new in the early 1940s and suggested that works of literature should be approached with an empiric, scientific methodology. Like cells in a test tube, poems should be analyzed in and of themselves, with a cold, dispassionate eye, dissected in the Platonic Petri dish in your mind. Forget the author! Forget the circumstances! Just read the words! Is the form reflective of content? Did you make it "new," like Ezra Pound told you to? And for heaven's sake, don't tell me about your life—just tell me how the text is what it is, not how it made you feel, or worse, how YOU feel about *it!* This thing—call it a poem, a story, a play, what have you— these words on a page, they are a thing unto themselves and as such don't have to excuse their behavior with anything as humanly, banally connected as an authorial explanation or biographical note. Let's just pretend that there is no author, no "I" to whom something has happened to provoke a response as ordinary as words on a page!!! Let's count syllables instead.

Oh goody!

Musso's. The Musso and Frank Grill on Hollywood Boulevard has been serving grilled chops and broiled sole and roasted duck to Hollywood insiders, since 1919. In the '30s, it was a hang-out for writers, trying to get away from the office and the industry executives breathing down their necks—F. Scott Fitzgerald, William Faulkner, Raymond Chandler, Dorothy Parker all hung out in the Back Room. With its mahogany bar, paneled walls and red-leathered booths, Musso's evokes restaurants of another time and era. It is cluttered with ghosts of the famous, the near-famous, and the n'er-do-well hangers-on. They are hungry, looking in from the street and the corners of the room, longing for entrance to the place they cannot get in and a table they will never have.

The Rainbow Bar & Grill on Sunset attained legendary status immediately upon opening in 1972, when Elton John played the party. It was a regular hang-out for rock stars, rising TV comics like John Belushi and Dan Akroyd, also everyone's groupies, and hangers-on, the Demi-monde of West Hollywood. The drinking club, self-named Hollywood Vampires, consisted of such luminaries as Alice Cooper, Keith Moon, Ringo Starr, John Lennon, Mickey Dolenz, and Harry Nilsson. Downstairs was the restaurant-bar and upstairs was the club, *Over the Rainbow*, where the super-stars clustered and The Hustle was more than a dance. I never saw any of those people there. It was dimly lit, I needed a flashlight to find my cocktail, and being new to the line dance moves, I mostly looked at my feet.

Far-Rockaway is a beach town on a peninsula that stands between the bottom of Brooklyn and the Atlantic. This toponym stands in for an urban beach boy from Brooklyn who spent summers in Far Rockaway. I went there with him once, in the middle of winter, when we were breaking each other to pieces like balsa wood. I could see this was the place that owned the better part of him—Far Rockaway and its frothy rolling ocean.

Cars And The Tales They Tell. Ok. I don't care how superficial this sounds—but it happens to be true: you can tell a lot about a person by the car he/she/they drive, within a reasonable margin of error. If a person is driving a beat-up, dented, multi-colored vehicle—VW bug, van, or generic American car, it generally indicates a lack of spare cash in the pocket to fix the cosmetics—or even just get a slightly better-looking car. Also, if the car is maintained—clean or dirty—as in cluttered with empty coffee cups, fast food wrappers, and stuff over-flowing the back seat vs. lovingly tended with a dusting mitt and a spray bottle of Armor All—you know something about how they live their lives and what their priorities are.

When I arrived in L.A., I drove one kind of car, a 1966 Royal Maroon Mustang Coupe, inherited from an older sibling. The Maroon Moose, as we referred to it, was perky and got the job done, transporting me from coast to coast, up and down both coasts separately, and back and forth from either coast to the mid-point, numerous times. The great thing about it was, you could break down anywhere and any old mechanic or even assistant mechanic, or just someone's brother who took the auto class in high school could fix it. Parts were easy to come by, even in the middle of nowhere.

I loved that car—it was simple, friendly, and a good sport, until I fell in love with something more complicated. I was infatuated with and then ultimately seduced by a 1973 Alfa Romeo, Bertone-designed, 2000 GTV Coupe in classic British Racing Green. The Italian job--dubbed LGC for Little Green Car by myself and the lover from whom I acquired this chariot which more closely resembled a magic turtle, with its head and limbs pulled tidily in. I could go anywhere in that car and often did, tossing the keys to the valet parking attendant at the Hotel Bel-Air, where I went to escape my grad school day-job and sat in a velvet glove of a booth in the piano bar, sniffing hot cognac and listening to female jazz vocalists sing standards. Sometimes the unexpected happened. One night, Bill Evans appeared, wraith-like, played a set of some of the craziest, deeply-emotional harmonically expansive piano improvisation I had ever heard and then vanished back into the night, to a bungalow beyond the garden where white ideas of swans were sleeping in carefully landscaped ponds.

This was the sort of thing that happened in the Little Green Car. It was also really easy to find a parking place anywhere I went, with its compact size sliding with ease into otherwise impossible spots.

As for breaking down in an Alfa Romeo—just don't. Don't do it, unless you have towing insurance that will take you to the closest Alfa dealer—which could be hundreds of miles in any direction. Off the shelf parts? Are you kidding?! If you sign on to an Alfa, you are in a long-term relationship and on a first-name basis with a foreign car mechanic in every city you live.

Mustang or Alfa, they each have their tales to tell. Sometimes the only way I can locate where I was in the time/space continuum of my frolicking adventures is by recalling the car I was in and who was at the wheel.

On the outing in question, it was the Maroon Moose and the stick shift with a sticky clutch were all mine.

Litotes and The Rhetoric of Sex. Say it again: Litotes. It is not a word you hear every day and yet you hear them, loads of litotes, every day. It is no small problem to define them as a figure of speech in which an affirmative is expressed by the negation of its opposite. Got it? No way! Way!!

How this plays out in the rhetoric of sex, in the on-going dialectic between the sexes or lovers of any combination, among humans in general, usually manifests in the attraction of opposites. Been there? Done that? Wonder why it didn't work out?

Also, doing or enacting the exact opposite of what you know you should be doing at that exact moment is another form of litotes in our daily lives. Sleeping with your girlfriend's boyfriend or vice versa can bring on a full-blown case of litotes in extremis, in hard to reach places.

Experience has taught us that defining yourself by what you are not, in and by the company you keep, which happens to be the opposite of your own natural inclination, may not foster the best, healthiest, or longest-lasting relationship.

But while it lasts, a good litotes can be very bracing, educational, exhilarating even, in a defiant sort of way, like illegal fireworks. And like fireworks sometimes do, they can blow your fingers off, bring down the rain that makes the flood, or just produce a lot of oooh's and ahhs from start to finish. And that's no true lie!

Mt. Pinos. Located in the Los Padres National Forest, the summit is 8,847 feet and the highest point in Ventura County. Known as *Iwihinmu ('a place of mystery')* in the Chumash language, the mountain was known to be the center of the world or *Liyikshup*, the point where everything is in balance.

Mythopoeisis, Mythopoeia. Hellenistic Greek μυθοποιία, μυθοποίησις, "myth-making," a narrative genre in which a fictional mythology is created by the writer. Sometimes falsely equated with the

242

state if being "a legend in your own mind" but compatible with a mock heroic epic lifestyle, painted in colors of bright hyperbole all about.

Pisco Sour. Pisco is a pale lemony-colored Peruvian brandy made from fermented grape juice, distilled and redistilled into a high-proof spirit, using copper pot stills. It is never diluted before being bottled. Flavor varies according to varieties and combinations of grapes used or by infusions of herbs or fruits. Pisco is distilled from the wine itself, rather than the leftover pulp of the wine which is the case with Italian grappa. Pisco was named for the place in Peru where it originated. The word means "little bird" in the language of the Quechua indigenous people. But there are those who contend the word means "mud container" and others say it means "boiled in a pot." It turns out all three of those definitions apply—the copper kettle it's made in, the mud container it is tradtionally aged in, and the little birds that fly round your head, tweeting loudly, the morning after you have consumed it in easy-to-down frothy cocktails.
Here's the sneaky combo that will take your castle by storm:

Three parts pisco brandy to one part simple syrup, to one part fresh lime juice; blend with one egg white and/or shake very hard in a cocktail shaker with ice; strain and poor into a glass, add a dash of Angostura bitters on top. You should eat food of some kind while drinking these, so as to be able to walk out the door afterwards.

Dithyramb. A passionate or inflated speech, poem, or other form of expression, sometimes associated with drinking songs for Dionysus, god of wine and fertility. Works well ironically in the context of a mock-heroic epic and hyperbolic fomentations.

Mushrooms. Psilocybin mushrooms have been around since the Stone Age—appearing in early cave drawings as early as 9,000 years ago. They have been used in religious rites and ceremonies from Pre-Columbian times to today. What is it about the experience that is religious? It is hard to describe unless you have been there and done that, but put as succinctly as possible, like the divine hot dog in the sky with all the toppings under the sun, the psilocybin effect induces a feeling of becoming "one with everything." Also, the feeling of euphoria is sometimes accompanied by extreme physical sensitivity in all the senses—sight, sound, taste, and of course, touch. Dry mouth and hallucinations are an additional side effect. If you are contemplating the magic mushroom experience, it is wise to be very sure that what you are taking is in fact, the right kind of genus Psilocybe. There are other varieties that look a good deal like the psychedelic variety, except they are deadly poison. So you really want to be careful about sourcing them appropriately. Once you have them and find the right time and place to ingest—a low stress environment with someone you trust is optimum—I do want to make the following suggested list of rules to be committed to memory before you begin your "journey":
No Matter What:
1) You cannot fly.
2) You cannot breathe under water.
3) Do not stare at the sun.
4) Don't forget to drink water, lots of it, throughout.
If you just stick to these guidelines and find a safe happy place to be, and nice people to be with, you should be fine.

Satori. Zen Buddhist terms for "awakening," "comprehension," "understanding."

NeoPoiesis: *a new way of making*

1) in ancient Greece, poiesis referred to the process of making: creation - production - organization - formation - causation

2) a process that can be physical and spiritual, biological and intellectual, artistic and technological, material and teleological, efficient and formal

3) a means of modifying the environment and a method of organizing the self, the making of art and music and poetry, the fashioning of memory and history and philosophy, the construction of perception and expression and reality

4) an independent publisher with a steadfast goal to print and promote outstanding poets, writers and artists who reflect the creative drive and spirit of the new electronic landscape

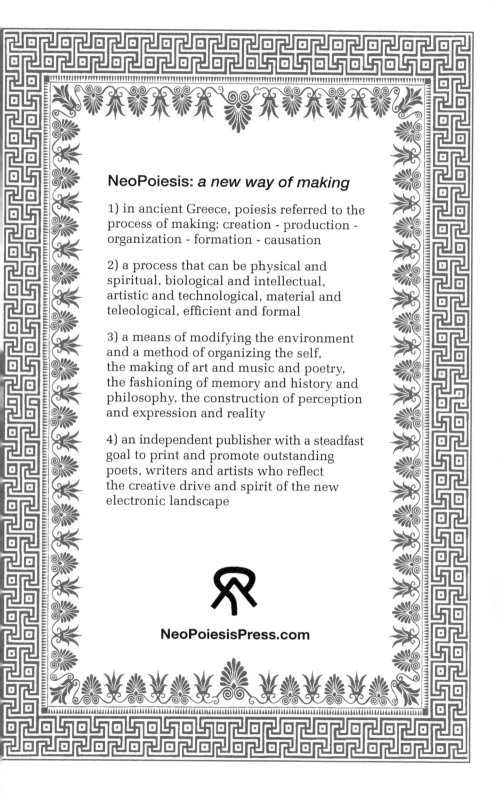

NeoPoiesisPress.com

CPSIA information can be obtained
at www.ICGtesting.com
Printed in the USA
FSHW022036050219
55507FS